CW00828896

GHOSTS OF MARS

The Adventures of Eva Knight

STUART WHITE

Cover Illustrator
JENNIFER JAMIESON

Penobi Press

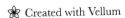

For my Eva

To infinity and beyond

Contents

The First

The world outside the window is infinitely more exciting than the colony nursery.

Drones buzz around, carrying small crates. Astronauts bounce around the landing pad, making final checks for the incoming rocket. A dozen or so maintenance workers are cleaning solar panels, test-driving the rovers, and checking the water recycling and moisture vaporiser machines. Far off, a dust devil whirls across the surface of Mars, like a fiery tornado, throwing dust and rocks around.

I ping the elastic band on my wrist, and my mind is back in the room.

The sudden snap on the skin increases blood flow and improves alertness. Apparently.

And I need both right now – a room full of young Martians and Earthlings gaze up at me, sitting cross-legged in four rows, making the nursery feel tiny.

The room smells of spilt porridge and sweaty socks, only slightly masked by Mr Quark's body odour. My nose wrinkles every time he walks past. The oxygenator isn't recycling the air fast enough to remove the lingering stink.

Seriously, I'd rather scrub solar panels out there, than stand here.

'Eva, tell us what it's like to be famous?' A kid, right at the front, a young Martianborn I recognise asks a question to break the silence.

I should have started talking already. Mr Quark introduced me, as everyone always does: Eva Knight, the first Martianborn. As if he needed to. But I haven't said any of the words I'd rehearsed with Dad last night.

There's a large image of me on the telescreen. Always images of me everywhere. This one from Halloween a few years, and I'd dressed up as a solar flare, my red hair styled up at an angle, like a fork of lightning. Warm reds and oranges in my little dress.

'Have you ever been to Earth?'

'What's your favourite planet?'

'Are you friends with Hercus Armstrong? I heard from my dad that she won the 2045 strongest person on Mars competition.' A loud chorus of 'wooooo' comes from the kids.

'The Martian Olympics,' I whisper.

Mr Quark moves to the front holding a finger to his lips. 'Settle down, kids, let Eva speak.' He smiles at me and nods. Probably trying to reassure me.

But I've never been less assured in my life. It's like the kids are growing larger, or the room is getting smaller. They're closing in on me.

I glance out the window, and it calms me enough to act.

'I'm sorry, I can't do this.' I run out of the nursery, and bump into the last person I want to see right now.

'And where do you think you're going?' Commander Darshi runs the base. Well, technically co-runs it with Dad, but she never acts like it, even though she's only been here a few weeks. She runs a hand through her greying, blonde hair.

I lower my head, wordless. Anything I say now will get me in even more trouble.

'This is classic, Eva. You're the biggest parasite on Mars,' snarls commander Darshi. 'You take and take and take and we all make sacrifices for you. And what do you give back? Nothing. You can't even speak to the kids in the nursery when asked.' She points through the window, and I see the kids' eager faces, their questions still unanswered.

I still can't find my voice, so I keep my head down and rub my sweaty palms together.

'Eva, are you even listening to me?'

I look up and nod.

'Good, now get back in there and watch the rocket land with them. The young Martianborn look up to you. They love talking to one of their own. Especially the first.'

Darshi marches away, and luckily my voice is still AWOL because I want to scream at her. I glance through the door again. A few small faces look up at me, their missing-tooth-smiles making me feel terrible for what I'm about to do next.

I run.

Far away from the nursery. In the opposite direction from the commander, back towards my apartment. Dad shouldn't be there as he'll be in the command centre for the landing.

I will be all alone. Well, almost.

I think you should go back, Eva.

'Quiet, T.'

Trust Thunderchild to take Darshi's side. I tap the tiny AI implant, in the tragus of my ear, to mute him…for the next five minutes anyway. I need time to myself – life up here is too much sometimes.

It's not just Mars or being the most famous person in the

Solar System, it's the way people treat me. They either ogle me like the Martian microbes we study down the microscopes in science, or they're like Darshi and wish I never existed.

Sometimes I wish that, too.

But there's no escaping it – I *am* the first Martian. There's reminders everywhere, and I hate it.

Or maybe I should say, the first human to be born on Mars. I mean, I'm not green or anything. But technically I'm an alien with human biology. But not all that biology works as well for me. I check my e-pancreas and sugars are in range.

As I move quickly through the corridors, I see the tele-screens are already playing the welcome message for the new colonists that are due to arrive today.

Welcome to Mars
You are now a colonist on Mariner Base
Birthplace of the first Martian, Eva Knight
Please report to your duty commander as indicated
on your space-pass

Amazing – another reminder. This is probably half the reason the new co-commander hates me so much. I ignore the photo-shopped image of me on the welcome message and hurry home.

The apartment is quiet – a different place to how it was this morning, during my argument with Dad.

'You will NEVER be an astronaut. Never. No type 1 diabetic, let alone one born on Mars, would ever pass the medical exam. Your insulin would take up precious space needed for oxygen, water, and food. And your Martian-body wouldn't stand up to the rigours of space travel. Please drop this absurd dream and take your responsibilities here, in this colony, more seriously,' he said.

'Mum would've let me take astronaut training.'

I winced at the memory – I knew it'd sting, bringing up Mum, but I did it anyway.

'Your mother would have agreed with me. Your path is here, on this colony, rising through the ranks, staying safe in command, or engineering, or food production, or whatever you have an interest in. Anything but out *there*.' He pointed out of our little window.

Red rocks and tall dunes and an endless sea of lifeless desert. Well, on the surface.

'I must go. We have many important supplies on that rocket, not least your new e-pancreas. That old one won't last until the next supply rocket arrives.'

As he left, I grabbed a small Martian rock that he'd given me as a present when I was four and hurled it as hard as I could at the screen, as it flicked through a collage of old family photos.

The rock still lies there on the floor, going nowhere, just like me.

My bedroom light flashes on as I enter, and I top up the insulin supply on my e-pancreas. My diabetes used to be such a pain in the butt when I injected, but now this wee machine does it all automatically for me. Technology is great. I don't want to be worrying about my glucose levels when I'm outside.

I change from my formal, all-white uniform, into my skin-suit, which we're all issued with to wear below spacesuits. Mine is barely worn, the orange sleeves and red core barely faded at all. Dad's barely has any of the colour left.

Once I'm ready, I grab Dad's spare multi-pass and head out again.

I will not be told what I can and cannot be.

I'll show him, and everyone else, that I belong out there.

2

Thunderchild

I run along the main corridor of our colony, past large windows looking out on the surface of the Red Planet.

Eva, are you listening?

'Thunderchild – I *always* listen to you!'

I said, 'your dad will kill you if you're caught.'

T might not have an actual brain, or even a head, yet he always has something smart to say. 'I've done much worse than this, T.'

Well, quite.

'Anyway, it's his fault I'm doing this.'

Not sure he'd see it that way, Eva.

'He sent me there, to talk to those kids. It's embarrassing and I hate it. I'm ready to be an astronaut and leave this dusty, lifeless rock. Not be stuck here forever, standing on display for the kids like those old rovers in the museum.'

It is part of your duty, as his daughter, but you also have a status. The young Martianborn look up to you. You have a responsibility. And you know it's impossible to become an astronaut. You've been told so many times.

T's voice does register but my mind is trying work out the big question: Where is the best place to watch a rocket land on Mars?

Where are we going?

I jog along the command corridor, the highest level in our base, knowing exactly where to go.

I would strongly advise—

'T, I re-programmed you to be there for me, to talk to me, not to question every single thing I do. I can take you back to Research and Development and you can get dusty on the shelves again.'

Well, really. The dusty shelves, indeed. And I question everything you do to keep you safe. If you listened to my advice more, I'm sure—

We arrive at airlock IV, which is almost never open, but it is tonight. I glance around. There's no-one on patrol. They must all be up in command.

'Good, we're alone.'

When you say good, why does it always turn out bad?

'When did you learn to be exasperated?'

I was programmed to imitate and learn from human emotions long before you stole me. Clearly, I have been exposed to a lot of exasperation since.

'Tell me about it.' I roll my eyes. 'Come on, we have a landing to watch.'

I pull an exo-suit down from the hanging on the wall. There are at least twenty in here but only a few academy ones, covered with ingrained dust and repaired tears. One even has duct tape on it. The badges are so faded I can barely see the outline of *Starship 3* and can only see a couple of the eight stars, on each one.

The one I choose has a small crack in the visor.

Eva, that one is not a wise choice. Exo-suit 7 has a better visor integrity—

'T, chill. I've worn this one before, it's comfy.'

Comfortable? You are about to enter a zero-oxygen, low-pressure environment, where you will risk your life if your visor breaks, and you are prioritising comfort?

'I honestly don't think exo-suit 7 is much better. They all belong in the museum.'

You never listen. I don't know why you bothered re-programming me.

'Me neither,' I whisper.

Heard that!

I get a sharp pain in my inner ear – the vibrations can't be heard by anyone except me, even if he shouts.

'Seriously, T. Lower the frequency.'

You mean the amplitude.

'You are infuriating!'

I walk quickly to the inner door of the airlock, swipe the card in my hand, and it swooshes open.

How did you open that airlock? That is level 5+ clearance. Command only.

'Let's just say, Dad can be a little careless with his multi-pass.' I wave the access card, which has a small photo of Dad, and **Level 7 access** printed on it.

Now, listen to me, Eva.

I press my tragus, on the inside of my ear, to mute him. Just for a few seconds until the lecture finishes.

And in those seconds, I pause. Part of me knows I should listen to T. I will get into trouble for this. So will Dad. But I need to show them. And show myself that I'm not a prisoner in this base. On this planet. That I can be free from all the adults' rules, for a while anyway.

A panel on the outer airlock flashes green, indicating the air and pressure are now identical to the Martian atmosphere. The outer door slides open and just like that, I'm outside.

I inhale a sharp, long intake of oxygen-saturated, artificial air, then take in the view.

This is Mars.

Red, rocky, and wild. Dust and dunes. Totally inhospitable to humans.

Deadly.

My planet. For now.

The change in gravity unbalances me. The colony uses Earth gravity—most colonists come from Earth—so the 38% gravity I'm feeling now has me bouncing.

Eva, are you there?

'Oh hi, T. Thought I'd muted you.'

Well excuse me! Muted, indeed. You do realise that a rocket is just about to land nearby, and weather sensors indicate—

'I don't care what they indicate. I've made up my mind and nothing can stop me.'

The suit is suddenly heavy. So heavy, it's pressing down hard on my shoulder and is almost crumpling my legs. I can't even lift my foot off the ground to take a step. It's like someone's turned on the gravity to ten times its normal force.

And I know who.

'T, now is not the time to try and stop me. I'll use the override, quit your algorithms' safety parameters, and you'll have no control. Release me. NOW!'

Sorry, Eva, but I simply cannot—

'Dcimos!' I shout the override command word, and my suit is instantly light again. I take a long breath and straighten my back. 'T, you need to relax a little. Trust me, when you see this view, you're going to thank me.' I do a small jump to make sure I'm fully free of his attempts to restrain me.

*Thank...you? Well, your life **is** full of firsts...*

'Don't remind me.'

9

The colony looks so still. The last time I was out, after I passed my junior Mars-walk test, it was buzzing with activity.

But now, it's almost…like a ghost-town.

Everyone else must be following orders and staying below the surface in quarters. The safety rules are so pointless, nothing ever goes wrong these days. Dad's just so over-cautious about everything and it drives me crazy.

'Oh cool, there's a MOXIE. They never let us near those.'

And quite right. The Mars Oxygen In-Situ Resource Utilization Experiment is worth more than you could possibly imagine.

The huge machine can apparently create enough oxygen for one person…when it works. It's looking a little weather-beaten – it's probably one of those they brought up with the Founders, all those years ago.

Eva, it seems your absconding has been noticed.

'Absconding? Come on, T. You're cooler than that!'

I really am not.

'Anyway, what are they going to do? Worst thing Dad can do is ground me. At least then I don't have to babysit a bunch of Martianborns. There is nothing they can punish me with that's worse than just being *here*.'

Yes, but if you're grounded, that means non-stop repeats of your depressing, 2040's, teen music. I'm not sure I can manage another week of that. Bring back the AI, synth music of the 2030's. We understand the patterns and rhythms much more than any Earthling. Or Martian…

Before us stands the tallest and most ominous vantage point close to the base. A large mound of dust and rock.

Parvos Tholus. Named for its…

'Are its name and history important right now? It's a hill. I need to climb it. That's all that matters.'

Well, I think it's important.

Despite the reduced gravity, the trek up the tall dune is

tough. The red gravel at my feet is like a landslide, and I fall on my front twice, scratching my visor the second time.

Eva, need I remind you that they know you are out here and are coming—

'No.' I ignore the small red dot flashing in the corner of my visor. Someone, Dad probably, trying to get in touch via the coms. Honestly, he doesn't speak to me properly for weeks and now he wants to chat. No way, I won't let him take this away from me.

I feel like I've scaled a mountain, like those famous Earth explorers did over a century ago. At this moment, I'm as close to being happy as I'll ever be on this planet. I sit down and dig my gloved hand into the soil, pushing the rust-red dirt around.

Just beyond the mountain peaks in the distance, the blue sun sets in the darkening Martian sky, and the Earth slowly rises. The small blue and green ball is barely visible, just the brightest star in the sky, but I know exactly where to look for it. I always know where Earth is, with all its life and vibrance; the place I *will*, someday, take one giant step.

'I'd love to go to the Earth's moon one day, too. Apparently, they have a big scientific research station up there and a space centre for ships to fly off to all parts of the Solar System. The Earth is so close, yet so far away for me.'

The Earth is currently 61.7 million kilometres away. This is the closest it's been in—

'Don't spoil it, T. Just look. Don't process, don't analyse. Just enjoy.'

And to his credit he does. Or at least, he goes quiet.

My life would be so different if only I'd been born on Earth. Not famous, not 'Martianborn', not desperate to be any place but where I am.

As the seconds drift past, my gaze glides to the setting

moons of Phobos and Deimos, just to the right and left of where Earth lies.

The scene reminds me of that old movie Dad loves. Luke Starkiller, or whatever his name was, staring at a binary sunset.

And we both wanted to get off our respective rocks.

Eva, I am sorry to disturb your moment. But a rover has now left the base and is approaching at high velocity.

'Can it drive up the dune?'

I doubt it. Even if the rover accelerated to double its current velocity, the mass of the rover would be unable to escalate the incline without intruding upon the sub-surface of the dune.

'So, it would sink and get stuck?'

Indeed.

'Did you enjoy the view, T?'

Well, I calculated the how long it would be until Deimos next eclipsed the Earth from this viewpoint. So, yes, I did procure 'enjoyment' by tapping into your retina's visual image stream.

The landing pad has been cleared. A few surface-walkers are dashing away in their suits, making for the safety of the airlock.

I have the perfect spot.

Landing countdown commencing. The lander rocket will arrive through the atmosphere in less than one minute. Telemetry has it on target for the pad.

'You hacking the command computer systems again, T? Naughty boy.'

I glance across and see Dad getting out of his rover, about to dash up the slope towards me. His exo-suit is much newer than mine, with distinctive gold stripes on the shoulders.

Eva, your heart rate is elevating rapidly.

I watch, rapt as the lander appears in the sky, hurtling through the clouds, parachutes slowing it.

Cortisol levels rising.

Rockets fire from the underside and it decelerates rapidly. Eventually, the rockets are firing so hard it's like the lander is floating above the colony, slowly being lowered, as though on a string. It might be almost peaceful except I can feel the roar in my whole body.

Dopamine levels are exceeding safe levels.

I can't keep my mouth closed and it's getting so dry, but every part of me is focussed on what I'm seeing. Tears prick at my eyes, and I almost feel like I'm out of O_2.

It's wonderful.

A rocket from another world. Proof that people can escape. They can fly away.

Then suddenly, lights flash red and orange inside my helmet like the Solar System's worst disco. It yanks me from my moment of awe, and my stomach clenches as the emergency computer's voice fills my helmet, loud and shrill.

This is a colony-wide emergency alarm. Surface staff return to base immediately. Colonists must remain at sub-level 2 or below. Emergency command staff report to the surface level. This is not a drill, incoming lethal weather phenomenon.

3

Losing Integrity

A series of twisting dust devils spiral towards the colony from beyond where the rocket has landed. Each reaches high into the darkening sky, whipping up the blood-red surface.

Eva, those tornados are strong enough to pick us up and deposit us far from here with 94.7% probability of death.

I look down at Dad, who has almost reached me, his long strides eating up the distance between us.

He missed the whole landing, took leave of his command, to come and get me. I swallow hard, tasting the salty sweat which runs down my face and soaks my underclothes. I never meant for him to come out.

His mouth is moving quickly inside his helmet, probably swearing at me. His wee moustache twitches like an angry caterpillar. I better switch my coms back on and face the wrath of Dad.

Eva, your adrenaline levels are spiking. Glucose levels also elevated.

'Eva, we must get back to the rover, NOW!' Dad screams down the coms, grabs me by the arm, and hauls me down the slope. I tumble once. He trips twice.

The dust devils move in so fast they surround us completely before we reach the rover. There is nothing but orange, flecked with darkness, and I can feel the power of the dust buffeting against my suit as the storm sucks up large rocks and throws them into the air. I freeze.

Eva, your heart rate is 180 beats per minute. Take a few long, slow breaths. Think of a happier, calmer place. Focus on what to do next.

Small pieces of rock and soil hit my visor, and, in the distance, I can just make out the shape of a solar panel, torn from its base. The wind snatches it, and it spirals towards the sky. Debris flies in our direction.

My jaw shakes, my chest thundering. This was stupid.

Best get into the rover now, Eva. It's just ahead.

For once, I agree with T completely.

Shards of metal and dust fly through the air.

Incoming debris detected. T is urgent.

'Watch out, Dad!' I shout, pulling him down with me.

We both hit the dirt, hard.

My visor now has a huge crack in it with small fracture-lines growing out, like a spider web, getting longer and longer. About to shatter.

Eva, you have approximately thirty seconds until your visor's integrity is compromised.

'Run!' I pull Dad up and we dash for the rover.

Shall I open the rover door in advance?

'YES!' I scream.

Ten metres from the door, it begins to open.

Ten seconds of integrity.

I see black spots in my vision.

'Quicker, Eva. Quicker!' Dad is just ahead of me now, pulling me along by my gloved hand.

The panic drives my legs forward, but they're getting heavier, and I stagger, falling to the ground. The wind decides it's done with the solar panel and drops it. It crashes to Mars with a thud and smashes into in a million pieces, right behind me.

Dad tugs me and we dive through the rover loading-door, sliding along the hard metal floor before it starts to slowly close behind us.

Five seconds of integrity.

I'm drowsy, everything blurring.

'CLOSE!'

Integrity failing.

The door finally seals, and I close my eyes, taking several long breaths.

Then I feel around for Dad, and relief hits me as he grips my arm, and I turn to him.

'Are you okay?' His eyes are huge and red-flecked as he squeezes my arm even more, to the point of pain. Even over the coms, his voice is such an assurance.

'Yes.' The guilt worm writhes in the pit of my stomach. 'Are you…okay?'

He pulls me into a tight embrace and whispers, 'Never do anything like that again. How are your glucose levels?'

'Fine,' I lie.

Then he's up and through the door to the cockpit. He slides into the driver's seat and accelerates through the dust towards the base.

I lie in the back of the rover, limp and exhausted, like T is weighing me down again. I *will* never do that again.

Integrity failed.

The visor crumples, the polycarbonate disintegrating like breaking glass. I carefully sweep away most of the pieces with my gloved hand.

And take a huge breath of recycled rover air.

'Dad, shouldn't we wait out the dust devils?'

'Eva, if you say one…more…word…'

I don't and instead remove my helmet and stare at the smashed visor.

Seconds away from catastrophe. You need to start listening to me, and when you do—

I mute T, knowing he's right. I have enough lectures ahead of me without one inside my head.

I go to the equipment rack at the back of the rover and replace the visor with a shabby spare. The whole vehicle shakes, and I crash backwards into the side of the rover.

'Another Dust Devil. Hold onto something!' Dad's voice crackles over the coms.

Winded, I crawl to a handrail and tether myself to it.

Our rover lifts off the ground, leaving my stomach behind. It spins through the air, making me dizzy, then crashes back to the surface. The impact throws me up, and my helmet smacks the roof, and, at the same moment, the rover flips over. A flying pneumatic drill strikes my shoulder, and I bite my tongue. The shoulder is painful, but the tongue feels worse, and the taste of blood follows. I spit it out, splattering the inside of the newly fitted visor with a crimson spray.

Instinctively, I grope my visor and suit, searching for tears or holes or cracks. My back feels like a meteor shower crashed down upon it.

'T, any ruptures?' I gasp, lying on the upside-down ceiling of the rover, still tethered to what was the floor.

Suit integrity appears to be maintained. Oxygen levels normal. Heart rate spiking. Please attempt to be calm.

'Are you kidding me?' I squint my eyes, but visibility is zero. It's just dust, flooding into the crushed rover. 'T, help me. What do I do?'

Get up. Return to base.
And don't die.

'Dad?'

No response.

'Dad? Are you okay?'

Still, nothing.

'T, can you get any readings on Dad?'

Negative.

I crawl to the front of the rover. The cockpit is empty, and the front window has been smashed. My vision is blurry, my eyes watering. Small sunspots appear every time I blink.

That must have been a huge force to break a reinforced polycarbonic window.

'T, seriously, I'm scared right now. What should I do? Which way should I go?'

Use the coms. See if anyone can hear.

'Dad? Anyone?' I switch on my open coms, crawling through the wreckage of the rover and outside.

Nothing. Either his line is damaged or…

My heart stops. All thoughts turn to one horrible possibility.

'I can't see, T.'

Every direction looks the same. Gusts of red dust spray my visor and suit, and the occasional chunk of rock fires past.

We should return. If he's not answering, we have no idea which way to go to find him. And it's dangerous to remain out here.

I spot something on the ground ahead of me and stumble towards it. 'Dad?'

Silence.

I kneel to see, but it's not him. Just a chunk of a broken wind turbine. For some reason, it looks out of focus.

I blink a few times, but my head is light and fuzzy.

Eva, blood glucose is very low: 2.9 mmol/L. You are hypogly-caemic and struggling to get glucose to your brain. You must return to base.

Somewhere in my head there's a crackle. 'No…wait.' My words slur.

You should go, Eva.

It's the coms. A deep and soothing voice delivers relief, 'This is commander Knight. There's been an explosion. I suspect it was the cargo rocket thrust boosters, but I can't be sure in this storm. Tell…whoever you can find…I'm trapped. And find my daughter. Find her first. Use my GPS signal if you don't have hers, as I'm not sure where I am. I'm fine, suit is intact. But they'll need a rover to pull me free. I'm trapped under…something…and get medics and recovery crew to the lander, see if anyone, or anything, can be saved. But first, find Eva.'

After the elation at hearing Dad's voice, comes the terror of knowing he's trapped and can't move. And the lander explosion…

'Dad?'

'Eva? Are you hurt? Where are you?'

'I'm fine. Just outside the rover. I'm coming for you.'

'Thanks goodness you're okay, but return to base, Eva. That's an order.'

'Dad. Where are you? I'm struggling to get a GPS hit.'

No reply.

A small rock hits my helmet. I frantically run my glove over the spot, but it's smooth. Unbroken.

But then another crackle comes across the coms. 'Help… send help…suit compromised…'

'Dad! Dad? Can you hear me?'

The line goes dead again.

This is my fault. My stupid decision to come out and prove something. All I've done is prove him right and put us both in danger.

'I've got to help him, T. Help me locate him.'

Affirmative. I will log into the base systems and see if they can track him, and I'll cross-navigate with your own suit systems.

'Hurry. Please. I don't feel so good.'

I'm not usually scared of anything, well, except the ghosts in my nightmares, but suddenly, faced with the thought of losing Dad, I'm sick with fear.

Beep

Eva, your glucose levels are dropping to dangerously low levels. I suggest—

'Dad?' No response. 'He's there, I know it.'

There's going to be two people needing rescue if we don't go back now.

The wind nudges me firmly and I stumble, imagining being swept off my feet and up into the Martian sky, then dropped again, like the solar panel.

I can't lose him, I can't.

Eva, return to base.

But T's right. Reality hits me harder than any lump of rock and I'm about to give up and head to the base when I see something. And this time it's definitely the outline of a person.

4

Sword in the Stone

I've only travelled about twenty metres, but it feels like a hundred.

The dust devils are even wilder than before, each gust nearly knocking me off my feet. Each step forward now takes twice the effort.

Dad would tell me to go back. He *did* tell me! But he wouldn't follow his own advice. He'd stride through a storm to rescue me. And that's exactly what I'm going to do for him.

I keep going, my legs burning each time I lift my boots and push forward.

Eva, your blood glucose levels—

'I know.' I only manage a weak whisper, before muting him. I need to be able to hear Dad.

I'm vaguely aware of another explosion before my legs give out and I hit the ground. The low blood sugar is making my head spin. Frustration rushes out of me in a roar but from my position, low on the ground, I see him.

Dad. Trapped beneath a solar panel. His visor is cracked but it must not be breached, or he wouldn't be breathing, and

I can see his chest moving up and down slowly, so he's still alive. For now.

'Dad?' I try the coms again but they're dead. The explosions, the dust, it's totally broken them. And now there's something else – dark smoke joins the whirling red soil.

Dad's right leg is jammed. The panel is too heavy for either of us to lift. Maybe if my friend Hercus were here…

Every muscle in me deflates with the realisation of my uselessness.

I clip onto Dad, lie beside him, and hold his limp hand. If I can do nothing else, I'll be here with him.

'Can anyone hear me?' Nothing.

'I'm sorry, Dad.' I grip his hand tighter. 'I can't do it. I…I can't save you.' What did I think I was going to be able to do?

Tears stream from my eyes, making my vision even more blurry. 'I don't want you to die out here in this bare, red desert.'

But it's not completely bare.

Something is there, something not right. Out of focus.

I blink repeatedly, trying to clear my vision a little.

Something—maybe the last explosion, or the swirling winds—has cleared the top layer of soil and a large piece of Martian rock is now visible with something metallic protruding from it.

It's probably a piece of debris from the rocket. I turn back to Dad, but now I can see it glinting, reflected in his visor. There's something captivating about it.

Is it a cross? No. I peer closer. More like a…sword hilt? Like in those ones in the old Camelot books I read.

No way.

I crawl to it. It's old, rusted and the colours on the metal are faded, but it does look just like a sword.

What's it doing out here, buried?

Maybe someone brought it from Earth, but it looks ancient.

I grab the hilt and tug, thinking I might be able to use it to cut Dad free. But it's stuck in there, totally secure.

Then there's a voice.

But it's not coming through the coms.

Eva...

My head snaps around as I try to locate the source of the sound. Through the haze, a figure is outlined.

'Hello? We need help?'

No reply.

The figure steps closer and I think I must be seeing things – the outline isn't right.

Too tall. No feet. White, glowing, and ethereal.

I shake my head and blink, rapidly. I'm breathing fast, my chest heaving in and out. I'm using up my oxygen like it's a race.

The figure is still there, approaching, impossibly bright, yet cloaked by the dark air around it.

'No!' I scramble backwards like a crab. 'No.'

Not a ghost…not in real life. My throat nearly closes, and I have to gasp in air. Cold sweat runs down my cheek.

'You are not here. Only in my dreams.' My lips tremble as I push out the words.

I must have really low blood sugar, or be in shock or something, because I'm sure I'm not dreaming. And besides, this ghost isn't screaming like they do in the dreams. It's saying something…it's saying my name.

Eva...

The figure is close now, but too bright to make out features. Despite my terror, I swipe my shaking arm through the air, trying to touch it, but I miss.

'You're not real. Are you?'

Eva...lift.

I look back to the sword hilt, firmly wedged in the rock.

'I can't lift it. I need to help Dad.' My fists clench and unclench beneath my gloves. 'No. No. I can't. I just...can't.' I squeeze my eyes shut as the tears come, sailing the hopelessness down my face.

Then the ghost's brightness dims, and a face forms. Familiar. Unforgettable. Same button nose, same wild hair, same dimples.

'Mum?'

How can this be?

Time seems to stand still, seconds passing like centuries. I reach out to her, but she points to the sword.

'I-I can't get it out of the stone. It's stuck.' I don't care about the sword. All I want to do is stare at her, at every little feature on the ghost's face. Is it my mum, or do I just wish it were? I can't look away.

Believe...lift. This blade is both the downfall and the saviour of Dad. His fall and rise.

'What do you mean?' Light-headedness causes me to sway, and I grab the sword hilt to steady myself. 'Will this really save him?' I ask the ghost. Mum. The ghost of my mum.

She nods. **His life will be in danger in the days to come. Only this blade can save him.**

I fumble at the hilt with both hands, plant my feet either side of the rock, and tug with the little strength I have left. And tug. And tug.

Come on!

For Dad. If this can save him, I must try. I grimace. For Mum, too.

Beep

My glucose monitor - again. I'm getting low. I put the last of my strength into a final pull.

I think of Dad. Every good moment we've shared: watching old movies, him falling asleep on the couch EVERY night and me putting my old, pink blanket over him, the time he took me out for my first surface walk. I held his hand so tight that day—

It slides out.

I fall backwards, hitting the ground hard. The sword lies beside me.

But it's not a sword. At least, not like I thought. Pulling it out seems to have brought it to life. The hilt now has a fresh, steel glint to it, like it's new. And where the blade should be is a humming, thin, glowing rod. Like a perpetual energy core reactor and a sword mixed together. Like a—

The ghost picks up the 'sword' and I refocus.

'Now what? How will this save Dad?'

The ghost smiles…then its face changes, suddenly twisted and too long.

It drops the luminous blade and as it strikes the dust, it rebounds and slices across my leg.

The red light on the inside of my helmet flashes, alerting me to the tear in my suit.

My breath comes in gasps. I know I need to be calm, but my lungs won't let me.

I switch Thunderchild back on.

'Help me, T!'

Eva, you have 15 seconds of oxygen left. Listen carefully.

5

Awaiting Death

First, seal the rupture.

I grab the utility tape from my pocket and strap it tightly around the small tear.

Eva, your adrenaline levels are escalated. Please take deep, calming breaths.

'You take deep, calming breaths!'

I only begin to calm when the red light stops flashing, then turns back to green.

Suit stabilised.

When I look around for the ghost it's gone. 'Please don't go.' I reach out to where she stood.

I try to memorise its face. My mum's. But it can't be her. As oxygen returns to my brain and logic kicks in, doubt shadows everything that just happened. 'Mum?'

'T, where has she gone?'

My scans of the apparition detected an intense cluster of electrons. But no living, organic material.

'So, ghosts are just electrons?'

It would appear so.

Beep.

The noise of the life support warning grabs my attention. Silly system. I've fixed the tear! But Dad is still stuck.

Maybe I'm just imagining it, but I do feel a bit stronger suddenly. And Mum did tell me to lift.

The sword sits beside me, still good as new, and still glowing.

I take it by the hilt, my arm shaking as I hold it up. Yay for low Martian gravity, I'd never be able to hold this on Earth.

Nothing.

'Have you ever seen anything like this, T?'

Nothing in the colony database. Let me scan it.

I thrust it towards the sky, hoping it'll be struck by lightning. Like Thor or Zeus or something from my favourite myths…I am ridiculous!

Still nothing.

It appears to be composed of some unknown elements, along with many of the core metals of both Earth and Mars. It has an energy output. A massive energy output. I would suggest putting the unknown weapon down.

'Define "massive",' I say. 'Actually, it doesn't matter. If it saves Dad, I don't care how dangerous it is.' But then the hilt begins to glow silver, then purple, then gold. Fluctuating through the visible spectrum of colour. Growing brighter and brighter. Sparks, like electrical impulses, surge from hilt to tip, then back and into my arm.

With each passing second, I feel stronger. I'm able to think more clearly.

I don't just think I could lift that solar panel now. I know I can.

Then the lightning strikes.

But in reverse.

Every bit of the electrical current that's moving back and

forth between the sword and my hand suddenly assembles at the tip. Then launches into the Martian sky like a beam, a continuous connection of electricity from me to the heavens of Mars.

In that moment, I feel all-powerful. I feel immortal, like I could lift every solar panel around us. Like I could fly across the Martian plains and look down on the ice caps at the poles. Like I could remove my helmet right now and breathe in the Martian air. There is nothing I cannot do. I could snap my fingers and save my dad and become an astronaut and leave this planet in a second.

But as quick as it happens, it stops, and I collapse, dropping the now dull, rusted sword. My breath is wheezy, coming in sharp waves, and my arms shake worse than a Marsquake.

But some of that strength from a moment ago is still there and I know I can lift the panel off Dad. I know it.

So, I squat, gripping as low on the panel as I can with this awkward suit on.

I take one, long, deep breath of oxygen and then jerk up.

It lifts.

Somehow, no idea how, but somehow, it's going.

Beep.

An inch. Followed by another.

Beep, beep.

I'm stronger than I've ever been. I'm going to rescue Dad!

Wait, what did Mum say about it being his downfall?

Beep, beep, beep...

And then I crumple.

I'm vaguely aware of dropping the metal panel. It crashes into Dad's legs. I peek open an eye to see him spring upright, this new pain causing a silent scream of terror which never escapes his helmet.

I collapse.

Beep, beep.

Warning, life-systems critical.

My suit's warning system is deafening, slicing through my failing consciousness and Dad's now awake and thrashing.

'Dad?'

His suit is torn open.

He's going to die in less than fifteen seconds.

Beep, beep.

Warning, life-systems critical, Eva. Glucose levels are detrimentally low.

I clutch the sword, unable to move, speak, or even think, my whole body shaking in hypoglycaemic shock.

6

Scarred

I wake in the emergency room, the flickering, faulty light blinking at me.

My mouth is as dry as the Martian soil, my head throbbing like it's never done before.

'What happened?' I try to sit up, but nope.

Dad's in the adjacent bed, the doctor leaning over him.

'Eva, do take it easy.' Dr Vane spins and helps me lie back. 'I've got a glucose IV drip going in and it's pretty much done, but need you to relax for now, pet.'

'How's D—…the commander?'

'Alive. Just. Brave or stupid, who can say, but it was lucky a rescue team made it in time. Found him and patched up his suit. You owe them your life. Your e-pancreas malfunctioned, both fuses were blown, and it flooded you with insulin. You suffered a severe hypoglycaemic episode. Lucky to be alive, to be honest. Can't install a new one as we don't have one – it was destroyed in the blast. All your diabetes supplies were on that rocket. I've got some needles for you to manually inject. Remember, like you used to?'

I roll my eyes and flop back down. 'Great.' But every muscle in my body has now relaxed knowing Dad is alive.

'And I have a small supply of insulin, but we'll need to work out a long-term solution quickly. Maybe I can have a look at that old fermenter your mum built.'

The mention of Mum gives me a shiver. First, I see her ghost, then the doctor brings up some machine she made. I'll need to ask Dad about that. I glance over at his motionless body and swallow a big gulp of worry.

'I'll see if we can maybe replace the fuses and get the e-pancreas working again soon, but a few days of manual injection won't do you any harm. In fact, it might make you think about your condition a little more. Your average blood glucose levels have been too high, and you've been relying on the e-pancreas to control things for you. Now, it's on you.'

I squirm a little, knowing that's she's right, but also outraged that she's lecturing me. People don't usually do that to me.

'Anyway, aside from the Lichtenberg scarring, caused by lord knows what, you should be free to return to normal duties later, maybe.'

'Lichtenberg scarring?' I look at my arms and see red lines running across my skin all the way from shoulder to wrist. Lifting my gown to the side, it's extended all the way across my front, too. I peer under the sheets, but it's not gone down my legs.

'They're scars which form in the shapes of fractal patterns. Looks like a weird tree tattoo, doesn't it? We usually see them as a result of a powerful electrical current through the body, like lightning,' the doctor explains, while trying to push me down into a resting position.

'Are they…permanent?' I trace a couple of them with my

fingers. It's weird, but also quite cool. I think maybe I like them. But it's also just another thing to make me different.

My skin tingles as I press on them, but suddenly I remember the lightning flooding through my body as I lifted the sword. That power. My head spins thinking about it, and I allow the doctor to place me back down on my pillows without resistance.

'Just take it easy, Eva.'

I decide not to mention the sword for now and since the doctor hasn't, maybe she doesn't know about it. I'm definitely not going to mention that it's supposed to save Dad's life. According to a ghost who looks like Mum. They'll think I've got a concussion or something if I tell that story. But surely the rescue team found it. I wonder what they've done with it.

I look around the ward at the other beds. Each has a curtain pulled around. Of course, the explosions. The shuttle.

'Dr Vane, what happened?'

'You just rest, Eva. I can't tell you—'

'No, please tell me.' I force myself upright again, despite the pain.

She smiles, but she can't hold it and it forms into a grimace. 'Fine. After the shuttle explosion, a series of oxygen tanks also blew. There was a chain reaction. Any small spark anywhere near the tanks and they go. Such a poor design, really.'

'People died?'

She nods. 'I'm afraid so. We lost twelve people today. One of the worst days in Mariner Base's history.'

She lowers her head and walks away to see other patients.

The thought of losing people makes me dizzy again. A dark, heavy feeling rises from my stomach to my mouth, and I want to get it out. But it stays inside, making me shiver. People died. And I was out playing astronaut, endangering Dad and who knows who else. My chest tightens and I close my eyes.

The image of the ghost—Mum—is burned into the inside of my eyelids. My breath quickens and I'm twitchy all over.

I consider resting, being a good girl, but the memory of what Mum's ghost said, about saving Dad, is overwhelming. If it really can help save him, I must get it back. But then, the same ghost tried to kill me. She cut my suit. Why would she tell me I need to save Dad, then try to kill me? Or did she? Was it a test? Or is she an evil ghost, imitating Mum…

Maybe she's just lying. And Dad is safe now.

But that power, of holding that sword and doing all those things that went through my head, is too much. It's the first thing that has ever happened to me that I know is important. I may have finally found a purpose, something that was meant for me, in a world where I wasn't meant to exist. It could be my way out of here and that's got to be worth a little risk, right?

I watch the doctor moving around Dad, treating his leg wounds. She spots me watching and pulls the curtain. I want to go to him, to sit with him and apologise the second he wakes up.

But this is my chance to escape.

I slide out the IV and put on the spare cadet clothes next to the bed. Then, I tiptoe away, trying not to gasp from the sting of my skin against the clothes.

As I pass each curtain I'm tempted to peek. But I'm terrified of what I'll see. Death. Or worse, ghosts. Or what if I saw my mum's face again?

The overpowering smell of sickness and burning is enough to convince me I don't want to see, and I sneak out of the emergency room.

The telescreens are playing Bick Clait's latest media

report, transmitting back to Earth as well as playing on a loop here. And guess who today's story is about.

Sponsors threaten to withdraw after latest accident on Mariner Base

Typical. No-one is ever on my side. Well, except Dad. And Thunderchild.

'T?'

No response.

I double-tap the ear implant to turn him on, but still nothing. I must've totally fried his circuits...poor T! How am I going to do everything I need to do without him?

I take a deep breath and think about what he'd tell me right now.

Focus on the solution, not the problem.

I have his memory and personality backed-up on my server. And a spare implant. I can fix this. This is something I can do right now.

7

Reboot

I suppress a yawn – it's been a long night re-installing Thunderchild's algorithm.

My room is silent. Usually, I'd listen to some Solar Sisters or the Moon Rockers, but tonight I'm on red alert for any sound of Dad coming home. He wouldn't approve, especially after all that's happened.

'T, can you hear me?'

Loud and clear. Systems functioning with optimal performance and capacity.

'Yay! I was worried I'd not be able to get you back. I've missed you.'

It's not been that long. You switched me off for longer than that when I commented on how you'd cut your fringe at a non-optimal angle.

I laugh. 'Well, a LOT has happened. I thought I'd lost you.'

Do I detect a small degree of emotional attachment towards me?

'Yeah, don't get too full of yourself, it's only a *small degree*.'

It's a start. I'll do a quick scan on the colony server to update my information log and synchronise my date/time settings. And link up with your e-pancreas.

'My e-pancreas is gone, so don't bother. But…while you're searching, find out whatever you can about what the science team have been studying this last week.' I hope T doesn't pick up on my no doubt 'elevated heartrate' as I casually drop that request.

I press start on the 3D printer, watching as it spools out a new back-up copy of the small chip that's currently in my ear and wait for his response

There HAS been a lot happening. And you're right, I can't seem to find the sensor for your artificial pancreas.

'Told you. Listen, I need to know where they took that sword. Where are they keeping it?'

Confidential.

'Yeah, but surely you can bypass that?'

I could, but the breach would be detected and located back to me. I have just come back online, and whilst I don't die like you, I have no desire to be completely wiped. Which is what they'd do to an illegal, unregulated, and unapproved AI interface.

'Okay, okay. But you know where the labs are, right? Where the science teams work?'

Sub-10.

'Right, we go tonight.'

Eva…

'Not now. I need to see if what I'm planning makes sense first.'

But isn't that my sole purpose? To listen to your ideas, tell you they are dangerous and ill-advised, and for you to do them anyway.

'Pretty much.'

'Eva? Are you home?'

Dad's back. I slide out of bed, awash with emotion to see and hear him sound so well. He didn't look as good earlier today when I sat beside him in the hospital wing. But he's still stiff and struggling to move. Bruises cover every part of his exposed skin.

He leans on the island worktop in the open-plan kitchen, letting his mechanical braces taking the weight off his injured legs.

'There you are.' He sighs and I'm steeled for a lecture, but I can't look him in the eye – the disappointment on his face is worse than any dressing-down. 'You need to accept that *this* is your life! Right here, on Mars, doing what you're told. You can't become an astronaut and go to Earth; you can't just do what you like and wander around without permission. You put yourself, and others, in danger.

Every time you defy me, defy the rules of our colony, it undermines me as a leader. How can I keep the colony in line if my own daughter doesn't follow the rules?'

I don't reply. Sometimes it's best to let him talk until he blows himself out, like the dust devils.

'I just received a notification from Earth. Just as they were attaching these.' He indicates the hydraulic metal legs keeping him upright. 'They know what happened here and now I have an official warning. Only one incident in fifteen years before this. And just when co-commander Darshi has started planting the idea that a single commander would be work better. The timing couldn't be worse.'

'I'm so sorry…I just wanted to show—' But he cuts me off with one angry look.

He paces, getting a feel for the prosthetics. Every step looks painful, and I grimace on his behalf. It's all on me.

'You are grounded for a month.'

'Fine.' I deserve worse.

He squints at me, probably wondering why I accepted the punishment so easily.

'Let's leave it for now. I'm tired.' He hugs me, too tight as always.

The creases in his face disappear and he sits on the couch and indicates for me to sit beside him.

'I am so relieved to see you're okay. I cannot believe it. I thought we both might have…well…we've been through enough, haven't we? First your mum, but losing you would have been…well, there are no words. I couldn't have coped.' A tear runs down his cheek.

I nod slowly. 'It's okay, Dad. We're both okay. I'm here and safe. You won't lose anyone again.'

He gives me a gentle hug this time, and I hold him for a long time. 'Are you feeling recovered?'

'Yes, thanks to you. How are you? Better? I've not stopped thinking about you since the second I woke. The thought of you being hurt or worse…'

'I know.' We sit, side-by-side on the couch, a mix of anger, disappointment, and relief flooding from Dad.

'Listen, Dad, I need to tell you something.' Time to come clean about what happened after the explosion.

'Have you eaten?'

'Yes,' I lie again. Can't tell him I've been reuploading my illegal AI to my unsanctioned ear-chip.

'Ah good, good. Computer, one adult portion please.' There is a small ding, and a foil packed meal slides down the food tube. Dad picks it up, tears it open with his teeth, and begins to munch the algal-jerky.

Yuck, I hate that stuff. Green, slimy and, worst of all, highly nutritious.

'Okay, what is it?' He pulls over a stool and sits, ready to hear my story.

I'm piecing it together in my mind when the door buzzer goes off.

'Hold that thought.' Dad eases himself up from the stool. 'Best see who's there.'

I nod and he presses the intercom.

'Sorry it's so late but I must speak with you.' A woman's voice. Cold as a Martian night.

'Yes, hold on, Belle,' he replies.

Can't she give him a moment's peace? We both just nearly died.

Dad presses the green button to unlock the door and it slides open.

She marches in, followed by a boy, I think his name is Jay, who looks even more miserable than his mother. I've seen him in class for the last few weeks, but he doesn't speak to anyone. Or maybe nobody speaks to him. It's hard being the commander's kid.

His floppy brown hair falls over most of his brown skin, hiding his kind, but sad eyes that I've seen before.

'Please refer to me as commander Darshi. Apologies for the late hour and for coming to your quarters, but this can't wait.' The commander's voice is even more harsh than usual.

'It's okay.' Dad's smile is warm and welcoming. 'No need for apologies today. It's been a tough one for us all.'

'Good. Well, I'll get straight to the point.' She looks at me. 'I've just come from the infirmary.'

'Would you like a drink? Something to eat?' Dad is putting on a very formal voice to be extra nice.

She shakes her head. 'No, I am not here for social reasons. That does no-one any good. I am here to inform you, as co-commander on the base, you have a second official warning for your conduct and negligence of duties. I warn you now:

I've been given strict instructions to get this colony back on track and back on budget.'

'But…but…'

'No buts or excuses or any more delays. We must keep moving forward, achieving the objectives set out.'

'But what is the additional warning for?'

'You broke protocol in taking an inexperienced cadet on a surface walk, while landing and refuelling was in progress, abandoning your post in command at a vital time.'

'But I was trying to retrieve my daughter. She went outside and we saw the dust devils on the tracker and—'

'Enough. I'm not sure this other story shines you in a better light. The warning stands.'

The room gets colder. Background sounds become clear and loud. I want to scream at Darshi. How dare she come in and speak to Dad like this. He is the commander, and this is his base, not hers. Who even is she? She's been here like five minutes. And if anyone should be punished, it's me, not Dad.

And I feel sorry for the boy, standing in the background, silent and ignored. What must it be like to live with *her*?

'I will work hard to speed up this base. It has become ponderous and costly in your tenure. Work with me, comply with the company orders, or your contract will be terminated. We have three months to send home a positive report.'

'But—' Dad tries to speak, but he seems too weak to respond properly. The pain meds are probably not helping.

She holds up her hand. 'We do not have the time for excuses. We need to be sending people up here in larger numbers, and sooner rather than later. Things are…not as good as they might be, back on Earth.'

'What is happening on Earth?' I say.

She looks at me, like I'm something horrible stuck to her

boot. Then continues to talk to Dad. 'Global warming…food shortages…famine…disease…'

I try to take in every word of their discussion, without showing too much interest, so I watch the boy as they talk. His head is slowly lifting but he's not focussing on the discussion at all. His eyes are on me. Then he turns away, more interested in the rest of the room.

I motion to him to come speak to me.

He shakes his head, nodding to his mum.

'Jay, time to go, it's very late.' Darshi motions to the door and he shrugs, then follows her out.

After they've gone, Dad turns to me. 'Come here.'

I walk over and he crushes me in a massive hug. 'Well, that was horrible. As soon as I'm a bit better, she'll see what I'm made of. And if she wants to try and push me out, then she's got another thing coming. Nothing stops your dad when he puts his mind to it. So, what was it you wanted to tell me earlier? Something good, I hope.'

'Never mind, it wasn't important. She's horrible, isn't she?'

Dad releases me. 'No. But she will learn that good leaders rule by example, not by fear.' He frowns. 'But decisions on this base seem to be made by executives more interested in money than people. It looks like she's the sharp point of the company's sword. Here to prod me and if need be, cut me away.' He balls his fists. 'After all I've done. All I've sacrificed for them. This is how they repay me.'

He snaps the elastic band on his wrist. The tension drops from his forehead. 'But this isn't really something for you to worry about. Get to your bed and rest. Do you think you'll manage tomorrow?'

'Oh yes, I'll definitely be fine for tomorrow.'

He smiles but his eyes paint a sad picture. 'You have a

strong will, Eva, and a big heart. Difficult at times, a *lot* of the time, but good underneath it all. Good night.'

'Good night, Dad.'

I go to bed, wriggling with liars' guilt. I grab an old photo of mum to distract me. That ghost really did look like her. Just maybe it *is* her. This could be the missing piece. If I somehow use the power of the sword again, maybe I could bring her back, and I'd be happier. Dad would be happier.

But if not…I go back to my hopeless current life. Imprisoned on a planet that traps me, destined to grow old and stay in the colony for ever.

'T, what do you think of her? The new co-commander, Darshi?'

She is a female, age forty-four, height approximately five feet, eleven inches—

'No, what do you think about her character? Do you think she's really here to replace my dad?'

Based upon her issuing him a warning, and her general tone and language, I would conclude her intentions to be…negative towards your father.

'Yeah, we'll need to keep an eye on her more from now on.'

From the other room, I can hear Dad watching something.

'Daughter of Linton and Ora Knight, two of the founding members of the Mars Discovery colony, Eva is a remarkable young girl.
The Martian conditions have done nothing to temper her physical or mental development, in fact her computer programming ability is extraordinary for someone of her age, however she suffers from the

autoimmune condition, Diabetes Mellitus, Type 1, and relies on daily injections of insulin to survive. Fortunately, her mother Ora is a top bioengineer, and has set up a small production fermenter to produce her daughter's life-saving hormone in sufficient quantities to sustain her. Ora told us more about Eva and her diagnosis…'

And then Mum speaks. I press my ear to the door remembering her voice again, the way she says 'Eva'.

'I keep forgetting what she sounds like, T. Does that make me a bad person?'

No. It does not. I could save an audio recording right now, so you can hear it any time?

'Thanks, T. I'd like that.'

I remain clamped to the door, listening, even though it makes me sad. Dad is crying again; this happens every time. He must miss her even more than I do.

I want to hug him, to remind him he still has me, but I don't think I make him happy right now.

Eventually the documentary switches back to Jeff Moon, and I hate his squeaky voice, so I slide into bed.

'T, play the recording of Mum, please.'

8

A friend and an enemy

I'm going to do it tonight.

I'll find where the sword is.

Dad's gone to work early. He always does in a crisis, and this is the biggest one yet.

Plus, he needs to show Darshi what he's made of.

His note:

Sorry, Eva, had to get started early today. I know you won't take the sol off but stay inside at the Academy. Do not go wandering. Dad. X.

Well, that means he's going to be late home as well, which gives me the perfect opportunity to get this done.

Eva, check your glucose before we go out.

'Why? You can just tell me.'

Excuse me, I am a highly sophisticated, and expensive, Artificial Intelligence. I am NOT an archaic continuous glucose monitor that will simply announce your sugar levels periodically, or at your whim.

'But T, that's exactly what you are.' I grin widely, knowing he can't see it.

T goes mute.

'Oh come on, T. I'm kidding. Fine, I'll go check it myself. It'll take more time, though. And we are in a hurry.'

Fine, you are at a steady 6 mmol/l.

'Ha, thanks. Knew you'd do it. Let's go.' I stuff some extra-sugary food into my backpack just in case my levels go crazy again, then I take my first insulin injection of the day. It nips. Oh well, only four more to go today…I really miss my e-panc!

As I walk towards the Academy, lost in thoughts of how I'm going to do this tonight, I bump into someone.

'Sorry.' I look up and see Jay. 'Oh, hey.'

'Hey.' He looks down when he speaks, avoiding eye contact.

'You going to the Academy?'

He nods.

'Cool, I'll walk you.' We march along together, but he's not talking.

'So, what do you think of Mars?'

He smiles. 'Freaking awesome. I'm going to learn so much. Once I get over my space sickness. My mum says not to overdo the excitement or studying for a few days.'

'Stick with me. I *never* overdo the studying.'

He smiles again, showing every one of his natural teeth. Usually, people from Earth have surgically implanted, straight, pearly-white teeth, so it's nice to see someone with teeth like me.

We walk in silence the rest of the way to the Academy. It's quiet today. The cafeteria and bar are closed, the walkways between the Central Hub and the wings are deserted. Those of us who are out are keeping a solemn mood, silently going about our day.

The accident seems to have affected everyone, whether people knew someone who died or not.

Dad says this sort of collective mourning is inevitable when we lose someone up here. That colonising a new planet not designed for humans will always come with a high death toll. I wonder if he'd say Mum's death was inevitable. He never mentions it.

'Morning, Eva.' Quasar Jones runs alongside us. 'Honestly, you just can't help yourself, can you? Anything to get even more attention and likes on SolarSocial.'

'I don't even have Solar anymore. Dad made me delete it. Said it wasn't good for my mental health. And I'm not trying to get attention. The opposite, actually.'

'Sure, sure.' She looks over at Jay, her eyes wide beneath her long, straight fringe of blonde hair, streaked with blue. 'Are you two losers coming to the protest tonight?'

'What's it for this time?' I roll my eyes at Jay, who smiles.

Quasar misses my sarcasm or else ignores it. 'It's the Mars against Meat protest. I think it's deplorable that we eat meat up here. It's bad enough on Earth but at least the animals can roam there. Up here, it's savage. It needs to end.'

'Not a fan of the burgers?' I joke.

'No, I am not. I'm vegan, thank you very much. And if you're not interested in my cause, you can just say so. I have plenty to do without you wasting my time.' And she storms ahead.

'Quasar is fun, huh?' I laugh.

'She's a bit intense, yeah. But she's passionate, which is pretty cool.' Jay watches her as we walk on, in silence.

Quasar and I have never been friends. She resents me, like Darshi. Probably for the same reasons. I'm just glad I never have to see them both at the same time.

'Oh no,' Jay speaks, giving me a small fright. Then I see what made him say it, and I echo him.

Co-commander Darshi is here.

She raises her eyebrow. 'Surprise, Jay!' She smiles, but Jay lowers his head and walks past her into our classroom.

'Hello, Eva. Nice to see you again. How are you feeling now?' She says the word 'nice', but her eyes are saying the opposite.

'Fine.'

'Really? If you feel like you need to leave class, do be *honest* and let me know the *truth*.'

I walk into class, seething at how she's treated Dad, unable to resist the question that every other silent, pensive cadet clearly wants to ask

'Why is *she* taking us?' I whisper to Hercus as I slide into my seat beside her.

Hercus is like my rock, ever since the Mars Olympics last year, when she squatted a rover to win a gold medal for weightlifting. And nobody, except Quasar, teases me in her presence.

She shrugs, twisting her corkscrew hair in her fingers, not daring to speak. 'I'm more worried about you. Should you even be here?'

'I'm fine.' I chew my nails and stare at the desk.

'Eva, you have scarring all over your skin. It's like tree branches. Doesn't it hurt?'

'It's called Lichtenberg scarring, but it's totally fine. Just stings. I'm used to it already.'

Hercus continues to stare at me, like I might explode any second, but doesn't ask again.

Darshi checks her watch and closes the door, then takes a seat behind the large desk at the front of the room. It's on a dais, raised above our rows of sparsely populated desks.

'Good morning, cadets.'

A few people murmured 'good morning' in reply. Again, the raised eyebrow, the same one she gave Jay.

'Hmmm. Clearly, I have much more to teach you than just the basics of life on a planetary base.' She stands. 'Good morning, cadets.' Her voice is as big as Olympus Mons.

This time we all reply together. It's always tricky when you have someone new teaching and have no idea how strict they'll be. I already know she hates me, but now I get the feeling she's going to be like that with everyone. It's the sort of feeling I get when I step into a cold shower. At least I won't feel singled out by her if she's cold as ice with the whole cla—

'STAND UP AND SALUTE!' she roars so loud every one of us leaps to our feet like gravity had been inversed. Except Jay, who slowly rises and lazily swings his arm up to salute his mother.

'Better. If I have to ask next time, detention will be… cleaning solar panels.' Her eyes fix on me as she finishes.

We all sit. Seconds pass in utter silence. Someone sneezes and it feels louder than the explosions.

I can't help but wonder why she's here, teaching us; doesn't Dad need her 'help' running the place? I thought she was soooo important and he couldn't possibly get everything back to normal after the explosion without her.

'In light of a very serious accident, we shall all maintain a moments silence in honour of those who lost their lives. Praise Ares for some peace for the families of those lost.'

For a whole minute, the room is silent. It feels eternal, and Darshi's eyes never leave me, even for a pico-second.

'The memorial for the those we have lost will take place tomorrow. You will all attend instead of normal lessons. Life is fragile, especially on Mars, and we cannot afford to have colonists thinking they are minor celebrities and running around doing as they please.' Her eyes narrow to slits as she stares at me. 'You would think those near the top of the command chain would have instilled discipline in those that they have responsibility for. But, apparently, not.' She pauses for several seconds, sucking in air like a snake. The hissing noise makes me quiver.

I shift around in my seat, staring at a map of Mars on the wall, ignoring the many sets of eyes now fixed on me.

'The most important thing I shall be teaching you is discipline – following orders and always maintaining rank and the chain of command. This base lacks control. Its leadership has become complacent, and lives have been lost as a result. That slack attitude extends even to this Academy. Cadets who do not follow every single instruction I issue will no longer be cadets. You will be expelled and either deported back to Earth on the next supply rocket or you will spend your days in a meaningless job in the depths of the Pits with oxide vipers snapping at your heels looking for their next meal.'

Well, really. Quite rude.

Hercus' deep breathing gets faster. Jay is facing forward, but his eyes are glazed over. Clearly, he's heard all this at home, his whole life. Behind me, Quasar gives me a big smile, enjoying my humiliation. I don't know who is annoying me more.

'Now, this morning, and every morning for the foreseeable future, we will start with the most basic principle in the Academy: health and safety procedures. Cadets, you will all fall in line.'

The moment her focus moves to the computer, eyes roll, and silent sighs circulate the room.

Health and safety! Oh good, my favourite!

Whose side is T even on!?

Academy will be great fun, Dad said.

Academy will teach you so many valuable skills, Dad said.

Academy will change your mind about Mars, Dad said.

Well, right now, more than ever, I want a black hole to swallow me up.

'Scribbo-Pads out. We'll be using the long lost, but remarkably effective art of handwriting. You will copy down the notes as they project on the screen, and I will be checking and assessing your work at the end of the lesson.'

As the first image goes up, I whisper to Hercus, 'When was the last time you hand wrote something?'

She shrugs, the muscles in her hands and wrists working hard to get every word down before the co-commander advances the slide.

'Hey, celebrity?' Quasar flicks my ear with her pen.

I ignore her.

'*Daughter of Mars?* How are you feeling after your little accident?'

I keep scribbling.

'Just another incident to add to your growing highlights reel. You love it, don't you? All the fame, all the attention?'

'Shut it!' My voice is super quiet, but hard, through my gritted teeth.

Others look over, in between glances at the screen. They're hoping for a spectacle. Waiting for me to blow up at Quasar.

'And of course, no consequences because your Daddy is commander … oh sorry, I mean *co*-commander. Shame he couldn't handle it on his own. But then I guess he's got his hands full arranging your publicity events, Miss Famous First Martian.'

The spectators get what they want.

'SHUT UP!' It echoes around the classroom.

Everyone's attention suddenly snaps firmly to their pads, scribbling down notes like nothing happened.

Everyone except Darshi.

I brace myself for the roar again, but worse – she speaks calmly and softly, the happy hiss coming from her again.

'Eva Knight, lunchtime detention. Bring your Scribbo-Pad. An hour of dictation and copying should do for starters. And you can join her Miss Jones.'

9

Plotting on the lower levels

'You been in here before?' Hercus walks alongside me, on our class trip, as we descend the stairs, one-hundred metres beneath the surface of Mars. On the way to sub-level 10.

'Yes, got the tour from Dad a couple of years ago. He's obsessed with plants and loves all of this. Wanted to encourage me to take botany as my specialty.'

'And will you?'

'No idea. I still want to be an astronaut, but Dad insists that will never happen. And I'm not sure Darshi is likely to allow it any time soon. But I won't give up that easily.'

Hercus screws her eyes up at me, then quickly looks away.

'You know what you want to do?' I ask.

'I think I'd like to work in the power station, with my dad. But, if I somehow graduate, they might let me train for the control room. Wouldn't it be cool if someone from the worker's wing went on to become a commander?' Then she shakes her head. 'But yeah, probably it'll be with Dad in The Pits.'

'You'll definitely graduate. You're one of the best in class.'

'Yeah, but they don't like us workers moving into control.

The company have never approved workers to become officers. No, I'll end up down there, with all the pipes and turbines and burners. It's pretty hot and grim, but it's an important job.'

'For sure.' Part of me thinks it would be cool to work with Herc one day, but I'll never end up in The Pits. As much as I hate how Quasar and the others talk about me, being the first Martianborn *and* the commander's daughter has a few good points. Even if popularity isn't one. And if I showed my face down there…Quasar's attitude is typical of what they think about me.

We pass the geothermal pipes, the rising heat radiating from them and making me instantly sweaty. Hot water pumped right up from the core of the planet, keeping us warm, providing us with electricity.

Commander Darshi stops us. 'These not only provide the heat energy to spin our turbines in the power station, but they also provide the heat required in the greenhouses. Nothing goes to waste here…or it shouldn't if it's run efficiently.' She looks my way. 'Let's move along, lots to do and learn this afternoon.'

She turns, and we chase after her moving deeper beneath the base. I take a mental note of all the levels we pass; engineering, food storage, fuel production, mining, even a floor marked nuclear bunker. I hope I never see inside that one.

But when we reach the next floor, sub-9, my left hand stings. It pulses. It longs to grip something nearby.

I check out the sign: *research and development.*

I've been in there once before. On the tour with Dad, when I stole the AI microchip that hosts Thunderchild.

Every hair on my body stands tall, crackling with current, telling me that the sword is in there. And that it's time to break in and steal something again.

. . .

'That hour long lecture on hydroponics made you want to specialise in botany any more than before?' Hercus nudges me and laughs.

I force a smile back, but my thoughts are upstairs with the sword.

'What's up with you?' She fixes me with a look. 'You've been zoned out since we got here. I totally get it during the lecture but what's up now?'

'The sword. I think I know where it is.' But I slap my hand over my mouth when I realise I've said it out loud.

'What sword?'

'I found it when I was out in the storm with Dad. It let me talk to the ghosts. They want me to find that sword. And they told me it will save my dad.' But the moment I say it, I realise it was a mistake. I'm still not totally sure myself, and I know Herc will be sceptic.

Hercus stares at me, her eyes widening. 'Ghosts? Swords? Okay…'

'Listen, don't tell anyone about this, especially Darshi! Or Quasar.' I prod her on the back to make sure she gets the message. 'I shouldn't have told you.'

'Who would I tell?' She shrugs and turns back to measuring her minerals for the plant feed. 'Hey everyone, Eva wants to get a sword so she can talk to Martian ghosts. They'd just laugh me out the room.'

'Seriously, not a word. But now you know, will you help me? I think it's just upstairs, on that floor we passed. If we snuck down here later, it would be quiet.'

'What is it with you, Eva? You nearly died in the storm. You're lucky to still be here.' Hercus shrugs and turns away again.

'And anyway, how do you propose getting into one of the most secure floors on the base?' She stops her work and moves closer. 'Darshi has the whole place under strict observation since you got out before the accident.'

My tummy wriggles a little at that. My fault, again.

'Well, my dad's the commander. I could take his access card. Though maybe I shouldn't, after all the trouble I've already got him in.'

'*Co*-commander. And on a warning.' Hercus shakes her head.

We spin round to see Quasar has snuck up behind us. 'How long have you been there?'

'Long enough to know you're up to no good again. You never learn.'

'Go away, Quasar. Whatever you heard, clearly, we were just joking.' I've never lied so badly.

'I don't think you were.' She moves forward and stands between us. 'And I want in. I want to see this sword. And R&D is where they do the animal experimentation. Maybe one or two of the guinea pigs and rabbits will escape.' She crosses her arms and sneers.

'No.'

'If you don't, I'll tell.' She turns to see where commander Darshi is. With the group next to ours. She'll be with us any moment.

'I don't trust you.'

'I don't trust you, either. You nearly got yourself and the commander killed. You constantly do as you like, and you get away with everything. You're such a special little celebrity.' She seems smug, her high, chiselled cheeks swelling.

But she's right. I've been teased by her for years, but I know she's honest. A pain in the butt, but she's no snitch.

'What about your Mars against Meat protest?'

'Perfect cover for us to sneak down.' She crosses her arms, as if I can't argue with her.

Just as I'm about to try, commander Darshi moves towards our group.

'Either, let me come along, or I will tell the commander right now.' Quasar turns to Darshi and opens her mouth.

'Fine, midnight. At the door to the Pits. Don't say a word.' I force the words out through gritted teeth. I have no choice.

She smiles and bounces back to her group.

The commander arrives. 'What was that about?'

'Nothing.'

She narrows her eyes. 'Were you telling her about your escapades? Your stupidity? After failing to follow instructions from your commander?'

I lower my head, biting my lip. Now is not the time to fight back, to say anything. The last thing I need is to get into trouble and be grounded for several more light years! I'll save that battle for another day.

'Yes, you should lower your head. You were lucky to be saved. It won't be long until I have this base back in order. And it starts both at the top and with you cadets. Only a matter of time.' She smiles and walks off, failing to inspect Hercus' work, or even acknowledge her like she did with the other groups.

Mouthing every single curse I know, I turn to Hercus. 'She needs to shut her mouth about my dad. I mean it, I'll lose it eventually. She's totally out of order.'

'I'm sorry.' Hercus stops her work and turns to me. 'I am. It's not fair to blame your dad for your mistakes.'

'Oh thanks. You're such a great friend. You *almost* said something nice.'

'Think that's as good as we'll ever get, E.' Hercus chuckles.

'You know what, if you're really sorry, you can help me tonight.'

She shakes her head. 'No way.'

'But you'll get a chance to do something very cool and very important. It could save my dad.'

'I don't care about cool. And doing something dangerous, willingly, is just stupid. And you're talking about ghosts and magic swords. It's a bit much, even for you. Eva, I've got to think about my life, too. Not just your things. I have plans of my own. How will I ever become the first Black commander if I do stuff like this. You know, I think Quasar is right sometimes. You do think the world orbits around you.'

'Fine, I don't need you anyway. I was just trying to reach out to you. You asked me if I was okay.'

'Fine by me.' She picks up the beaker and thrusts it into my hands. 'There you go, concentrations should be right. We're done. Or should I say, I'm done. If you were actually my friend, you'd understand why I'm saying no.' She walks away, as Darshi signals the end of the lesson, before turning. 'Eva, do take it easy. You've been through a lot.' Then she ambles towards the stairs, shoulders slumped.

The commander spots her but doesn't call her back. I'm already feeling bad, but I have to do this, and if Herc won't help, I'll need to just do it without her.

'Well, T, looks like it's just me, you, and Quasar. What a trio!'

We're not actually letting Quasar come along? I already think it's an illogical, and hugely flawed plan.

'If we don't, she'll just snitch. Right, let's feed these plants and get back up for dinner. It's on. Tonight.'

10

The Museum

The alarm goes off.

11.45pm, Eva. Fifteen minutes until you meet Quasar.

'Thanks, T.'

Eva, I must state my opposition to your plan. It seems reckless.

'Noted. Now, are you going to help me, or should I switch you off?'

Well, really. You know my first priority is always you. But it would be against all my logic-programming not to tell you how illogical your idea is.

'When you start seeing ghosts and pulling super-powered swords from the surface of Mars logic starts to go out the window, T.'

Point taken. But each of those phenomena will have scientific explanations.

I pull off the duvet, and as I'm fully dressed and haven't slept at all, I can be out of here in less than five minutes. I grab my bag, but just as I enter the kitchen there's a beep from the front door.

DAD!

I charge back to my room and close the door behind me as the front door slides open. I hear him speaking to someone.

NO! Now I'll never be able to get out without being noticed.

I look back at the clock.

11.47pm.

I'm going to be late.

Quark!

I take a long breath. Okay, maybe the chat will be quick, whoever it's with. Maybe they'll go away again. Maybe Dad will go straight to bed.

I place my ear to the door.

'Linton, I must admit that things are much worse than I first thought. The power production is too low, the food storage is dwindling, with crop production too low to compensate. We have so few natural resources, minerals, and metals coming up from our current mines. In short, with all those supplies lost in the rocket explosion, we will not survive with the base operating as it is. We need to cut back on almost everything. Lights-out needs to be earlier, except for essential operations, and we need to start food rations.'

'Okay, the lights-out is a good idea, but we can't cut back any more on food. The people, particularly those in the Pits, are starving. They're already unhappy – a ration could cause a strike. Or worse.'

'If it does, so be it. I am here to ensure this base survives. That things are run as efficiently as possible. I have sacrificed a lot for this and if others must sacrifice, too, then that's how it must be. I am not here to be popular.'

I want to scream at her about how much people up here have sacrificed. I lost my mum to this planet and its radiation. People have died. Lots of them. The base isn't more important than people.

'Okay, okay. Give me the night to think on it. We can decide on the restrictions in the morning. How were the cadets today? Enjoy teaching again? I read that you trained astronauts with the NASA programme in a previous career.'

'Abysmal. They are just like this base. Undisciplined, naïve, and with limited survival skills. They've been overindulged and are soft. They need hardening up. They need better instruction than they've received. I will continue to oversee the discipline side of their training, although captain Pulse, and others, can continue with the specialist's skills. I don't think you'll be needed to teach anymore.'

'I do love teaching, but if you'd prefer to spend more time at the academy, I can take charge in the control centre.'

'Not a chance. Let me be clear, Linton. I am co-commander for now. But if I don't see an improvement from you, and the base overall, very quickly, you will be dismissed. Good night.'

The front door opens and closes.

'Who does she think she is, T?'

She thinks, and is, the co-commander of this colony and—

'Oh, be quiet.' I check the clock.

11.56pm.

I need a distraction – something to get Dad out of here.

I stagger into the living room. 'Dad?'

'Not now, Eva.' He is staring at the wall. I must do something.

'Dad, I need the doctor here. Now.'

I feign a stumble and then sit down.

He leaps up from his seat, wrapping his arms around me and lowering me into a lying position. 'What is it? Is it the scarring? Diabetes?'

'Diabetes. I'm hypo. I just need some glucose gel – can you get me some?'

'Take it easy, I'll run down and wake the doc.'

He sprints from our apartment and the pounding noise from his footsteps slowly disappear.

I follow him out but run in the opposite direction.

11.58pm.

Eva, you are taking this too far. You've faked a medical emergency. There will be consequences.

'Dad will forgive me if it saves him at some point. It's important.'

Is it? Or are you only thinking of your own wishes, Eva?

I ignore T. He's right, obviously. There will be consequences. I swallow hard. But if this sword can save Dad, then I've got to do it.

I hope Quasar is ready to go – or better still, doesn't show – Dad is going to come back, find me missing and send out a search party. As well as being endlessly disappointed and furious at me.

So much for being grounded. I glance up at the cameras as I pass each one. I can pretend to be going to the protest if anyone stops me.

Quasar waits for me at the stairway door on the ground level, which leads down to all the sub-levels, and eventually The Pits.

'You came,' I say, unsure what feeling to have about that.

She shrugs. 'Couldn't resist. The protest will just be ignored anyway. Plus, I'd love to see what else is going on down there. We're breaking into the experimental science lab – apart from your sword, there's bound to be loads of cool things in there. Maybe some Martian things. And a chance to do some real activism.'

I can't help but suspect she's going to get us in even more trouble, but I don't have the time to argue. I decided earlier I had to trust her.

But the door to the stairs is locked. I turn away from Quasar and whisper to T. 'Can you bypass the lock?'

Affirmative. But the question is not if I can unlock it. It's if I should unlock it.

'Just do it.'

Quasar is staring at me. 'Why are you whispering to yourself?'

'Just trying to work out how to open this door.'

'I thought you said you had a pass?' She shakes her head. 'Oh never mind, I'm off to the protest after all. If you can't even get past a door, this is a waste of my time.'

I'm relieved and happy to let her go, but just then T unlocks the door. It pulls apart with a swish.

It's like staring down into a black hole, as all the usual lighting is off. To save energy, I suppose – like Darshi said, it's essential usage only now.

'Wrist-pads on. Turn the light on full and we can at least light up the stairs in front of us. Quick.'

'Why are we taking the stairs anyway? The lift would take us down,' asks Quasar.

'Lifts have camera's and are tracked when they move floors. Stairs not so much.'

The pounding of two sets of feet, half-running, half-jumping, down the multiple flights of stairs, must be loud enough to alert anyone to our presence. But there's no-one here. Absolutely no-one.

'This is uber creepy,' Quasar says, her voice echoing slightly. 'Mwwwwwaaaahhhhhaaahhhaaaa…' She laughs.

'Quit it,' I whisper.

'What's wrong? Scared of the dark?' Quasar shines her wrist-pad light in my face.

'Not a big fan, no.' I shrug and run on.

I stop, thinking I saw someone above us, following us down the stairs. Quasar also pauses.

'What's up?'

'I thought that I saw something…never mind.' And we continue down, but every so often, I see movement in the corner of my eye. I'm sure we're being followed.

Quasar stops and shines her wrist-pad at the sign for this level. 'Sub-7. One more to go.'

Then I see a shadow. A definite outline. 'Who's there?' I ask, shining my light up to the stairs above.

Someone tall, with a slightly hunched back, moves forward. 'It's just me.' He steps into view.

'Jay? Have you been following us? Is your mum with you?' Quasar can't stop talking.

He holds up his hands. 'It's fine. I'm on my own. I was just sitting in my mum's office, and I noticed two unauthorised colonists heading into the stairwell on the security camera. And you did it without even using a pass. I had to come and see how you bypassed the system without setting off an alarm.'

'Does your mum know we're here?' I ask.

He shakes his head. 'Off talking to the protesters.' He turns to Quasar. 'Talking of which, why aren't you up there? After your speech this morning, I thought you'd have been at the head of the rally.'

She shrugs. 'Yeah, didn't fancy it tonight.'

He frowns. 'Really? What's so interesting down here that you'd miss the protest. I'm really intrigued now.'

'None of your business,' quips Quasar.

'She's right. Best not to get involved,' I add, still not sure if he's spying for his mum or is actually telling the truth. If his mum was literally anyone else, it would be fine.

'Well, I'm here now. You either tell me or I go back upstairs and let mum know what you're both up to.'

I shake my head. 'We don't have any choice, do we?'

He shakes his head. 'Nope. But you can trust me.'

But I'm not sure I can. Anyone related to Darshi can't be good news. And if he is spying, bringing him along is the worst thing I could do. Maybe we could still turn back.

Someone opens a door below us, their steps echoing up.

'Quick, in here,' I whisper, pointing to a nearby door. But it's locked.

'Don't worry,' says Jay. And with a swift swipe of a pass, the doors open, and close behind us in a moment.

We all remain frozen, holding our breath as we hear the steps on the other side of the door. They stop, centimetres from where we are hidden.

Jay quickly does something to the lock.

The person outside scratches at the swipe pad with their pass, but it's not opening.

Then the footsteps move away.

We relax.

'What did you do?' I ask Jay.

'Just cleared it with my magnet.' He holds it up, smiling.

'Good thinking,' I say, patting him on the shoulder.

'Yeah, good one, noob.' Quasar turns away. 'We'd best stay here a minute in case they're still out there.'

'So, where are we?' Jay asks.

Behind Quasar a sign says: *Sub-7: The Museum.*

'Museum? Oh yes, I read about this. Soooooo cooooool.' Jay's almost dancing with excitement.

'Okay, we can have a quick look, then back on task,' Quasar says.

'Really?' I give them a stern look.

'Why not? He's like a new puppy or something, isn't he? May as well keep him happy, as he does seem useful.'

'Plus, we can't go back out that way for a bit. It will take a few minutes to reset the lock,' adds Jay.

He swipes the next door, and we step inside. The overhead lights flicker on, bringing the whole museum into marvellous reddish light.

'Wow, it's like being outside in here.' Jay runs to the first exhibit.

Quasar and I have been in here before, on school trips, so know it well. I remember being as excited as Jay when I first came.

'PERSEVERANCE!' he shouts.

'Alright, nerd, keep it down.' Quasar leans against the railings beside him, pretending to show little interest.

'You realise how much scientific data this rover provided for us? We wouldn't have been half as prepared for colonisation without its work. There'd have been no funding if it hadn't found the first signs of ancient life on Mars.'

'Duh. We all know this, Jay.' Quasar starts twirling her hair in her fingers.

Jay runs around the museum, from exhibit to exhibit. The old rovers, the first few supply pods, the ancient insulin fermenter my mum made before the company sent up something better – which then broke. And broke again. And no-one could fix it.

'Pathfinder! How cute is that? He's so tiny. Oh, I am so coming back here tomorrow after class.'

'Seriously Jay, get a grip.' Quasar tuts but moves closer to him.

'Wow, I didn't know this.' He points to a plaque which has the names of all the colony Founders. The first fifty to land and start building the Mariner Base that we now call home.

'Amazing to think that was just fifteen years ago. And now there's more than two hundred of us.'

'The first dome they lived in is now the ground level cafeteria.' Quasar looks pleased with her fact.

'That's kinda cool,' says Jay, smiling at her.

'Look Eva, there's your parent's names.' Quasar points to the seventh and eighth names – Ora White and Linton Knight. 'Wait, your mum's surname was White?'

I nod. It's not something I remember or think about too much.

'So, you're telling me that your mum and dad were the White-Knights?' Quasar smiles.

'That is a-maze-ing,' says Jay, scanning the names more thoroughly now. 'Like the defenders of the first humans on Mars.'

He spins round, holding an invisible sword. 'Stay away aliens, the White-Knights are here. And they will kick your alien-butt if you come any closer.' He laughs, and so do the rest of us.

But I have an underlying hollow feeling that I don't get to share that joke with Mum. Not now, or ever.

And him holding a pretend sword has focussed my mind back, razor-sharp, to the real mission tonight.

'Quasar. Jay. I need to tell you something.'

They both come close.

I'm not sure they're ready to hear this, Eva.

I ignore T. It's time to tell them. 'When I was out in the storm, something happened.'

'Yeah, you got your butt kicked by Mars, unsurprisingly,' Quasar says.

Jay frowns at her. 'Harsh, Quasar! Go on, Eva, what happened?'

But before I can continue, a second door opens. Not the

one we entered through, but a second one. 'Who's down here?' shouts a voice.

We tip-toe back to the door but when Jay swipes his pass, it still won't open.

'Hello? Who's in here?' It's a different voice this time. Two guards, on patrol. As I wonder how they found us, and how we're going to escape, a message comes through on my Wrist-pad.

I quickly type a reply.

Stuck in the Museum. Can't get door open.

As the guards' footsteps get closer, I look around for somewhere to hide and spot a small gap between Perseverance and Curiosity. I make a move, indicating for the other two to follow.

We slide between the two antique rovers, crouch low, staring back into the red glow, searching for movement. Minutes pass, and only the occasional flash of light or sound of a heavy footstep comes to us.

I barely breathe.

The guards come into view, shining their lights across the room in a circular motion. It's only a matter of time before they get close enough and see us.

Just a few more steps and we're done for.

Several heavy thumps come from the stairway. T confirms in my ear that the noises are coming from two levels below.

The guards run to our door, which now opens with a wave of their pass, and they disappear outside and run down the stairs. As the door lies open, about to slide back into place any moment, we emerge from behind the rovers, everyone breathing a sigh of relief.

'That was close,' Jay says, wiping his sweaty brow.

'We'd better wait in here until the guards are definitely gone,' I say, and the other two agree.

For once, a sensible decision.

But as we're about to settle down for a short wait, someone runs through the closing door.

11

Breaking in, breaking everything

'Hercus!' I shout the moment the door closes. 'You came!'

She smiles as she jogs over. 'Couldn't leave you stuck down here.'

'Did you distract the guards?' Jay asks, looking impressed.

'Yeah, chucked a chair down the stairwell, so it crashed at the bottom. Waited one level up until they ran down, and then I snuck in here.'

'Genius!' I say, and I give her a quick hug round her waist.

As I step back, she shrugs, her cheeks going red. 'Well, you're my friend. And you were in trouble. Anyone would do it.'

'Nope,' says Quasar, shaking her head.

'Well, maybe not you…' I start to dig at her but stop myself as I need them all on board now. I don't want to mess up this chance.

'Okay, so we wait a few minutes until it's all clear outside, then we go down to sub-9 and see what's happening in R&R.'

Everyone nods.

I want to ask Hercus what changed her mind, but for now I'm just happy she's here, so I don't spoil the moment and let Jay tell her all about the Perseverance mission. She nods politely as he recalls facts that Hercus probably already knows.

She's a great friend.

T's confirmed to me that the stairway is clear – he can sense vibrations of the footsteps on the metal stairs - so we leave the museum and move downstairs, our wrist-pad lights back on.

We reach sub-9. Still alone. Still silence all around. Jay is rubbing his arms and shivering. Darshi is really cutting back on things.

'Hurry up and let us in, then,' Quasar says, nudging Jay.

He pulls out the multi-pass and swipes it on the pad.

The door to the experimental science lab slides open, and the slicing sound makes me shudder. The sterile, chemical air is different from the artificial, recycled air in the rest of the base. It stings my nose a little. Another warning that I shouldn't be here. That this is both dangerous and stupid. I don't need T to tell me that right now.

I scan the various bright yellow signs around the lab.

Flammable.

Corrosive.

Highly explosive.

Seems to sum up this whole situation pretty well to me.

The space is massive with long lab benches, Perspex screens, and signs hanging down from the high roof, indicating each section in the open-plan lab. The signs sway. Must be the ventilation.

Each of us is drawn to different sections – Jay to *Technology*, Hercus to *Engineering*, and Quasar to *Animal Testing*.

I go straight to *Martian Artefacts*.

This section is incredible – behind glass containers I find a floating, cloudy orb, a small skeleton (non-human?), and a large, decaying book.

I want to open the cases to every one of the objects in here, especially the book. Who wrote that? And why is it on Mars? It looks ancient. And the cloudy orb is a bit creepy. Maybe for another time.

And could the skeleton be an animal…or something else. We've found some sub-terranean species up here; Oxide Vipers, Titanium Terrors (don't ask!), Chromium Caterpillars (which the vipers love to eat when they can't get any human!), and Magnesium Peckers (small bird-like creatures which peck at the magnesium deposits in the Pits).

But no matter how fascinating everything is – and I could spend weeks down here looking at them - I'm drawn to one object over all others.

In the final case, the largest of all, is the blade I pulled from the Martian rock. I notice so much about it that I missed the first time around; the metal shimmers, a morphing, ever-changing, rainbow colour, and yet silver at the same time.

The hairs on my arms begin to spark again. Or maybe I'm imagining that. But the fluttering in my stomach is definitely there. I remember the feeling of flying high above Mars. Of the power and the energy. It felt…more than Human… more than Martian…more than anything I could imagine in this whole galaxy...

Adrenaline levels spiking. Please step away from the sword.

A small note in the case says: 'Martian Excalibur?'

Eva, I really, really think you should reconsider. The energy readings coming from the blade are beyond most measurable scales. I also detect large doses of gamma radiation – prolonged exposure to the blade is dangerous.

I'm past the point of debate. This is happening.

My fingertips spark as I move my hand closer and closer to the glass case, like mini forks of lightning. Like the Van De Graaf machine in science.

I lift the sword off gently. It's vibrating. It hurts the bones of my hand to hold it. A piercing, high-pitched squeal, comes from the blade. I can't see properly – there's a fog, like water vapour or …

Ghosts. They appear all around me, closing in, slowly. They grow brighter as the room dims, their shapes becoming more defined. Like bioluminescent people, but the wrong shape, and much smaller. Alien. Definitely alien.

Ghosts of Mars.

They close in.

Around me, I'm vaguely aware of red, flashing lights. And shouts from my friends. A loudspeaker announcement drifts into the room, too. But all this sensory input has been filtered.

Every neuron in my body is focused on two things only: the ghosts and the blade. They are connected.

As I step closer, the connection deepens. Electrical impulses surge back and forth, from tip to hilt, fluid and co-ordinated.

I am one with the sword, and the sword is one with me.

I grab the hilt and my hand is all crackles and singed hair, and the power returns, even stronger than before. I can see beyond this room, the whole base, the whole planet. I'm connected to every living thing; the humans, Martians, plants, bacteria and even the ghosts…their spirits are connected to mine through the sword.

And then she's here…almost exactly like the photo in my bedroom.

'Mum?'

She smiles but shakes her head slowly.

'But…but…you look just like her…'

Bring the sword to me. This blade is the downfall and the saviour of Dad. His fall and rise. You must get it to me.

I lift the blade up, electricity swarming the multi-coloured metal. 'Why?'

I need your help. Dad needs your help. You're my only hope. You're Mars' only hope.

'Who are you? And how can *I* help you?' The sword starts to vibrate in my hands, suddenly feeling heavy, where before it was light. My arms shake and drops of sweat fall from my face, sizzling on the blade.

She shakes her head.

Come to me.

'But how will I find you?'

The sword will guide you...once you learn to control it.

'I can control it. Look.' The sword begins to slip from my grasp, tendrils of electricity spiralling out, all around the room, like reverse lightning, coming from me and my blade.

Control.

Then she's gone.

I'm suddenly conscious of the room again, and what's happening around me. Hercus, Jay and Quasar are huddled beneath the large central workbench, holding each other, and shielding their eyes from the blinding light emanating from the sword.

The red lights still flash, the voice still blaring from the loudspeaker.

Oh no.

It's Dad. Guilt rises from my fingertips up to my heart and when it settles, my connection to the sword severs.

For a millisecond, everything is silent, dark and calm.

Except for the energy surging from the blade and from…me.

Then the whole world explodes, and I'm lifted from my feet and slammed into a wall.

And everything becomes truly silent and dark.

12

The Decline of Dad

'Her e-Pancreas isn't just broken now. It's welded to her surrounding organs.'

I keep my eyes closed but focus beyond the cloud of drowsiness that's swamping me. I want to hear every word of Dr Vane's. I need to know just *how* much trouble I'm in.

'How?' Dad asks.

'High current. High resistance. Her body became so hot on the surface, she burnt through most of her clothes. So, imagine the heat on the inside. Melted away the metal and the nanocarbon elements and fused them to tissue and organs. Her liver and intestine, especially. We will need to do a procedure to remove the broken e-Pancreas and to repair the damaged tissues. But not immediately as there's been too much internal bleeding - I've stopped it for now, but she needs to heal and reduce the swelling before I do the procedure.'

'Will she be okay? You know, with her diabetes?'

'Well, it's a worry because our supplies of insulin are low. The entire stock they sent up was destroyed in the explosion. The GM bacteria have served us well, but the fermenter was irreparably damaged last night. We need new cultures and new equipment, which aren't scheduled for another two years.'

'But will she live?'

'For now. Once I perform the procedure, she can resume her old treatment of manual injections and blood glucose testing. But until then, she must take it extremely easy and let her organs heal. The inflammation will be bad for at least a week. And very painful. No duties, no academy.'

'I'm not sure she'll accept that.'

'Her life could be in danger if she does not rest. I'd suggest keeping her here, but I worry she'd sneak out again.'

'Okay, house arrest it is. I can control her a little more there. Fewer ways to escape and I can revoke her access card for now.'

'Very good, sir. And maybe we could take the old fermenter from the museum, the one that her mum…that Ora built. If I can get someone with mechanic expertise, I'm sure we could get it up and running again.'

'Do it. Listen, I'll be back shortly – I have a disciplinary meeting now with our new Co-commander.' Dad lowers his head.

If my abdomen wasn't in such agony, I'm sure it would tickle with guilty, rampant butterflies.

'Why you, sir? What did you do?'

'She is my daughter. And I have been a poor dad. I have to take responsibility.'

I want to scream out that he's not a poor dad. That this is all my fault. But I don't have the energy. But I will make it up to Dad. By saving his life.

'I have to say, sir, that you're looking remarkably good, and sprightly considering your injuries.'

'Well, these braces have helped very much, but I'll also be delighted to get them off soon.'

After a moment of silence, Vane continued. 'Do we know when full power will be restored? I'm struggling to keep things running here on back-up.'

'Sorry, I don't know, doctor. But be assured, the medical wing will be one of the first to get full power restored.'

He brushes hair from my face and smooths it back over my skull, repeatedly. I enjoy the contact, the tenderness, the attention. The warmth in his hand is nice.

Then it stops.

'I must go. Alert me if anything changes.' He marches out and I hear the door open, then close.

I risk opening my eyes a little, straining to see where Vane is. She's at her desk, typing into the terminal.

Glancing around, I realise I'm not the only one in here. There are twelve others, in varying states of consciousness on their beds. Three of them are awake and staring at me like they want to kill me. I have a private booth, but the rest are all in the main ward.

I clamp my eyes closed again. What have I done? Is the power out and all these people hurt because of me?

'T?'

No reply. I hope I haven't fried the chip again. Poor T.

I just want to escape here. Shut out all my thoughts about the sword. Get the next shuttle to Earth. Start a new life. I've spent my whole life feeling trapped here, but never more than right now.

I lie for a long time, eyes closed, pretending to sleep, pretending that nobody is staring so hard and with so much hate, they're practically scorching me with it. The solar radiation outside must feel like a gentle tickle compared to this.

I wonder if they know I can hear what they're saying.

'Such a priv.'

'No regard for any of us workers.'

'Her or her father.'

'First Martianborn. Big deal. No regard for any of us, the way she acts.'

'Lucky the whole station didn't blow.'

'Nearly killed her friends, too.'

The last comment makes me gasp.

I resist the urge to sit up and ask immediately. If they're injured, they must be in here somewhere. They'll never forgive me either. I dragged them all with me. All for that stupid sword. It's done nothing but cause me, and others, harm.

And yet my mind is thinking of very little else.

There must be a reason I found it. That it speaks to me.

There has to be a reason I'm here. Stuck on Mars. The first Martianborn, the best-known person on either Earth or Mars, yet I have no purpose, no reason.

I just leach resources and money and cause trouble and endanger others.

A negative reel of images flicker through my drowsy mind as a soft swooshing noise indicates another IV dose of morphine...and I slowly drift off.

My friends float in and out of my unconscious mind.

But wait, if I'm unconscious, how can I see them? And now, Mum. Why her? Why always her? My heart pangs, again weird if I'm sleeping.

Mum takes off from the surface of Mars and flies high above the base. I follow and realise I'm still in my hospital gown...a sharp panic and elevated heart rate are sharp reminders that I can't be asleep.

This isn't real...the sword in one hand, I glide behind the

ghost of my mother, soaring over the Martian terrain. I've no idea how long we've been flying but there's a mountain range ahead and Mum descends. Following with an unnatural control of flight, I land next to her, at the mouth to a huge cave, at the foot of one of the mountains.

She points inside.

I try to speak but can't. I shake my head.

She nods. **I need you. Only you can save me. The fall has begun, but you need the sword for the rise.**

She holds out her hand and I take it. Every single atom in my body vibrates with overwhelming euphoria and I want to freeze this moment, to encase it in carbonite, and hold on forever.

I am touching my mother's hand! It's so smooth, and warm, but strong and firm.

She leads me to the dark opening…then the ghosts pour out, faces a mix of human-like and deeply alien. Some are laughing, delighted, others fill me with fear. They surround us, closing in, pushing us further from the cave.

Mum's outline becomes less clear, and starts to dissolve, like she's being blown away.

I yell at her to stay as the ghosts keep coming, their faces turning into feral, angry, alien beasts.

I run, then fly. They don't follow, remaining by the cave opening. Luckily, I have the sword, or I'd never have escaped.

Then I'm falling. The sword is gone, and I flap furiously, like a bird in a storm. Terror rips at my shrunken lungs as I try desperately to breathe. My body curls and every muscle hardens, preparing for impact.

I scream.

'Eva?' A large hand shakes me.

'Hey, wake up. You were dreaming.' Hercus' voice penetrates my frightened brain.

She stands over me, in a medical gown. Then tilts her head, eyebrows close. 'What is happening with you?'

I can't speak and gulp down some water from my bedside table, taking a few seconds to ground myself back in reality.

'I don't know, Hercus. I really don't know…'

'You mean you can't tell me?' She crossed her arms.

'No, I would tell you. I just don't know myself.'

'Really? You seemed to know exactly what you were doing just before you fried us all. Before you fried the whole damn base.' She shakes her head and takes a deep breath. 'Listen, just rest. The fact that you're alive is a miracle. But I won't lie, you're in big trouble and so are we. My dad went berserk, and poor Jay has been getting it bad from the commander.'

'Co-commander. My Dad is still jointly in charge.'

'Yeah, but for how long after this? Anyway, I only came in because you were screaming, and no-one else wanted to go near you. You're okay now, so I'll catch you later.'

'Wait…Hercus?'

She turns at the door. 'Get some rest, Eva.'

She closes the door to my cubicle, cutting off the noise of the machines outside. The constant beeping was a comfort. The dead silence is not.

Suddenly, I grab the bedpan and empty my stomach into it. My throat burns, my tongue feels hairy. The contents are green, with white specks, like mould growing on algae.

I lie back, my body soaked from the nightmare, the confrontation and the sickness. I twist to sip more water but the sharp tug from my catheter is too much, and I flop down and close my eyes.

I am the first Martianborn. The Daughter of Mars – the most famous person in the Solar System. Everyone knows my name, but no-one wants to know me.

Earth won't have me.

Mars hates me.
My colony blame me.
My father is losing everything.
Because of me.
And I have never felt more alone.

13

The New Normal

The last few days have sucked.

Actually, that's totally understating it. It has been the worst few days of my whole miserable, Martian life. Quasar and Hercus managed to avoid any major injuries, but I wasn't so lucky. Stuck in the hospital wing, with a surgery scheduled for next week to unfuse my metal e-pancreas, which is welded to my internal tissues.

Pain meds are keeping me from doubling over in the meantime.

But yesterday was the worst day. I saw Jay in the hospital wing, and he was in a wheelchair, his legs completely crushed by a MOXIE machine that fell on him. Multiple fractures, torn ligaments. It'll take months to heal, and he'll need electronic braces fitted in the meantime so he can get around. The base is not very wheelchair friendly.

Everyone stares, and I don't know if it's because of what I did, or because of what I've become: a resident of The Pits. Proper hero to zero stuff. I never wanted to be a celebrity for the right reasons, and now I'm famous for all the wrong ones.

So, yeah, my break-in nearly shut down the entire base and killed everyone. But of course, Dad somehow made a deal to save me, but the consequences were harsh. On him, I mean. I totally deserve it. He got demoted so we had to move out of the command accommodation and into a tiny pod in The Pits. And I have to do this apology, live on a transmission across the base, and back to Earth.

I've barely seen Dad – he does what he always does in a bad situation – he buries himself in his work. And this time, he is literally burying himself in it. Because he's working in the mines. And I'm sure that's fine, I'm sure he's safe, but still …

I have no-one to hang out with because all four of us who broke into the research lab are now grounded. Classes and meals only. No other wandering or "deviation". Well, except to do the detentions Darshi has promised.

And to make sure we comply? She's made us wear ankle trackers until we can prove we're trustworthy. She insisted, despite Dad's protests. Except Jay, for obvious reasons.

T is gone. Forever. Well, unless I somehow get the 3D printer back. And the laptop—with all my programmes, including T's personality algorithm—is gone, too. Darshi took everything from us, and the consequences keep coming.

'Eva, it's time to face the music.' Darshi smiles as though she's savouring every moment of this.

I follow her to the door of Bick Clait's studio, the media room on the ground level. To my surprise, I see Hercus. Don't tell me she has to do this stupid apology, too?

'This is your way to repay the colony. Make a good impression and we may well bring the investors back and regain their confidence – that your accident lost for us!' Darshi has a mixture of amusement and anger on her lips. This is the worst punishment of all, and she knows it. She also knows I can't refuse. 'Hercus Armstrong, as a co-conspirator, and another popular figure for our sponsors and the people back on Earth, I think it would look good to have you at Eva's side.'

I notice that Quasar isn't included in this ridiculous live apology. Or Jay. But after what I've done to him, that's fair. And Quasar didn't do as much damage as Hercus and me.

Shoulders slumped, we trudge inside to see Bick Clait, official photographer, editor of Solar News, and the head of the colony's social media channels, looking as self-satisfied as Darshi.

I've been the subject of far too many of Clait's reports already, especially when I was younger. 'Dad's had at least twenty arguments with Bick about things she's written about me,' I say to Hercus.

'Same.' Hercus shrugs like it's nothing, but I can see she's as reluctant as me to do this.

'And she lies. Or at least twists the truth.'

'Always.'

'What's up?' I ask. 'Apart from having to do this cringe.'

Herc shrugs again, but this time she stops and looks at me. 'I dunno. I just wish sometimes someone would say something good about me that isn't only about my strength. Like, I can do so much other stuff. I'm clever, always work hard, and I'm a good friend. But nobody ever mentions that or says, "well done, Hercus" for anything except lifting stupid rovers!'

'You are a good friend. You came and saved us in the Museum. And the other stuff, too. You always stick with me, even when I do thoughtless stuff. I'm sorry about it all, by the way. The stuff in the lab. I don't know what happened.'

'It's fine,' she replies.

The crushing feeling of the last few, lonely days begins to

lift. 'And trust me, I know what it's liked to be labelled and never get rid of it.' I smile, and she returns it.

'True. If anyone knows how it feels, it's you.' Her mood seems to lift as walk on – her shoulders high, her strides longer, her neck straight.

'So, what ridiculous photoshoot will she come up with this time?' Herc asks.

'Dunno but anything has to be better than that Christmas one!' We both laugh.

'Yeah, I thought it was bad when she made me Santa.' Hercus smiles. 'Ho, ho, ho.' We laugh again. 'But when you came in dressed as Rudolph with that big, flashy red nose…it nearly killed me.'

Darshi returns and snaps her fingers, and we silently fall in line behind her.

Bick Clait has two chairs set up about a metre apart and facing each other. Ring-lights sit above each as do four cameras, facing the chairs from different angles.

She smiles widely as we enter. 'Do come in.' She pats the chair next to her. 'You sit here, Eva.'

When she smiles, her tongue sticks out between her teeth. She's dressed in non-standard clothing, like fancy people on Earth wear. They call them dresses. And it's a particularly ugly one, with bright red flowers.

'You can change into these in a moment, girls.' She points to two more dresses, hanging just behind her. Both similar to hers, one with small rovers patterned on it and one with small astronauts.

'No thanks,' Hercus says politely, clearly unimpressed by the rover pattern.

Darshi steps in. 'You will wear those dresses and you will

act like you enjoy it, too.'

'I'd rather clean the sewers,' I say, crossing my arms. I don't care how much trouble I'm in, I won't be dressing up for Darshi's amusement.

'Well, we can arrange that, too, Eva. But first, please take your transmission script from Bick. You will read it word for word. No alterations. Or else sewers will be considered a light punishment compared to what I'll do. It seems like you don't care what happens to you, but what about your friends?' She smiles again, sucking her breath between the gap in her front teeth. 'Or your dad?'

I turn away from her, clenching my shaking hands into fists and pressing them into my thighs. I know the astronaut dress is for me. She knows it's what I want, and she has the power to decide if I get it. I hate her.

'Here you are, dear.' Bick hands me a sheet of paper, entitled **Eva's Humble Apology**.

I want to rip it up into tiny pieces and throw them into Darshi's face, and I grab it so tightly the sides begin to crumple.

'Softly does it, Eva. We don't want to you destroy anything else.' Darshi narrows her eyes.

Every word from her poisoned mouth makes me want to storm out, but the threat of consequences for Hercus, and even Quasar and Jay, as well as Dad, keep me quiet.

Hercus and I sit with our dresses on, and I hold the paper, ready to read. I can barely open my eyes under the big, bright lights shining on us, and all the cameras are making me dizzy.

'I feel sick.' Hercus lays a steadying hand on my shoulder, and I swallow down the bile which is rising into my throat.

'Now dears, nice big smiles for the cameras, sit upright

and keep your eyes on me if you're unsure. I'll direct you as we go.' Bick turns to Darshi, who nods. 'Okay, my lovelies, we go live to the Solar System in five, four, three, two…' And then she stops speaking and I see her hold up one finger, then none.

She holds her thumbs up.

I freeze. I know I should be reading the statement, but I stare at Darshi instead, tempted for a second to refuse and spoil her game.

But Hercus nudges me in the ribs, and nods. So, I stare down at the paper and begin to read. For her, not Darshi:

'Good sol to all humans, both Earthborn and Martianborn alike.' I know she put in the Martianborn bit just to remind everyone I'm different.

My mouth is so dry, but I swallow and continue. 'My name is Eva Knight. Many of you know me as the first to be born on Mars. I take that responsibility seriously, and as such, my recent actions, which have brought dishonour to Mariner Base, my father and the…' I swallow hard again. '…exemplary commander Darshi, who has helped show me the error of my ways in the last few days. I fully understand now that my choices reflect poorly on the whole colony, and I wish to take full responsibility for the recent power failure, and the number of lives I endangered with my own selfish actions.'

The bile shoots up my throat again. It's in my mouth and my cheeks expand, struggling to hold it all in.

But somehow, I manage and swallow it back down. My mouth tastes disgusting, and I want to get out of here. Sweat is running down my nose from my forehead, and as it drops onto my lips, I taste the slightly salty fluid.

I spot Darshi, aggressively pointing at me. Hercus stares at me, worried. Bick keeps pointing to her mouth and indicating for me to smile.

I worry if I open my mouth again, I won't be able to keep my lunch down.

And I'm live to whole base. I'm live to the whole of planet Earth.

Hercus takes the sheet of paper from me and continues to read. I hear her voice saying the words meant for me. More apologies. More humiliation.

Darshi looks like she could burst, her face turning more and more red with each passing second of my silence.

'…Eva and I are both deeply sorry. And we can assure everyone back on Earth, and on the base, that this will never—'

And then, in the middle of the live broadcast to every human in the Solar System, I vomit.

A purple and yellow stream of half-digested cabbage and potatoes erupts from my mouth and sprays the floor in front of us, splashing the camera lenses and the bottom of my dress. No shame there.

As I force out the last of the bile, I suddenly feel better. I use the sleeve of my dress to wipe the sweat from my face and I stand up, smiling.

I know I'm going to regret what I do next, but it's going to feel so good to do it.

Every person in the room is statue-still.

I move closer to the camera, staring at Darshi.

'I am not sorry. Not even a little bit.' And I walk out of the media room, throwing off my dress as I leave.

But with every step I hear whispers of regret. I've only gone and made things worse for me and everyone else involved, including Dad. That last thought extinguishes the last bit of angry fire in me, and I run into a bathroom, sinking into a small ball, hoping no-one ever finds me.

14

A New Assignment

The class is silently copying down the step-by-step procedures for a safe surface walk, and everyone knows it's because of me. It's like the new commander wants everyone to hate me as much as she does. And it's working.

She walks back and forth, upright, and rigid. Inflexible and unmalleable, like the metals we studied in Mars geology class.

Jay sits in the front row with Hercus, and I'm glad they've become friends. She's been helping him around the base since they installed his bionic legs. I can't look at him for more than a second, as the shame threatens to engulf me like a black hole. I know he'll be able to walk again one sol, as I imagine the pain he's gone through, I swallow and turn my head aside.

Quasar sits near me, not saying much, but that feels bigger than Jupiter right now. I wish it was because she was being a friend, but since the accident, none of the kids want anything to do with the four of us.

But I am enemy number one. Darshi has made sure everyone knows we've had funding cut because of my outburst on the live transmission, and so every shortage of power, heating, supplies, and food is blamed on me. They've even threatened to abandon the whole base, or replace the command, if it doesn't get sorted out ASAP. Yet another reason for Darshi to hate me.

Everyone else on the base gives me evil looks, every minute of every sol. I wonder for how long, but I suppose it's forever. I'm stuck here, on this red, dead planet. No mum, no dad and no T. Mars has more life on its surface, than I have inside me.

There's a growing panic inside me about losing Dad. I don't know why, it's not like he's going anywhere. The commander's evil glares increase that feeling of impending doom.

And so, my mind is never far from the sword. It's eating me up inside, since the accident especially, that I must get that sword. It has the power to help me do…anything. If I want to get out of stupid detentions and cut off this ankle tag. Done. If I want to escape Mars. Done. If I want to save Dad. Done.

It's not logical, and T would say so, but I trust that Mum-Ghost and what she said. She looked different to the others.

I pack up silently and leave the classroom and take the lift back down to my lonely, silent pod in the Pits, my head down, my favourite album (T plays it for me, grudgingly – he doesn't appreciate modern music) drowning out any noise or comments that might be coming my way. I learnt that first sol out of hospital - what you can't hear, can't hurt you.

But I can see their lips moving.

'Our biggest celebrity, off home to the Pits. Where she belongs.'

'Superstar Eva Knight. Super jerk, more like.'

It's been the same comments for sols, and they do hurt, but I won't let them see it.

I burst into our pod and bury my face in my pillow, crying and then punching it because I'm annoyed at myself for letting them get to me. At Darshi for making it all worse, and blaming me. At being stuck on this stupid planet and never being able to leave.

I wake up from a nap I never meant to take and hear people talking quietly. The door is slightly ajar and from my bed I can see two figures. I keep my eyes closed enough that they'll think I'm still asleep, but open enough to see their outlines.

Commander Darshi stands just on the threshold, speaking to Dad.

'Linton, I am truly sorry about all that's happened in recent sols. It gave me no pleasure whatsoever to demote you. However, I have an opportunity for you. Which could help you make some amends. To show your value as a potential leader again in the future.'

'Anything, commander, anything. My loyalty lies with Mariner Base, and I'll always do whatever I can to serve it.'

My heart sinks knowing it's my fault he's in this position.

'We've received strange readings from a location a few sols drive from here. From inside a strange network of underground tunnels, which indicate the possible presence of ice and higher than usual oxygen levels. Plus, a strange power source. We need someone with your experience to lead an away team to investigate. Are you up for it?'

His chest swells as he stands as straight as a rocket. 'Absolutely, commander. You can count on me.'

'Good. Assemble a team. You leave immediately. There's still reports of that dust storm coming in, so it will be a quick turnaround to get back to base. Not a moment to lose.'

He salutes. She nods and leaves.

When he turns his head, he's beaming. I've almost never seen him so happy. Or is it relief at getting a second chance? Either way, I'm so, so happy, too.

He immediately leaves the apartment, picking up the colony directory list, which sits on the back of every door. He must be off to pick his team.

I remain still on my bed for a long time. 'I wonder why she came down here and didn't tell Dad upstairs.'

I say it out loud, hoping for a response from T. But I only get silence and more time alone with my own thoughts. Maybe it's better for Dad to get away. If he's not around, he can't be blamed for the things I do.

A message pings on my wrist-pad.

Eva Knight – report to sub-level 11 waste recycling for your colony service detail

Detention. Great.

I push myself out of bed and take the stairs down to waste recycling, imagining being knee deep in human waste for the next few hours.

I am not disappointed.

When I arrive, Quasar and Herc are already there, in the lime green wading suits that they use down here to walk in the sewage pipes. One of the hole covers has been opened and the smell that comes out makes me retch. My mouth opens wide like a fish, over and over.

'Welcome, Eva.' I recognise the person who's supervising us. She's spoken to me a few times and is always asking me how I am. I think she was friends with Mum.

'Hi Rosie.' I wave awkwardly, knowing I shouldn't smile as this is a punishment.

But she smiles back. 'Just one more to arrive and then we

can get started. One hour of good old colony service. We don't get too many kids down here. Your dad was much more lenient than the new commander. Here, Eva, put these on.' She hands me a wading suit.

I grit my teeth at her saying 'new commander' but ignore it. No point in arguing with Rosie. She's nice and I don't want to make this detention any worse.

The straps sit on my shoulder and the suit itself covers me from my feet up to my chest. I really hope I'm not in chest deep human excrement today.

Herc and Quasar haven't spoken to me, nor even looked in my direction. It's my fault they're here, so yeah, that figures. Plus, last time I saw Herc I vomited on her feet, live, in front of the whole solar system.

'Hey,' I try.

Hercus turns and nods but then turns away again. Quasar smiles, but then walks a few steps further away. It's been awkward like this since the accident. And then my outburst, which just made things even worse for us all.

The elevator beeps, breaking the awkward silence, and out comes Jay.

As he struggles into his wading suit, I have to look away.

'How do they work?' Quasar asks.

Jay's eyes widen. 'I'm glad you asked. People haven't asked and I am getting annoyed as I've learned everything about them.'

Quasar smiles and puts her hands on her hips. 'Well?'

'Oh yeah, right. So, they are essentially fixed to my legs via microscrews that they drill into my femur, tibia, and fibula bones. I think I have sixteen on each leg.'

'Ouch,' says Quasar.

'No, it was fine, all done under anaesthetic, and I've hardly felt it since.'

I squirm as he talks, genuinely desperate to get into the sewer to avoid hearing about what my stupid actions have done to Jay.

'And then they insert tiny electrodes that connect with the nervous system and synchronise my legs to move when I fire a neuron thinking it. Pretty cool, huh?' He looks over to me and his smile disappears. 'It's nearly as good as walking to be honest. I just get tired more easily as my legs are still healing.'

I can't even look back at him as he's being so nice about it. I think I'd rather he was angry with me.

In the end, they find an extra-large set of waders for Jay, as the leg-fixations are too wide to fit into normal ones.

Quasar nudges Hercus. 'Hey look, it's the not-so-jolly, green giant!'

Jay laughs and we all join in, breaking the tight silence.

'I can't believe she gave you this detention duty, considering,' Quasar adds.

'Well, my mum isn't known for her kindness. Said it would be an abuse of her position to give me a different task as I'm equally to blame, apparently.' His eyes rest momentarily on me, and I look down.

'Well, let's get started then,' chimes in Rosie, clapping her hands together.

After a lengthy explanation on how to unclog the sub-pipes that branch from the main one, we descend the ladder into the main sewage pipe, which is about six feet away and seems to go on forever in either direction. Dull lamps reflect on the dark surface of the sewage, which flows slowly along, transporting the sludge towards the machines that will eventually extract the liquid, sterilise it and recycle it for our water supplies. The solid left-overs are compacted, dried out and taken to the hydroponics and farming levels to be used as fertiliser.

The hole cover closes above us. Rosie has come down, too. 'I'll just clear some of the pipes this way. You four can head downstream. Be easier for you. Back here in thirty minutes.'

And we're left alone, with half an hour of pipe de-clogging ahead of us.

'She's way too happy about working with faeces every sol, isn't she?' Quasar says, scraping some clogged waste from a narrow pipe.

It splashes in the river just in front of me, and I retch again. Even with the nose clips we were given, only taking tiny breaths through the mask over my mouth, I can taste the rotten, decomposing waste of a two-hundred-person colony with each gasp.

What's worse than wading through sewage is that no-one is talking to me. They occasionally mutter to each other, but I'm never included. There's a huge hole inside of me with T gone and Dad about to leave. I need to win back my friends.

'Did you feel that?' Hercus asks.

'What?' asks Quasar.

'The sewage level. It's rising!'

I look down and I think she's right. It seems a little higher. I stare ahead, and then behind where the sewage comes from. A small wave splashes into my waist.

'It's definitely rising,' I say. 'We should get out of here.'

'Oh, should we lightning girl? Who put you in charge? The last time you told us what to do, we all nearly died. How about you let us decide what we want to do from now on.' Quasar turns to Hercus and Jay.

'She's not wrong.' Hercus turns to me. 'We should get out, it's about ten centimetres higher than when we started. I'm okay but you lot are not as tall as me.'

'Fine, let's go.' Quasar leads us back towards the ladder we came down on.

'Hey, something just moved past my leg,' Quasar shouts.

All four of us freeze and stare at the sewage flow closely.

'Might just have been a big piece of poo, Quasar.' Jay smiles.

She narrows her eyes. 'Yeah, maybe. Let's go.'

Each step is harder now, going against the current, which seems to be getting faster. And the sewage thicker. Jay is really struggling, with his new leg-fixations probably not designed for this.

But when I stop, it's not because of the current.

A bright silhouette rises behind me, and as the others round the bend away from me, I slowly turn on the spot, my right hand shaking like a Marsquake.

The sharp features slowly round and become more human-like, and then there she is. The same ghost who told me to lift the sword.

'What do you want?' I whisper. 'I've lost everything because of that sword. What was the point?'

You will know when the time is right to reclaim the blade. And then find me. It will save your father.

'How will I know when? How will it save him?'

But her features dissolve and the silhouette sinks beneath the rising sewage.

'EVA!' Hercus' voice echoes from round the corner, as she sloshes into sight. She spots me standing, still shaking, staring at something which is no longer there. 'Are you okay?'

I turn to her. 'Hercus, I'm seeing things. Ghosts. One of them is telling me to do things.'

'There's no ghosts here, Eva. Come on, we have to leave.' She's gentle with her response, but it's clear she doesn't believe me.

She's my closest friend. I must make her believe me. I

can't deal with this alone. 'It was the ghost that told me to get the sword. It said it would save Dad.'

Hercus shakes her head. 'We don't have time for this, Eva. There's no such things as ghosts. You can't blame them for what you did.'

'Why won't you believe me?' I shout. 'I won't move until you say you believe me!'

'That's enough.' And Hercus grabs me round the waist, flings me on her shoulder and starts to wade back to the ladder.

I don't have the strength to fight back, and it would be pointless anyway.

'Hercus, you need to listen…'

'Enough, Eva. No more lies.' She sets me down and stands behind me to force me to walk forward.

'I feel something. And it's not a big piece of poo.' Whatever it is, it's circling my legs, bumping against the waders. 'Is there anything down here? Anything that lives in the sewage?'

Hercus shrugs. 'Come on.' And she grabs my hand to haul me forward, but as she does, something pulls her under. The movement is so hard and forceful that her face smashes off the surface.

And then she is gone. The sewage ripples and twice her arm crashes through the surface before being pulled back down.

I force myself under. As I do, something wraps around my arm and I get such a fright, I momentarily freeze.

I can't breathe. I kick and my feet brush the bottom of the pipe, then I dig in my gloved hands, trying to get some grip on the sloppy pipe, but it's no use. They have me too tight and are dragging me somewhere.

Panic kicks in, and my chest feels ready to burst open, I get a surge of energy. Maybe it's adrenaline or maybe they've loosened their grip, but I get free and rip my arms and legs away from the slithering snakes.

Then a strong hand grips my arm, then another loops around my waist. It must be Hercus. So, I grab her back and push upwards. At first, we don't move, but then slowly we begin to move up, finally breaking the surface and I take the best breath ever. My head spins like I've been in a 3G rocket simulator.

Hercus rips two snakes from her knees, pulling them off like they are toys rather than strong, living animals. She throws them far down the tunnel.

Finally, we splash back to the ladder and we both climb out and back into the clean air outside the pipe.

'Thank you,' says Hercus as we lie on the ground.

I nod, hoping this will help her forgive me.

As Rosie puts the cover back on, the stench lessens slightly. We're all still covered in it though, and I watch as the others slide out of their waders.

'Oxide Vipers in the sewage. We've never had that in my time. Are you all okay?' Rosie is as white as a sheet of sub-surface ice, and mostly directs her gaze at me. 'Eva and Hercus, take a decontamination shower, then please report to Doctor Vane and get a check-up. You'll have been exposed to all sorts of microbes down there. I mean, it's been treated and diluted, but it's still not nice. Lucky you had the masks and nose clips.'

'Yeah, really *lucky*! I am *never* going down there again,' declares Quasar. 'Not if they made me commander of this whole base or queen of the whole universe. Not a chance. Worst detention ever!'

'Agreed,' Jay sits down, resting his bionic legs

'Did none of you see or hear it?' I ask quietly, conscious of Hercus staring at me and narrowing her eyes.

'See what?' Jay asks.

'The ghost?'

Quasar laughs, Jay raises his eyebrows, and Hercus just shakes her head.

'You're kidding, princess. We're imagining ghosts again, are we?'

'Not imagining it. They're real.'

Quasar laughs again. 'You've got to be kidding me. We nearly got drowned in human poop, got attacked by oxide vipers, and you're talking about ghosts. You need a time out, Eva, seriously.' She walks away to the showers.

Jay also leaves, heading the boy's side to shower.

I walk silently with Hercus, shadowing Quasar, when she turns to me. 'Eva, I've been your friend for a long time, but I don't know what's got into you recently. You know you can tell me the real problem, right? What's causing all this stuff? Is it about the astronaut thing?'

'No, honestly Herc. There are ghosts. Lots of them. It's not the first time I've seen them, but this one keeps speaking to me. And she looks just like…my mum.'

Hercus eyebrows unfurrow. 'I know you wish you knew your mum, Eva, but her ghost isn't here speaking to you. You need to accept how things are, and that's the astronaut thing, too. You can't change the past or things that aren't in your control.'

She marches off, but then slows at the door to the changing room. 'Thank you, again. That was scary back there, and you could easily have run and left me.'

I shrug. 'That's what friends do, right?'

She smiles and disappears.

I decide to stand in the shower for a while after the others leave. I don't want to spend any more time with people today.

After I've been given the all-clear from Dr Vane and taken

the handful of antibiotics she hands me, I arrive back home. I'm relieved to see the pod is empty, dark, and quiet. Has Dad gone already? Without saying goodbye? Maybe I should stay awake and wait, but I'm too tired.

I flop down on my bed, fully clothed, stinking, and exhausted, and fall straight asleep.

15

We all have Ghosts

I wake the next morning to find the pod empty.

Except for a note.

Dad loves a note. It means he can avoid any difficult conversations. Any time we argue, or I asked more about Mum or going back to Earth, he always leaves me a note afterwards.

Eva,

I had to do something big. I need to make sure the commander knows my worth. Both our positions in the colony are at stake. I've volunteered for a scouting mission. This is my chance to make amends. When you were young, I made it to commander after several successful missions as a mining and explorations officer. I think this makes it better for you, so I hope you'll understand. With me out of the picture, she'll be nicer to you, too. I also need some time on my own, concentrating on the one thing I was good at, so stay at home and recover. I'll be back soon, in time for your surgery. Lieutenant Boson is just next door if there's any emergencies, and of course commander Darshi is there for any bigger problems.

Love you infinity…plus one,

Dad

My heart hammers as I read the words a second time. He's gone. He's really gone. But I actually understand. I can't be mad because this is my fault.

He'll be fine. I repeat it over and over in my head to stay calm. Maybe this isn't what Dad will need saving from. Definitely not this.

And Darshi be nice to me? Come on, Dad. More chance of an oxide viper jumping over Deimos.

I'm disturbed by a knock at the door, and I stuff the small piece of paper into my pocket. 'Hello?'

'Hey, Eva. I'm supposed to take you up for our next detention. Let's check out your new place.' Quasar walks in, straight past me.

I'm tempted to stand my ground and tell her no, but the fight has gone out of me, and I'm still raw all over from the accident. And she's probably still mad at me, too.

She turns in a circle, in the centre of the pod. 'Wow, this is even suckier than ours.' She laughs. 'Must feel pretty different from that palace you had upstairs.'

And it sparks a small flicker of fight.

She holds her nose. 'Yuck, it still smells of auld Grady. That dude used to work in the sewage recycle, and he carried that whiff around the whole place with him. But he's left it bad in here.' She smiles, clearly looking for a rise. 'Though maybe it's just from you.'

I take a breath. I remember how much trouble I got her and the others in to, and I shrink a little.

'I don't mind it.' I shrug and sit down on my bed.

But then, without any chance of stopping them, the tears flood.

I bury my head in my arms, trying to stop Quasar seeing me like this. The last thing I need is people talking about Eva, the cry baby. I'm getting all that I deserve.

The bed sags a little on my left and an arm curls round my shoulder.

It catches me by surprise, and the tears stop.

I lift my head off my arms and take a breath, sucking a whole bunch of snot up my nose.

Quasar hands me a handkerchief. Or a really dirty piece of cloth, used to clean who knows what.

'Thanks,' I manage.

'Listen, why don't I show you around this palace? Show you the spots to avoid and the spots to really avoid? Before we go upstairs. We've got a bit of time.'

I laugh, and a little more snot comes out my nose.

Quasar jumps off the bed. 'Come on, then. Stop moping about here and let's see the world!'

'But don't you still hate me?'

'I spoke to Hercus. She told me what you did to help her in the tunnel. You're alright, Eva. Not great. But alright.' She laughs. 'Come on.'

We've been assigned to clean rovers for our next detention. Jay and Quasar got Rover 4 and Herc and I got Rover 5. Dad took Rovers 1 and 2 on the scouting mission – I couldn't help checking the log when we first came in here.

'This is drone work!' Jay moans. 'Honestly, first she puts us in the sewer and now we're cleaning dusty rovers that a drone could do in half the time. She's the devil!'

'That makes you the antichrist then,' Quasar laughs, spraying Jay with her hose.

He soaks her back and they begin a water fight to the death.

Herc and I focus on our assigned rover.

'Just as well they found that ice sheet, so we have plenty of water!' Hercus smiles, but I barely hear her. 'Hey, Eva, what's up? You've been rubbing the same spot for about five minutes now.' Hercus puts down her hose and walks round to me.

'It's nothing.' I've decided I'm not sharing anything with anyone from now on. I only get mocked and told I'm a liar.

I am not a liar. Well, not anymore.

'Okay, but I am here if you need to talk.' She moves back and continues washing her side.

The next two hours are spent cleaning the outside, the inside and the underside and tyres of all eight rovers in the bay. We also restock and repack all the food and water crates, the equipment packs, and the exo-suits (which are considerably nicer than the ones I've used before).

Lieutenant Boson has been watching us carefully and now wanders over. 'Okay, cadets, just give the floors a quick hose and that will do us for tonight. And get in under those grates there, too.' He points to the underfloor spaces where all the dust and muck has collected. It's going to be horrible in there.

'I'm going to get a coffee from the cafeteria, so I'll be back in ten minutes. Don't destroy the place while I'm gone.' His eyes rest on me, before he turns and marches out.

We lift the grates and start spraying the sunken spaces below the rovers, cleaning the concrete walls, and pushing all the dirt towards the tiny drainage hole in the corner.

Suddenly Jay drops his hose, and it starts spraying in all directions, soaking us all.

'Hey, watch it!' Quasar is about to spray him back but when she follows his gaze, she also drops her hose.

Hercus and I move closer and see what has frozen them.

'You're all seeing this, right?' I glance at each of them, the white, ethereal glow reflecting in their eyes, as they nod.

'Seeing, but not believing,' says Jay.

At least ten bright ghosts are flowing up through the

drainage holes beneath us, floating up and then hovering only a few feet away, towering over all of us, even Hercus.

For a long time, none of us speak, and they also remain still, only their long, oval heads moving from side to side, as though searching for something. Their mouths open and close, showing sharp, reptilian-like teeth. Their eyes blink with a double eyelid. Their seven-fingered hands point to the rovers.

They lead us to Rover 5 and then phase through the closed door.

'Now that is cool,' says Jay, his open mouth curling into a grin. 'Let's follow them inside.'

'Wait, we've just cleaned it,' says Hercus, putting an arm across him.

'Seriously, Herc? We shouldn't follow the mystery of the Ghosts of Mars, just so we don't mess up your cleaning?' Jay raises an eyebrow.

She shrugs and moves aside as Jay and Quasar slowly move to the door and open it.

I wait back with Herc, still unsure about the ghosts. Sometimes they seem helpful, particularly the one that looks like Mum. But other times they're dangerous and sinister.

'Wait!' I'm not sure which ghosts we're dealing with.

But they ignore me, and Jay and Quasar disappear inside. For a few seconds there is silence. We creep closer and peak into the rover.

The main lights are off, but the screen on the control panel emits a bright glow, even brighter than the ghosts themselves, who seem to be dulling. Jay and Quasar are standing over the screen staring at a map of Mars.

As I get closer, I see the ghosts are all pointing at one location.

'Where's that?' I ask, as much to the ghosts as my friends.

But the ghosts are silent and within a few seconds, they've disappeared, like fallen ash erupting from Olympus Mons that doesn't settle.

'I'm just checking,' Jay replies eventually. He jumps into the driver's seat, a little awkwardly on account of his bionic legs. The guilt worm squirms inside me again.

He looks so at home with a computer in front of him. He loves solving problems, unlike his mum, who just wants to get rid of any problems. I wonder how he grew up so different.

Although I suppose I'm not that much like my dad either. At least I don't think I am.

Jay interrupts my thoughts. 'Okay, this location is where the drone-copter found some unusual readings a few sols ago. It's a 'site of interest' apparently. It says your dad is leading a team there now, Eva?'

I nod. 'Yeah, he left earlier. That's why two of the rovers are logged out.'

'My dad's gone with him.' Hercus pops her head between us and looks at the screen. 'Said he'd be back in a few sols.'

'But why did the ghosts point at it?' I ask. 'Is it warning, do you think? Should we tell someone?'

'Eva, who would we tell? We can hardly tell my mum that ghosts pointed at a screen.' Jay runs his hand through his hair and lets out a long sigh.

'Yeah, he's right.' Quasar turns to me, looking serious for once. 'Eva, I'm sorry I didn't believe you.'

'Me, too,' adds Jay.

'And me.' Hercus puts her hand on my shoulder.

'Not important. What's more important is finding out why the ghosts think they're in danger and what we can do about it.'

It's only a few words from my friends, and Quasar, but I'm

already feeling infinity-times better. Someone else has seen them. I am not losing it. They are real.

'Wooooah, hold on Eva.' Quasar crosses her arms and looks more like her usual self. 'We don't know anyone is in danger and we're definitely not doing anything about it. We're already in enough trouble. My parents are this close to packing up and going back to Earth. I am staying out of trouble for now.'

'Yeah, but Eva's right,' Jay says. 'I think we should find out more.'

Quasar frowns at him.

'I don't mean do anything stupid, but we can find out things without anyone knowing. We can be space-detectives!' He says 'space-detectives' in a dramatic voice like a movie voiceover and even Quasar smiles at that.

'Yeah, I'd like to know more too if it might affect my dad.' Hercus nods. 'Let's get finished up before auld Boson comes back and we're here another hour.'

Next morning, I wake up in our...I mean my...pod, alone.

Dad has started his mission, but ours is only just beginning. Once we get this last detention out of the way, the space-detectives can get on the case!

I meet the others upstairs on the surface level where a tired looking lieutenant Boson waits for us. 'Good job last night, cadets. Maybe I'll ask the commander to have you come over once a week to give the drones a rest.'

Everyone groans at that, but no-one argues. We just need to keep quiet and get this last punishment out of the way and then we're free. Well, as free as you can be on a small colony base on Mars.

We're taken to the commander's office, and I'm guessing

it's not so she can say all is forgiven and well done on cleaning the rovers.

She meets us outside her door. 'Ah, thanks for bringing them, lieutenant. I must rush out for an urgent meeting on the coming storm, so no time to chat, but you need your last colony service detail, don't you?'

She looks around, like she's going to make something up on the spot.

'Let's give you something with less potential for…messing it up!' says Darshi, narrowing her eyes at us. 'How about an essay on the life and trials of Eva Knight, first Martianborn human. That little celebrity tale will keep you all busy and out of trouble for a while. Like a very special homework.' She licks her lips and gives me a toothy smile.

16

Homework

'Can you believe she's making us do this?' I slam my hand on the list of questions we need to research. 'This is worse punishment than the sewers and rovers put together!'

And almost as bad as manually injecting insulin five times a sol. I shift around on my bed – my butt still stings from the last jab.

'She *is* punishing us!' Hercus sighs and continues scrolling through the digital textbook, *A short history of humans on Mars,* by Phoebe Deimos.

'And me most of all – this is humiliating! "Give an account of physiological differences in humans born on Earth versus those born on Mars, citing examples." In other words, citing myself. Ugh!'

Hercus raises her eyebrows and slowly turns to me. 'Sorry, Eva.'

She knows why this is a particularly cruel punishment. 'She is actually the worst – putting *that* question in. The main reason they're not letting me become an astronaut. I'm not doing it.'

'But Eva, it would save me looking it up.' She laughs.

'Fine, but that's the last time I help you with homework. Seriously.'

She silently scrolls, occasional making a few notes on her scribbo-pad. Every so often, she accidentally reads a sentence or two aloud. Not loud-aloud, but just above a whisper and I don't think she notices she's doing it.

When she sees me staring, and smiling, she turns red and clams her lips together tightly.

'Aw, you look so cute!' Hercus turns the digital book so I can see. 'It's an extract from one of those programmes they made about the colony but were basically about you.'

A full-page picture of me, age eight, in my first spacesuit, holding my helmet under my arm. I'm smiling, a big gap where my front two teeth are missing, and I look so naively excited. Dad's smiling next to me, looking like a giant, in his suit.

We're holding hands, the headline reads:

The costs and rewards of being born on Mars

Eva Knight, pictured here with her father, commander Linton Knight, is the first human to be born on another planet.

But this story is about much more than the challenges that she will face. This is a story of heartbreak, of the fragility of human life and the cost of maintaining it.

Eva's mother, Ora Knight, who was the Martian colony's chief medical officer, died as a result of the extensive exposure to solar radiation during the trip to Mars and the early sols of the colony, where lead shielding was less extensive and effective.

When we interviewed Eva for our recent documentary, and we asked her what her greatest ambition was, it brought a lump to the throat to hear:

'To be an astronaut and an explorer. I want to go to Earth, and to other planets. Or to Titan. They're sending people to Titan soon. And to go beyond the Solar System. I want to be like my dad.'

I throw the tablet to the floor, the screen cracking with a satisfying crunch.

'Sorry, Eva. I didn't realise it would get that personal.'

'No, but the commander did when she set the homework. I hate her.'

'I didn't know some of that. I remember seeing the documentary, but don't remember it all. I'm so sorry you had to read it.'

'I'm done. I don't want to be famous for being born on Mars, or for being an expensive burden. I don't care if I get detention every sol for the rest of my life, I am not doing this. And I hope it annoys the hell out of the new commander.'

'Wait, so we're not doing the homework?'

I smile. 'C'mon, let's go chuck our homework into the Abyss.'

I grab my scribbo-pad and the smashed tablet and laugh hard at Hercus' wide-mouthed expression as I make to leave. 'And don't forget to bring a camera to record this – it will get so many views. If they want me to be famous, they've got it!'

'Not a good idea, Eva. If we want to investigate that place our dads are going, we need to be sensible. Do the homework and stay under Darshi's radar. If you're grounded again, you'll probably be thrown in the brig and then you'll never find that sword!'

I stare at her for a moment. Part of me wants to rebel, to see the look on the commander's face when she hears where my homework is. But another part of me sees Herc's intensity, and her dad is out there, too. I can't mess this up for her by getting us all into more trouble.

'Yeah, maybe,' I finally say. 'But ugh! I hate this. She's making it so personal.'

'We know she is, Eva. But we can't let her get to you. Come on, let's just get it done. Jay and Quasar are heading along in a bit. We can split our time between the homework and the mystery. Deal?'

I nod. 'Deal.'

Grudgingly, I finish my essay, but I can't stop thinking about Dad and I open the transmission archive, using Dad's password – my birthsol, of course, and play one of the updates Dad has been sending back to the base.

Dad's face appears, absolutely delighted with something.

**Commander…errr, Linton Knight checking in.
We are on sol 4 and we think we've hit the jackpot.
Professor Wěi has not stopped shouting and jumping around. Of course, chief-engineer Armstrong just wants to drill more. I think he's keen to get the job done and go home.
But honestly, look at this.**

Dad picks up the camera and pans round. They are in a huge cavern. It looks like it's been carved or built. He zooms in on what looks like a hole in the middle of the cavern.

We took samples from the wall of the lava tube and found life in these small pools on the walls. Yes, life. Alive, right now. Not ancient remains or fossils. Not the results of our experiments. Real, Martian life. The liquid, Wěi calls it the Primordial Soup of Life, is teeming with microbes.

We've also found some evidence of small invertebrate-like organisms. We've not seen them directly, but we found shed skins or webs from place to place.

This is very exciting, both for this mission, but also the colony. When Earth hears about this, the funding is sure to go up again. Our futures will be more secure.

Anyway, I must go. More arguments between Wĕi and Armstrong I believe. Will check in again soon.

Knight, out

'Woah, did you hear all that, Herc?'

'I did. Interesting, but didn't Perseverance find signs of ancient microbial life in 2022.'

'Okay, but still cool to think there's actual life on Mars, right? I mean, not just the weird, accidental life of the vipers and spiders. And did you see that cavern? It didn't look natural, did it? More like someone made it…or something'

'Let's not get carried away. It's a big leap from microbes to ancient Martians.'

'Well, I'm glad he seemed okay in that last transmission. He seemed okay, right?'

'Yeah, he did.' Herc's face also has longing in it, and I scan the files for a message from her dad, but there's nothing.

'I'm sure he's fine,' I say. 'Come on, it's movie time.'

And with that, I put down the photo, grab a packet of cricket-chips and relax to watch a movie.

'What will we watch?'

'I know which one.' Hercus presses a few buttons.

The projector screen flickers to the movie.

'A classic,' she says, smiling.

The camera focuses in on a few astronauts, on the surface of Mars.

'Matt Damon!'

But before we even get started, someone's at the door to the pod.

I open it, and in rushes Jay, followed by Quasar. He's breathing heavily, the physical exertion of moving around with the leg braces.

His eyes are wide. 'Eva, we were doing the homework and we found something!'

17

The Lost Knight

'Eva, you were definitely born on Mars, right?' Jay asks.

He lounges on my bed as I pace around our tiny pod. Herc and Quasar listen in.

I wipe sweat from my forehead and jam the door open, trying to get some air circulating, and to let out heat.

'Yeah, pretty sure. I mean, that's literally what this stupid homework is about!' I laugh, but something about Jay's tone feels off. 'So, come on, stop teasing us. Tell us what you found out.'

'Alright, keep your spacesuit on! How come there are three Knights on the passenger manifest when your family first arrived from Earth?' He shows me his screen.

Linton Knight. Ora Knight. Celeste Knight.

'Celeste?' I frown and look at Quasar and Hercus. 'You ever heard of a Celeste up here?'

Both shake their heads.

'It could be like a gran, or an aunt, or a cousin or something. And they left to go back to Earth maybe? I'll check the outgoing manifests for the name Knight.' Jay goes back to searching.

Something is churning inside me. Have I got more family than I once thought. But also, I'm annoyed it's Jay telling me, not Dad.

'No Knights have left Mars according to the records, but I did find a picture of the Knight party on arrival to the colony.' Jay hands me his pad.

It's a picture of Mum and Dad looking much younger, with a young girl in between them, maybe five or six years old. Bright red hair, like mine, though hers sits neatly on her shoulders. And a smile wider than Saturn's rings. I'm stunned. Is she … my sister? I always wanted a sister or brother, but I knew it was never going to happen.

'She looks so happy,' I say. 'I wonder what happened to her. And why Dad never told me?'

'Let's find out,' says Jay. 'Grab a pad everyone and get looking!'

We spend the next hour looking for any hint of her in the base records, working our way through a month's worth of snacks, but there's none. Not a whiff.

'It's like she never existed.' I throw down my pad.

'Or more like she's been deleted,' adds Jay, smiling.

'Why is that so funny to you?' I narrow my eyes and ball my fists, ready to whack him.

'No, it's just really clever. Someone has managed to delete all record of her, but they've not been clever enough.'

'Come on then, genius, tell us how?' Quasar folds her arms and stands behind to view his tablet.

'Well, when you delete something, that thing is gone. You can't find it. But you leave gaps behind. And those can be seen.'

Quasar shakes her head. 'I don't follow you.'

'Well, imagine you're writing a story, or singing a song. You can take out words or lyrics from them and no-one will know what they were, but you can't hide that there's now a gap in the story or song. And it's the same when information from the records is deleted. There are gaps and if you know as much as I do, it's obvious.'

'So, someone has deleted all the information about my sister and Dad never told me about her …do you think it was him? I mean, he can barely remember his password sometimes.'

'I doubt it. It'd have to be someone skilled in our computer systems. It's too good a job. And they'd have got away with it if I wasn't here.'

'You know you actually are a genius, Jay.' Quasar puts her hand on his shoulder.

'Yeah, you are,' I say, knowing I have a LOT of making up to do with him. With all of them.

'I know,' says Jay, tapping his skull.

'And modest, too,' Hercus quips. And we all share a laugh.

'What do we do next? How do we fill these gaps?' I ask.

'They may have deleted the computer records, but people have memories. Especially those who have been here as long as your dad. And there may be written records – people back then wrote things with pen and paper.'

'Retro!' Quasar laughs.

'Right?' Jay smiles. 'But it might be a good place to start. There's a records room on the same level as the Science and Research lab, so that's a good place to start?'

'Okay, but we're all totally on your mum's watch-list right now – I mean, I'm stuck up here, so I can't be sent back to Earth, but you guys and your families could.' I nod to Quasar and Herc. 'And she probably could make my life even worse than it is right now. And I dread to think what she'd do to you, Jay.'

Jay shrugs. 'I've been dealing with her all my life, I'll be fine.'

'I've got an idea,' I say.

The others look to me, and guilt floods me as I tell them the plan.

'Eva, you know that if it doesn't work, we'll be in detention for the rest of our lives!' Quasar smiles.

'That's why I'll take the biggest risk.' And I prepare to go to see the last person I want to speak to on this base.

'Come in, Eva.' Commander Darshi's sharp tone tells me she's busy and not in the mood for a chat. She continues to read something on the screen as I scrape my chair and sit.

For about thirty uncomfortable seconds, we sit in silence, and usually I'd start feeling edgy, but today this is exactly what I want. To waste her time. To make sure she's here in her office, so she doesn't see what the others are up to.

Finally, she stops, interlinks her fingers and places her hands on top of her desk.

'Did you enjoy your final assignment, Eva?' Her smile is the same temperature as winter at the poles.

'I did.' The lie makes me so happy. 'But I have a question.'

'Oh, you have? Well, be brief. As you can see, I'm *very* busy. Someone must keep an eye on the expedition group, as well as patching up a seriously damaged base.' Her eyes dance, like the tips of a naked fire.

'What is out there? Where you sent my dad and the others? Why did you ask him to lead the expedition?'

Darshi arches her right eyebrow. 'Interesting question. Let me tell you something, Eva. You are currently bottom of my

list, in fact so far down my list, you're sub-terranean, below
The Pits, beneath even the very bottom of the depths. You are
the least trustworthy human, if I can call you human, on this
base. I don't have time to justify myself to anyone, let alone
you. Close the door on your way out.'

I can't breathe. Even for Darshi, that stung. My stomach
has flipped even more times than it did when I was upturned
in the rover by the dust devils. I lick my lips, trying to bring
my dry mouth back to life.

Nothing comes out.

'Good sol, Eva.' Darshi goes back to reading her screen.

But I picture the ghost's warning again, and I know some-
thing isn't right. Dad could be somewhere dangerous. And
Darshi might even know about it, and she's sent him anyway.
My fingers dig into the arms of the chair.

'Not until you tell me something. What is out there? I
know there's something. You wouldn't send the most capable
person on this base to find out if it was nothing.'

And I cross my arms, refusing to move until she speaks.

She sighs. 'Detention. Every night after classes. Lieutenant
Boson will assign you wherever your labour is required on the
base. Now, get out of my sight.'

I shake my head slowly.

She stands up, her chair crashing backwards and thundering against the back wall. 'GET OUT! NOW!' Her
shaking finger points to the door.

I grip tighter to the chair to hide my own shaking hands.

Darshi continues to stare at me, her bloodshot eyes drilling
deep.

Eventually she presses a button on her desk. 'Derek,
please come in and escort Miss Knight to Lieutenant Boson
please.'

When Derek enters, the fight in me finally leaves and I let

him guide me out the room of the most vile, hateful woman I've ever met.

I have to bite my tongue to stop screaming back at her that I'll find out anyway. I don't want to blow Jay's cover.

Derek takes me to lieutenant Boson, who gives me a schedule for the next week, with a list of names and departments that I must visit after class each sol.

Once I leave him, I go straight back to the pod, as agreed with the others, even though every part of me wants to go and find Jay and see what he's found with his hack.

But I wouldn't put it past her to have me followed, or to watch the cameras to see where I'm going.

'Check this out.' Jay shows us what he found when he hacked into the base's collected data systems.

He shows us a series of satellite images taken from the orbiter, showing the place that Dad's investigating, ranging from one year ago until just a few weeks ago.

In the first few images, the oldest ones, the mountain looks normal, but on the last couple there's a hole in its side.

'What is it?' Quasar asks.

'Could be a meteor,' Jay suggests. 'Or something falling from orbit.'

Then he brings up the same images, but this time they're overlayed with a sort of blueish filter. 'These are the thermal readings for the same place on the same dates. Purple and blue means really cold, red means warmer, and yellow means super-hot. Watch this.'

He flicks through the images as before, and at the same time the hole appears in the mountain, the whole mountain gets redder and redder, with a yellow point in the centre.

'So, something hot crashed into it? What, like an alien spaceship?' Quasar laughs.

'It doesn't even need to be hot. Something cold would give off heat with that impact. But why not a spaceship?' Jay nods. 'We've just seen Martian Ghosts. Why wouldn't there be other intelligent, space-faring species out there?'

Even for me, Jay's being a bit out there. I mean, I want to believe, but it's also scary to think about.

'Probably just a meteor.' Hercus speaks. 'They're just going to find a meteor and then come home.' She sits down.

'Yeah.' I nod, not sure I fully believe that either. It's too much of a simple explanation for Darshi to be hiding it. 'But surely they wouldn't send a whole expedition for a meteor?'

Quasar shrugs. Jay pouts his lower lip. Hercus scratches her head.

'Well, that's killed the mystery a bit, huh? I mean, if it's aliens, then cool. But if it's just a super-hot meteor, that's a bit of a big freeze. I'm tired.' Quasar gets up to leave.

'Wait.' Jay clicks on something else. 'Check this out.'

An image from the orbiter shows the base over the last few sols, including the sol I blew up the science lab, but lack of electricity that sol isn't what's interesting. When Jay zooms out, and then out further, something comes into view.

'A dust storm. It's huge. Looks like it might even be a planet coverer.' Jay bites his lip as he tells us.

Hercus moves closer, just as Jay keeps zooming out on the images.

It does look huge. None of Mars's surface can be seen on nearly half the planet.

'How long until it gets to us?'

'A few sols. We'll be okay. They already know about it and will be preparing. But Eva, look at this.' He zooms in on a small convoy of rovers, showing Dad's expedition as they head towards the mountain. 'I tried to work out how long it would take them to get there and come back, and how long they'd have at the site before they had to come home.'

'Yeah, and how long do they have?'

'Two more sols at the site and then they'll have to leave.'

'Well, that's not so bad, is it?' suggest Quasar.

'No, but with a storm this size, you never know. It might come in faster than we expect.'

'And Dad would be trapped.' I turn to Hercus. 'And your dad, too.'

She puts her head in her hands. 'They would have known when they left. They'll be back. I know Dad will always come back.'

I put my hand on her shoulder. 'They will.'

'So that's one mystery partly solved,' says Jay. 'We know why they were sent out to that mountain. But I still can't find anything about your sister, Eva. I tried, but it's all been electronically wiped, even from the private servers that I hacked into.'

I miss T – he'd be able to hack in and restore the information.

I sit down next to Herc. 'Well, there will be time to find out about that later, *when* our dads return.'

Hercus smiles back, but it quickly disappears.

'He will be fine, Hercus. I promise. They'll both be fine.'

'You can't know that. It was stupid of them to go out with that storm coming in. I guarantee they knew about it. And your mum sent them out.' She points at Jay who inches backwards on the bed.

'I don't think any of us love Darshi, Herc. But they chose to go, so it's on them I reckon.' Quasar steps between Herc and Jay.

'Easy for you to say when you don't have anyone out there

with their life at risk.' Hercus moves closer to Quasar, towering above her.

'It's time for sleep.' I step in and guide Quasar to the door, Jay following silently. He looks wary of Herc, and I'm not surprised. She's hyperventilating.

'You want to stay here tonight?' I say to her. 'I think we could both do with not being alone. You can sleep in Dad's bed.'

Her eyes finally sync with mine, and she nods, lowering herself onto Dad's mattress.

Jay gives me a small nod as he leaves and the door swishes behind him.

The lights are off, and neither Herc nor I have spoken in a while, but I don't think she's asleep either.

'Eva, why do you want to leave Mars so badly?' Hercus voice gives me a fright.

'I dunno. I don't like people telling me what I can and can't do, I suppose.'

'My Dad has always talked about Mars, ever since I can remember. And when we came up, he was so happy. And I was, too. I don't think I'll ever leave. Going back to Earth is a no-go.'

'What's it like? Earth? The way Quasar goes on, it's amazing, but then Dad says it's full of problems and problem people."

'Horrible. Honestly Eva, it's much better up here.'

'How is this dead rock better than a planet full of life? Where you can breathe outside, and swim and fly, and walk for further than just the capacity of an oxygen tank.'

'It has some nice parts. But up here is different. Everyone has a job here and is welcome. And I know Darshi is a pain, but you must see it her way – she can't have you running around destroying the place. She's harsh but fair.

'She's not fair. She's got it in for me. Says if I step out of line again, she'll make sure I never become an astronaut.'

'You need to keep your head down then, Eva.'

I decide not to argue with Herc. I've got too many things swirling in my head already; I don't need to add falling out with my best friend as well.

Finally, I hear snores coming from Herc and know I'm alone, with my thoughts. And it's the first time I've been alone all sol. I have friends now … like, plural.

Pretty great for someone who normally pushes people away. I won't mess it up this time.

18

Moxie

'Where are we going?' Hercus trails behind me as I'm marched down to engineering.

'I have more detentions. You don't need to come.'

'May as well. There's no-one to go back to the pod for.'

I used to think Hercus and I were so different. But right now, we've never been so similar. We don't agree on everything, but we do need each other.

Boson is showing his clear annoyance at being given the job of taking me to detention every sol. 'Down there, ask for old Senex. He'll put you to work.' The lieutenant doesn't wait for any kind of acknowledgement and is already halfway back up the stairs.

'You ever been in here?' I ask Herc.

'Yeah, a few times. Never met Senex, though.'

'Neither have I.'

I've obviously been given clearance to be here, because my key card gets past the big door with 'authorised personnel only' written on it.

'This is exciting,' I say, as we pass through the doors into the darkness of the engineering level – bright red and orange glows come through the grated walkways beneath our feet, along with a mixture of smoke, steam, and the smell of gas.

'Exciting is one word for it.' Hercus moves ahead and goes down the stairs to the right, avoiding stepping on the raised, grated walkways for now.

'It would be like walking through the clouds or something.' I stare ahead, thinking about the clouds of Earth that I'll never see or fly through. Mars almost never gets clouds. And definitely not as thick as these.

'Come on, Eva.' Hercus shouts up to me, and I follow her down.

Below the level of the steam and smoke, the engineering floor looks huge. Maybe even bigger than hydroponics and farming. Rows and rows of various machines are chugging away, some of which I recognise from class, and others I have never seen before.

'Wow!' Hercus stands beside me, turning in a small circle to take it all in.

'Big, huh? It's easy to forget that this is what is keeping us alive in here. All these machines recycling our air, our waste, and turbines producing electricity; it's all kinda like a living thing. Remember when we learned about ecosystems and how each part depends on the other?'

'Yeah. It *is* like that. Looks like there is a point to Earth-science class.' We both laugh.

'Hello girls, what's so funny?' A small man with grey hair slides out from beneath the machine we are passing.

'Oh nothing, sorry to disturb you, sir.' Herc salutes and I take a step back to let him stand.

He smiles, and as he does his large ears wiggle. His crin-kled face is one of the kindest things I've ever seen. 'Haha, no need to call me sir. I'm not the sir of anyone. I just fix the machines and keep things going down here.'

'We're looking for Senex. We've been told to report to him for detention.

He laughs. 'Oh, in trouble, are we? Send the trouble-makers to Senex, is that what they think now?'

'No sir, we're not troublemakers,' says Hercus defensively.

'I'm kidding, kid. No offence meant. Come on and I'll show you a few things then if you're stuck with me.' He hobbles further into the heart of the machines.

It's a maze of equipment here and without Senex leading us, we'd definitely get lost. The cloud of steam above us makes me feel like I'm in a metal city, floating high above the surface of the Earth. I've watched videos of planes flying into and above the clouds, and I reach up, trying to touch the white vapour but fall short. Herc could probably touch it, but she's more interested in the machines, gazing at each like it's her favourite thing in the world.

'Come here, kids. Let me show you how to clean these and then you can try yourself.'

'What is it?' Hercus asks. We stare at a huge machine, with giant pistons either side of a large, metal box.

'A MOXIE. You not studied these in class?'

'Yes, but the ones we looked at were much smaller.'

'Ah right, like the ones on the rovers probably. I've been working these MOXIEs, and water recyclers and vaporisers over there since I got here as one of the founders. These big ones produce much more oxygen but need much more main-tenance and power.'

'If you're a founder, you'd have known the Knights? When they first arrived?' I try to keep my voice steady.

'Aye, I did. All three of them. Lovely family. Tragic what happened.'

'You really knew them? What happened?' I ask, shoving my hands into my pockets to hide how much I'm shaking.

'Not sure exactly. Linton and Ora were as decent and good people as you could ever meet. They never recovered from it.'

'FROM WHAT?' I take a step closer to Senex, and I can't keep the volume out of my voice.

He narrows his eyes, perhaps knowing he's said too much. 'Have you kids met that Eva Knight? Now there's a trouble-maker, if there ever was one.'

I turn to Herc, rolling my eyes. 'I think you've met her, haven't you Hercus?'

She frowns. I wink.

'Oh yeah,' she stutters. 'Yeah, I've met her. Seems nice.'

'Caused chaos down here. Had to reset all the systems and we nearly lost life support. Luckily the back-up generator is in good condition, thanks to yours truly.'

'Do you like working down here, Senex?' I ask.

'Love it. The machines are my life. I never bother with anyone else. My pod is just at the back there.'

'But don't you miss people? You must want to do other things sometimes. Have some fun?'

'Mars isn't fun. I have a duty to keep everyone alive here by making sure everything works perfectly, all the time. Duty is my friend, and servicing the machines is my fun. Now, do you want to know how to repair a clogged-up MOXIE? It's the most fun part of the job.'

Two hours later, with sore hands and sweaty feet, we're climbing back up the stairs and through the clouds of steam, escaping Senex's strange world of metal and machines, and I can't stop thinking about how he's given his life to keeping all of us alive, and I've barely even thought about another person, ever.

'What's up, Eva?' Herc nudges me.

'Nothing.'

'You sure?'

'Yeah, I wonder if we should do something for Senex. He must be lonely, despite what he says. I would ask Dad if he was still here. He deserves an award or a party or something for what he does.'

'He does. I think I'd like that job, though I'd definitely not live down there.'

'You wouldn't want to be away from the best friend ever!'

'Who? Quasar? Nah…'

We both laugh and head back up for lunch.

As we climb the stairs my mind is focussed on Celeste. Who was she? Why was she hidden from me? And how could Dad lie after losing Mum?

'No way, they have cheeseburgers today!' I run excitedly towards the queue in the cafeteria.

Hercus strides after me. 'If there's one thing we can always agree on – it's that cheeseburgers are out of this world!' She smiles, a small slither of drool escaping her mouth as she stares at the burgers on the counter.

'Only five left,' I say, panic counting the number of people in front of us and hoping most of them will choose something else.

'Disgusting.' Quasar pushes into the queue beside us, looking disgusted at the burgers. Jay slides in, too. Several tuts come from others behind. She spins and gives them her death stare, and nobody comments further.

'Cheeseburgers are heaven.' It's a known fact, like that Mars has two moons, or that a sol is 24 hours, 39 minutes and 35 seconds.

'You are barbaric.' She turns to everyone seated with a burger in their hand. 'You're all barbaric.'

'Judge much?' Hercus laughs.

'It's not a judgement – it's true. The conditions for animals up here are totally against nature. They don't get to roam free and wild like they do on Earth. They are all cooped up and then slaughtered every few months to give you your treat. Horrible lives they lead.'

'I agree with you. But we hardly treat animals that well on Earth either,' Jay adds.

Quasar whirls around and burns him with her gaze. 'I cannot control how every human treats animals but I am here and I think it's horrible. End of discussion.' She exits the queue, grabs some fruit from a communal bowl and marches off to sit at the table and wait for us.

'I take it you didn't find anything?' I ask Jay, remembering where they'd been while Herc and I were in engineering.

'Hey, it's me. Of course, I found something. I'll show you at yours once we've had our dinner.' He smiles. 'Oh, and Eva I've been working on something for you. And it's ready now.'

'What is it?' I'm so surprised I forget all manners.

'An insulin pump. I found it amongst some of the ancient medical supplies. I managed to rig it so it can sit outside a spacesuit as well. In case, you know, you become an astronaut one day.'

I have no words. So, I nod instead. Then after a few seconds of awkward silence, something comes over me and I give him a quick hug. I can't believe he did this.

I turn the pump over in my hand. It will be nice to not inject all the time. Jay is smiling, and all I can think is – I don't think deserve this. Especially not from him.

Then I realise this is the same one Mum made all those

years ago for me, slightly modified. I swallow hard as I think about her helping me now, so many years later.

Quasar interrupts the moment. 'Right, enough with all the emotions, let's get out of this room of animal-eaters and talk about something interesting.'

After twenty minutes of Quasar staring at us like we're oxide vipers, Herc and I finish our burgers and head down to my pod.

'Do not even breathe on me.' Quasar holds up her hand to Hercus' mouth, who's next to her in the lift.

'It's not like I'm going to breathe cow onto you.'

'You're disgusting.'

'Trust me, you and Jay's corn, radish and onion breath is hardly any nicer.'

I quickly push the mess off the chairs and my bed as we enter the pod, clearing a space for everyone to sit.

'This place is such a palace.' Quasar carefully picks up a half-eaten algal-jerky and chucks it in the recycle tube.

'Don't need to be here, Quasar,' I say, before turning away. That was a bit cruel.

She crosses her arms. 'Nothing else exciting happens round here. And this is kinda interesting. So, I'll stay. Whatever.'

Jay pulls out of some paper files from his beneath his t-shirt. The first file is covered in sweat. 'Sorry, that top one was against my skin. Only way to sneak them out.'

'It's fine.' I grab the files, hungrily.

Scanning through them, I can see the others staring at me, quiet, and waiting for my response.

'So, I did have a sister...but she went missing. These are all reports about search parties and statements from Mum and

Dad.' I continue to read them, the rest of the room silent. But their silence is annoying me.

Finally, I look up at them. 'You can ask questions, you know?'

They all seem to breath out at once.

'Well, tell us more.' Hercus is the first to speak.

'Her name was Celeste, as you know, and she went missing when she was five. Nobody knows where she went. There was a spacesuit checked out, but no rover tracks or footprints to follow. She disappeared…like a ghost.'

'Wait, so no one noticed a five-year-old girl taking a space-suit and walking out onto the surface and then just…vanish-ing?' Quasar looks sceptical, and I share her opinion for once.

'It is weird. They did loads of searches and scans, with drones and with people going out. It looks like Mum and Dad logged hundreds of hours on the surface looking. Thousands of rover miles in here, too.'

'No wonder they buried it,' adds Jay. 'Who would believe it back on Earth? And how could they explain it? Funding would be cut and the colony in jeopardy. My mum's worst nightmare. It's all she ever thinks or talks about.'

'Maybe she became one of those ghosts,' suggests Quasar.

'Impossible. All the ghosts are huge. None of them look like a young girl.'

'Maybe she went back to Earth?' suggest Jay sensibly. 'After running away, they found her, but kept it quiet and just sent her home?'

'It's possible, I suppose.' But that doesn't seem right. I don't think Dad would send his daughter away. Although, he didn't even tell me I had a sister.

'We should investigate,' says Hercus, rising from the other bed.

'What's the point?' I say. 'If they found nothing, why would we find anything fifteen years later?'

'Because it's us, Eva.' Jay points to himself, and then to Hercus. Then reluctantly to Quasar, who throws a pillow at him.

We share a nice moment of laughter, then I make myself refocus my mind on the problem.

'But how are we going to get to where we need without being tracked? We've still got these on, remember?' I point to my ankle tracker.

'Simple. Same way Quasar and I got into the records room without anyone knowing.'

Hercus and I stare at him as he enjoys a dramatic pause.

'We use magnets to disable them. It's simple science, Eva. It's only a short-term disablement, but it will give us time to get in and out. Let me show you.'

Halfway between being irritated at his arrogance and awed at how annoyingly brilliant he is, I listen to him as he explains how to do it.

I have a sister.

And I will find out who she was and where she went.

19

Saving Dad

When I sleep at night my unconsciousness goes into overdrive. The ghosts visit me relentlessly. The dreams are so vivid that I think they're real. Mum is always in the background while the other ghosts whisper to me. Sometimes they sound in pain, other times they are excited. But it's always in a language I don't understand. I ask Mum what they mean. But she just smiles, and I wake up.

Seven sols since Dad left. He's checked into base control every sol, and to be fair, commander Darshi has told me each time. It's the highlight of my sol, arriving home to see the flashing green light on our console. Hearing Dad's voice, with his distinct tones and pronunciations, even if it is just to relay boring mining updates, is comforting. The one time of sol I feel less alone.

He doesn't address me directly. No apology for abandoning me. No apology for the way he left things. Just the steady, sober voice, full of authority and distinction. The one I've heard addressing our base all my life. I've heard it through a speaker more often than from his lips. But I miss it and, even with the impending operation to remove all the debris from my now-defunct e-Pancreas, it's helping me through these solitary sols. His message tonight is similarly regimented and procedural.

The door beeps.

I tip-toe to the door and tap the ID screen. Commander Darshi.

I try to back away, silently, but her voice drills through the door, sharp and sure. 'Open, Eva. I need to talk to you about your dad. It's urgent.'

I shrug and let her in, avoiding eye contact. I can't look anyone in the eye anymore.

'Have a seat,' I say, like I have any authority. But she sits.

'Eva, I need to tell you something about your dad. And the mission.'

My heart plummets into the Abyss. 'What is it? Is he okay?'

She sighs. 'Our satellite has detected a large dust storm approaching our location. We will be fine in the base. We have enough supplies, power, stored oxygen, and water to survive if we ration.'

'But Dad and his crew are out at the mine. And they don't have enough supplies? Order them home. Now!'

She looks annoyed for a moment, then nods. 'They are calling it The Great Dust Storm, possibly the largest in our Human-Martian experience. Your dad and his team have enough food to last a few weeks out there, but they'd have no power, as dust storms—'

'Dust storms mean no solar power can be produced. The MOXIE and WAVAR machines need power to produce oxygen and water.'

'Indeed.' She stands. 'You're a smart girl, there's no doubt...but the discipline...ahhh, I guess we'll never agree on that. Our world views are too different. But perhaps we can be civil for your father's sake?'

I open and close my mouth several times, unable to find the words.

She really needs me. I guess it would look bad if her orders were defied and she lost an expedition team. I'm not sure how much she actually cares about the people, it's more about her reputation, her career, her shot at becoming permanent commander. I know she'd push every last one of us out of an airlock if it meant furthering her career.

'I need you to come to command and be there when I ask him to return. To make certain he does.'

She doesn't wait for me to agree, and strides ahead of me into the corridor, occasionally glancing over her shoulder to ensure I'm still there.

'Oh, and a reminder that you have your career interview coming up. I'll expect you to be fully prepped with all realistic options and ideas.' She gives me a curt nod.

How can she even be thinking about a stupid careers interview at this time? The last thing I want to do is to sit with her, in her office for an hour, and discuss my future. If she had her way, I'd have no future at all.

We reach the command centre, and the door slides open for the commander, as if the heat radiating from her body acts as her genetic signature. I've seen Dad use the retinal scanner, but the commander has ascended beyond mortal security methods. I'm sure it suits her god-complex perfectly.

As we enter the circular room, everyone stands and salutes. She indicates to me to sit down with an open hand - a very Dad move, and not like her at all. Is she trying to be more like Dad to get me onside? Ha!

She sits in the throne-like chair in the centre of the room, flanked by flashing buttons, facing a tall, wide screen (even bigger than the one in our colony cinema). It has smaller, individual screens surrounding the outline of the main one, like a cell wall, providing a ton of additional environmental data, from both inside and outside the colony base. If Jay was in here, he'd get lost in those numbers for sols.

'Corporal, contact mine-commander Knight.'

A young man at the front of the room glances back and begins to punch some codes into the panel in front. 'Yes, Ma'am.'

The view on the large screen changes, from an external view of the whole colony to a blank screen. Every four seconds a beep sounds.

Seven beeps mark out time passing in the agonising silence.

The commander tuts and everyone else is tense and tight-lipped.

Why isn't he answering?

He's always preferred being on his own, but he's never shunned *me*.

Then the screen changes, and I breathe out, quietly, so the commander doesn't hear. Flickering images at first. Then Dad's face appears in clear HD, fifteen metres tall and thirty wide. I almost laugh at how big his nose looks. But then I register the desperation in his eyes and the pulsing vein on his forehead.

'Dad?' I shout it before anyone else has a chance to speak.

He squints, the lines on his face clear on the big screen, age, and stress all over his otherwise young-looking face. Well, he's young-looking compared to a lot of the other dads.

'Eva?' He blinks several times, edging closer and closer to his screen and becoming bigger and bigger in ours. 'Why are you in the command centre?'

'Come home. There's a dust storm on the way. The biggest ever.'

'Not just yet, kid. We're so close. Honestly, you should see it here – it's magnificent: wall to wall precious metals and minerals. Enough to keep stocked up for fifty years. Some of it looks almost unlike anything else I've mined on Earth or Mars. I can't leave now. This could secure our future on the planet for a long, long time.'

'Dad, I need you to come back. I won't stop worrying.'

'Eva, I've seen the report for the storm, we've assessed the risk and are happy with it. We still have two or three sols before we have to leave. It'll be fine. How are you?'

I'm tempted to ask about Celeste and why he lied. Why everyone lied. But I leave it. Darshi would enjoy it, and that's enough to stop me. 'Fine. I mean, it's not been totally fine but—'

The commander interrupts me. Her patience has gone. 'We don't have time for this, Linton. Those metals can wait. Report back to base immediately. We will resume mining in that mountain once the dust storm clears.'

I never thought I'd say this, but I'm actually agreeing with the commander.

'Dad, come on. I need you here. My operation is in the next few sols.'

There's a long pause and Dad looks around the large cavern he's standing in. A rover sits in the background beside a tall flashlight.

'Okay, okay. You're right. It's not worth the risk. And I really can't leave you alone for the operation, Eva. I'll wrap things up here and then…'

A high-pitched scream of terror echoes through the cavern and across the video transmission.

'Linton, what was that?' Commander Darshi has an unfamiliar pitch to her voice. Almost like she's worried about him.

We can only see the back of Dad's head as he frantically looks around, looking for the source of the scream. He's shouting orders. 'Dalton, what was that?'

'It's Io, sir. She's been bitten.'

A second scream. Dad runs out of view.

The transmission continues to run, but we can only see the rover and the light. We hear more shouts and screams, both increasing in frequency, but nothing is clear.

Then something long and thin darts across the picture and smashes into the light, plunging the screen into almost darkness – just two thin beams of light remain, coming from the front of the rover.

The lit strips show only the ground. Then, something crawling. The outline of a colonist. Their suit's torn and they're shouting at the camera, but it's muffled.

The person shouts, 'There are too many of them...'

Then the screen goes blank. The transmission has cut off from Dad's end.

A buzz of panic rises from the less senior officers, and I know I'm scared because I actually look to Darshi for comfort. I'm anticipating a flurry of commands to come from her, to rescue Dad and his team. To get to the mine immediately.

But she ignores me. I am no longer useful to her. She sits down and says nothing.

'Commander, any orders?' asks the corporal, wide-eyed.

'Keep monitoring the communications channel in case they come back to us. Keep hailing them, too. In the meantime, resume normal duties. We must also prepare for the incoming storm.'

'What?'

I want to shake her, yell in her face, but I know she won't listen.

So instead, I slowly back away towards the door, hit the green exit button and slide out. She barely notices.

I run back to our quarters – actually, my quarters now – planning as I go. I need to save Dad, I need to get to those mines, and I need to get the sword. I feel it stronger than anything I've ever known – this is it; this is what the ghost meant. Whatever is in the mine is what I have to save Dad from.

But how do I do any of those things? I don't even know where the sword is, or how I'd get to Dad in this storm, or even how to drive a rover!

I need help. And I know I don't deserve it, but I must try.

If they'll help me. Herc, Jay, and Quasar have already been a better friend to me than I deserve. And this is a lot to ask but I can't do this without them.

And we're gonna need all the help we can get – we might need to overload systems, or hack into the satellites, and we're definitely going to need all the knowledge we can get venturing into the unknown - I need to bring back T.

The Resurrection of Thunderchild

'Wait, so you have an AI friend who lives in your ear and gives you unwanted advice all the time?' Quasar laughs. 'Sounds like my mum.'

'I'm serious. He's like my best friend,' I say, honestly. 'Well, he was my only friend for a while.'

Hercus clears her throat.

'Well, you've always been nice to me, Herc. But I've never really let anyone in, and I was alone before you arrived on Mars. Before any of you came. And then when the other kids did come, I always thought that if I made any close friends here it would get in the way of me leaving Mars.'

'Well, that was silly,' Hercus replies. 'Everyone needs friends, even if they're not hanging around for long.'

Now, more than ever, I couldn't agree more.

'So, you want us to help you steal a computer, so you can download your friend into your ear again?' Quasar gives me the wide eyes.

I haven't even got to the worst part yet, but I'll save that for later.

'My dad is in danger. Darshi took me to command where he was transmitting. He was about to agree to return home, but something attacked them all, and broke the lights, and people were hurt.'

'*My* dad…' Hercus' face becomes white as a ghost.

'I'm sorry,' I say, gently rubbing her shoulder. 'We can save them both, then.'

'What do you mean save them?' Quasar crosses her arms.

'Well, we need to get out of there and rescue them. But first, we have to steal a computer, and find my slightly annoying AI implant.'

'What? But surely there are other, better people than us can go? Like the adults? I'm sorry about your dads, but it's not up to us to rescue them.' Quasar arches her eyebrows.

'Commander Darshi won't rescue them,' I say. 'There's a large dust storm coming, and she won't risk the rest of the colony to save them. She says it's too dangerous.'

'So, let me get this right. The people in charge, with years of experience and expert knowledge, say it's too dangerous for them, but you think it's a good idea for a couple of barely-teenagers, with no experience, to go out there instead?'

'Yes.' I stand as tall as I can.

She laughs for a second and turns away. 'Herc, you can't possibly be thinking this is a good idea?'

'It's a terrible idea, but if what Eva says is right, we have to try.' She stands beside me.

'Honestly…right, I'll help with the computer, Eva. But no way am I going on that death mission. That's crazy talk.' Quasar actually looks scared.

'Fine, we'll take your help to find Thunderchild,' I say.

'Thunderchild? You gave him a name?'

'Well, T for short. It's from a book…but you probably don't read…'

Quasar's eyes widen.

'I mean, you haven't read it...'

'Whatever! He can be called R2D2 for all I care. What's the plan?'

'I need to get the laptop. When they took it away, Dad said it would be safe in the digital supplies room.'

'Cool, where's that?'

'On the command level. Next to the commander's office.'

'So "you think" it's in the room next to the number one place we don't want to be sneaking around in this whole base? I tell you what, Eva, you don't make things easy for yourself, do you.' Quasar smirks and shakes her head.

This is going to be hard sell for them, especially Quasar, who has nothing to gain from helping me.

'So where do we come in? Do you need us to help get you into the room or something? We should definitely get Jay involved. This seems like something he'd be able to help with.'

'No, we'd best leave him out of it, as it involves his mum and he's probably in enough trouble with her already. I think I can get in the room, but I can only do it if the commander is not sitting next door. There's a window on the wall between the two rooms.'

'Of course there is.' Quasar rolls her eyes.

'Listen, Quasar, quit all the digs. Let's just help her. Listen to her plan.' Hercus stares at me, waiting for something good.

And I should have something awesome. Something really great, considering how much trouble I'd get them into...but I just...don't.

'Okay. So, how about you set off a disturbance in the Quad? Like, start a big argument, or a fight or something?'

'But why would the commander come and deal with that personally?' asks Quasar. 'No, listen I have a better idea. Hercus and I will start a fire in her apartment.'

'Oh, yeah. Much better idea, Quasar. Let's set the colony up in flames. It'll distract her as the base explodes and if we survive that, we're sucked out onto the surface.'

'No, wait. Quasar, that's a really good idea actually.'

'Eva—'

'No, listen. We won't set it on fire, but you can set off the smoke alarm. Burn something really small just below the alarm at her apartment door. That will get her running that way, even if the emergency team are dealing with it.'

Hercus looks unconvinced. 'Okay, we'll try. Where will we meet you after? To plan for the rescue?'

'Sub-19. I'll get down there as soon as I've downloaded the software onto the chip.'

We all look at each other for a moment.

Then I nod and we begin the journey up in the lift to the command level. Hercus and Quasar move left towards the command apartments. My old home. I move right, towards the commander's office.

'Good luck, Eva.' Quasar smiles. 'You're gonna need it.'

I climb up into the ventilation shaft about twenty metres along the corridor from the digital supplies room, carefully replacing the cover to hide any trace of my break-in.

I grip the slippery sides of the air-vent and slide forward.

The vent is mostly dark with squares of light where branches lead down into a room. The digital supplies room is the fourth room along. The commander's office is the fifth, so I try to move silently.

I keep holding my breath, but then the exhale is even noisier, so I switch to keeping my breathing slow and steady. The condensation is unreal in here. Exhaled, recycled air flows through these vents, all being drawn towards the huge MOXIEs.

Right now, I'm breathing in carbon dioxide-rich air, and it's making me light-headed.

My hands are soaked in what is basically hot, human breath. Totally yuck, but I have to do this. I need T if I'm to rescue Dad.

I claw my way closer, much more slowly now. I have passed the third room. Digital supplies is next.

I pause above the vent, waiting for the smoke alarm to go off, and to hear the commander leaving her room.

As I wait, I go over the steps of the plan: get T, get the sword, and steal a rover. Drive to Dad's mine and rescue him (and anyone else). I think of the images on the commander's screen and just hope there are people to rescue.

The alarm sounds.

I hear the commander's door slam, and move quickly, lifting the vent cover and slowly lowering myself down. Luckily there's a desk beneath me and it's a short fall.

Quickly, I rummage through all the scattered computers and hard drives, monitors, tablets, and wrist-pads.

'Where is it? Come on.'

The seconds lengthen into minutes, and I still haven't found it.

The alarm stops.

And at the same moment I look through the glass screen and see the laptop sitting on the commander's desk.

'Noooooo!' I bang the screen. If I go in there, she'll know. But I have to risk it.

I slide the screen to the side and gently step into the office, slide the chip into the laptop, flip it open and find the software.

I click download. The screen says it will take five minutes.

No. She'll be back soon. What can I do?

Footsteps outside the door. I turn around wide-eyed, expecting to be caught, but then I hear Quasar's voice.

'Commander, come quick.'

'What is it, Jones? I have had an irritable evening already.'

And the footsteps start to move away.

I release my held breath. Three minutes left. But I don't think I can risk it again. Quasar can't distract her for long.

I'll need to leave the chip downloading.

I crawl back into the digital supplies room, slide the screen back, and exit, leaving a small wrist-pad in the doorway to wedge it open. I'll go back later.

As I slip out of the doorway, I hear footsteps. I freeze, no way out, except past the person coming.

'Commander…' My mouth dries up so fast, the next sound is something between a grunt and a squeak.

'Eva? Why are you up here?' She narrows her eyes and looks around to check if I'm alone.

'Umm…' If only I had T to give me a good reason.

'Ah, wait. Are you here for your careers interview?' She smiles.

And my body relaxes, as does my tongue. 'Yes, that was it.'

'Well, you're early! It's not for a few hours yet. Go home and have your dinner and I will see you at our appointment time.'

'Thanks commander. And when was that again?'

'2000 hours.' But then she frowns. She's staring at the door, and the wedged wrist-pad. Then she shrugs and pushes the wrist-pad inside the room, and it slides shut. A green light flashes on to indicate it's locked again.

Dammit.

'2000 hours, Eva. Looking forward to it.'

'See you then.'

I walk as casually as I can until I turn the corner, then I don't stop running until I'm taking the lift down to The Pits.

That did NOT go well. But the interview does give me another chance to get T, if she hasn't used the laptop and found him by then.

Quasar and Hercus wait for me outside the lift on Sub-19.

'Well?' Quasar asks.

I shake my head. 'We have a problem.'

'What?'

'I didn't get T downloaded. And I have to go back to her office in a couple of hours to do a careers interview.'

'Skip it,' says Quasar, shrugging.

'I can't skip it. She'll know something's up and keep an eye on me if I do. In fact, I wouldn't put it past her to send people down here to find me if I don't go. We can't let her suspect anything is up. Plus, I think I can still get my chip and T back.'

'But aren't we supposed to be leaving at 2100? We'll have to change the plan.' Hercus looks worried.

'It'll be fine. I'll play it cool and just agree with her and get out of there well within an hour, and I'll steal the chip with T on it. We'll be fine. Promise.'

Hercus doesn't look as confident. She has as much riding on this rescue as me and I can tell she's worried I'll mess things up.

'Herc, it will be fine.'

'Okay, but we better start planning. Let's go to yours and chat about what we need to bring with us.'

21

Careers Interview

I knock on the door to the commander's office.

For so long my father was on the other side of this door, and I'd never have to knock before entering. Now, I'd give anything for it to slide open and to see him at the chair, smiling and chatting to someone important back on Earth, pointing me to a big bowl full of sugar-free snacks that sat on his desk, just for me.

He gave up sugary foods, all those years ago, when he found out I have Type 1 Diabetes. Not that there's much to spare up here, but we always get a small supply with each shipment, mostly for celebrations, like birthsols and Founders' Sol.

Today, as the door hisses open, a cold draught creeps out from the office.

'Enter.'

I take a few tentative steps forward. The four walls are the same. The desk, also the same. But almost everything else that made this place Dad's has been removed and replaced. Like he never existed.

She points to a metal chair across the desk from where she's scribbling down a few notes on old-fashioned paper. The laptop sits where I left it, still closed, with the tiny chip poking out the side. Luckily the side facing me. She must not have seen it earlier.

I stare, and she notices.

'Yes, some of us are dinosaurs and still use paper. The systems up here are not always one-hundred percent reliable and handwriting really is a lost art amongst your generation.'

'We write, too.'

'Yes, on those unwieldy scribbo-pads. Half the effort, half the outcome.'

I sit down, wondering what her life must been like until now. How did she come to be here? And why? She is so anti-tech; she hates Mars and all of us. I've never seen her be warm to anyone.

Dad only cared about those things – the base, the people, the science. He loved them all, and encouraged everyone else, too.

'So, Eva. Next year you will begin your specialised academy learning. You will need to consider and choose the classes carefully, based upon your desired career. Which for you, is sadly confined to this base, only. Your Type 1 Diabetes, and Martian gestation, both preclude you from any role outside the base, unfortunately. However, there are so many fine ways to serve the colony. Have you given it any thought? Cleaning the sewers, perhaps?'

'Not really. Dad wants me to become a commander, or at least to join the command programme and take a role with base command.'

'An admirable, if challenging, ambition. Commander training is the most demanding and intensive route. It is for the most able and determined of students. Not for the likes of you, Eva.'

'I could do it! If, you know, I wanted to do it.' A small fire of determination to prove her wrong wells up inside me. But this isn't the time to argue. I only have one task, and it's not discussing careers.

'Indeed, as if we could all become brain surgeons if we simply wished it.' She makes a few more notes, smirking a little.

'I thought about maybe doing the astronaut programme, and going back to Earth, and other places in the Solar System. The Titan mission looks amazing and—'

She laughs. It's wicked and high-pitched. 'Out of the question, as I'm sure your father has explained to you.'

'Yes, but—'

'The specialists have been very clear, you would be unlikely to survive the trip to Earth, let alone the wildly different atmospheric pressures of our…sorry, *my* home planet.'

'But maybe there could be a facility built on Earth, equivalent to the conditions here, where I could—'

She snorts. 'A facility! Just for you? My goodness, you have been indulged with notions of ridiculous celebrity all your life.' She turns away to get a tissue to wipe her eyes and I take my chance, snatching the chip from the side of the laptop. 'Simply being born on a different planet does not give you any extra credit with me, nor does it give you special importance that would mean funding a multi-billion-dollar facility to be built exclusively for you, Eva. Do you really believe you are that special and important?'

I am so happy to have T back in my hand, that I barely hear her.

'Do you really believe you are that special and important?' she repeats.

I don't have an answer for her. I shift a little in the uncomfortable chair, and almost begin defending my suggestion, when it hits me.

She's right.

This woman, who I hate, who has replaced my dad, and turned our lives upside down. She has said something truer than anything anyone else has ever said to me.

I don't believe I am special or important.

I've been told by others my whole life, that I'm different, that I am a spectacle, even a celebrity.

But they don't treat me like I'm special or important. And they shouldn't.

'Well?' she peers over the top of her small specs.

'You're right.' I stand and move to the door.

'Where are you going? We need to finish this consultation, Eva.'

'No, I don't. As you say, I am not important. But I'm also not going anywhere. I will let you know what I want to do once I've talked it through with my dad.'

I press the button, the door swishing open.

'Eva, you may never see your dad again. You know that, right?'

I stop in the corridor and turn, just as the doors are sliding closed.

'Wrong.'

I slump down on the chair in our room, staring at the one family photo, taken of me and my parents, moments after I entered this world, and eight years before Mum left it. It's the one thing I want to take with me from this pod.

My heart is so empty without Dad.

The only thing that matters now is saving him.

I need to feel something, so I lie on the couch, wrapping myself with a blanket, staring at my picture of Mum and Dad, trying to recall the best moments with him. I only have a few minutes before I need to get upstairs and meet the others, but I take a quick moment to remember what all the risk I'm about to take, is for.

I try to imagine what life would be like if Mum had survived. I know she'd have been brilliant, and with her around, Dad would have been even better.

But then again, maybe not.

I slip the tiny chip inside my tragus and double tap it, to initialise.

'Hello?'

Well, hello there.

'T! I am so happy to hear your voice—'

Technically vibrations.

'Oh, shut up! There's so much to say, but we don't have time. T, is there anyone in the cafeteria?'

There's a moment's pause as he no doubt gets synchronised with the base systems once more.

No, most people are asleep, Eva. Perhaps you should try it, instead of another night-time excursion, which is no doubt, unauthorised.

'This is going to be much more than an excursion, and it will definitely be unauthorised. About as unauthorised as you can get.'

Oh dear, what now?

I quickly message my friends. Friends. It's weird to use that word, after all that's happened recently, but I hope after all my years of keeping them all at a distance, mentally, they'll still be willing to help me and to do the biggest thing anyone has ever asked them.

It's time. Use the magnets – we can't let anyone know what we're about to do, or where we're about to go.

22

Gathering the Team

The cafeteria is ghostly quiet.

While I wait for the others to, hopefully, show up, I stand at the surface-viewing bay. The blue sun is slowly descending beyond the mountains. The moons are rising.

In the distance, about as far away as I can see, a thick red cloud is forming. The Great Dust Storm. It looks big, rising from the ground to the very top of my view, and to both sides, too. T says it could last months or even a year. Dad won't survive that. Nobody could.

Not without my help, and the extra supplies we'll take.

I'm going to find and bring him home. But I need to get that sword – the ghost was certain I needed to use it to save Dad. Its power is…beyond anything I can understand. It scares me that I might hurt myself, or my friends again. But something tells me I must take it with me.

I'm about to go into the unknown. But hopefully not alone.

'Hey, Eva.'

I spin round and see Hercus striding in, with a steely focus on her face, ready for the rescue. And then, just behind her, I hear someone.

'Hello?'

Quasar bounces in. 'It's me.'

'You came?'

'How could I say no to this unauthorised, and highly exciting, meet-up? Especially after all we've done already. What's one more detention in the sewers.'

'I think we'll get more than detention for this next one,' I say, nerves launching into orbit from inside me.

'Well, maybe I just want to come along rather than hang out in a tiny pod with my annoying family. Nothing wrong with that, is there?' Quasar looks annoyed, but her face changes when someone else arrives.

'This *is* unauthorised.' Jay ambles into the cafeteria, leaning on the wall next to the door. 'I should report you all. The whole base is under strict curfew, unless on official duty, because of the incoming storm.'

He smiles and walks slowly towards us, his bionic legs still bedding in.

Quasar and I both become rigid. But I guess for different reasons.

'What up, space nerds!?' he says, his face breaking into a smile.

'Why are you here?' I ask, knowing one word from Jay to his mum and the rescue is over before it's started.

'Well, I couldn't help but notice you all sneaking up here.'

'How did you know? I mean, not that you're not welcome,' I tread gently. 'We disabled our trackers with the magnet like you showed us.'

'I know, and so I know how to track you even when you do that. Look, I get that it's hard to trust me, with who my mum is, and the way she is. But I was in Mum's office. After

Eva's careers interview. She lets me sit in there. Better wi-fi signal.'

I remember that from when it was Dad's office.

'And she has a monitoring screen – like a blueprint of the whole base and each of your tracker's blink in red if they leave their quarters. All three of you were stationary in here, outside of mealtimes, for far too long. I knew you were up to something.'

'What? So, she personally tracks us? I thought the trackers were monitored by like security or something.' Quasar moves towards Jay, like it's his fault.

'Yeah, it was me who re-jigged the monitoring system to allow it. She asked me to, and I was bored, so I did it. She said to keep it between us, and I was to keep an eye on it, while she was busy in the command centre, planning for the arrival of the storm. Funnily enough, I think she suspected it might be you, Eva, who'd be breaking curfew. That, plus the suspicious fire. I knew something was up, and it was likely to be you.'

'Well, you hardly need to be deGrasse Tyson to guess it would be Eva,' says Quasar, with her wicked smile.

Everyone laughs at that. Even I struggle to keep a straight face.

'I can't believe she's personally spying on us. Like she doesn't have anything better or more important to do than watch we're up to.' Hercus is back to being annoyed. 'I'm sorry, Jay, but you're just as bad for helping her with that and not telling us.'

He lowers his head. 'I know.'

I have a sudden urge to hug him.

'But you want to get involved with this? The misfits and delinquents?' Quasar raises an eyebrow.

He shrugs. 'I guess I realised you're all actually alright. Sometimes...'

Quasar laughs and the tension drops, and we all share a smile. 'Yeah, we're alright. *Sometimes*.'

'So, you're in then, Jay?'

'What is this? Why are you meeting up? Is it about Celeste?'

'If you're in, then you must swear that you'll not say a word to anyone, especially not your mum, and that you'll be willing to do even more "unauthorised" things?'

'It's not like I haven't already done a bunch of stuff with you nerds. And if there's a good enough reason, then I would do more unauthorised things?'

'How about saving my dad?' I ask. 'And Herc's.'

'Wait, he's way, way off-colony. Like, as far as anyone has gone on Mars. And he's holed up in a mine, with basically the biggest dust storm this planet has seen since humans arrived, and you want us, four kids, to go out and save him?'

'Yup.'

'But he doesn't even want saving! My mum mumbles about it all the time. Says he wants to become a martyr or whatever. The first Martian saint.'

'Well, he doesn't have a choice. That's what I'm doing. I just need to know from all of you: are you in, or are you out?'

Hercus steps forward immediately. 'In. Always in.'

Jay stands. 'Well, I know if it was my mum, pain though she is, then I'd do all I could. So, I'm in, too.'

Quasar is still standing away from us.

'How about you?' I ask her.

'Well, I don't think I could stand your sad face around here all the time if your dad didn't come back, so why not. Besides, anything to get out of that pod for a few nights.'

'So, what is the actual plan?' asks Hercus.

'Well, first of all, we need to steal the sword.'

'NO WAY!' all three of them reply.

Couldn't have said it better myself.

'We need it. I don't know exactly why, but we need it.'

'Eva, we nearly destroyed the base and killed everyone the last time you tried to take that thing.'

'You just need to trust me on this one. The ghost was adamant I needed it, and just know, deep down, that it's the right thing to do.' I don't think mentioning the ghost looking like my mum will help right now.

They look to each other, like they're vying to be the one to argue.

'Look, I know it seems crazy, but you saw the ghosts. I'm going to do it, with or without your help.'

Hercus shrugs. Jay puts his head in his hands.

But Quasar smiles. 'Well, if you're going to do it, you're going to need our help. Someone has got to keep you from doing the most stupid thing in every situation.'

Actually, that's my job. Though, clearly, I'm not very good at it.

'Thank you.'

'We need a team name. And nicknames, too. I refuse to do this unless we all have cool nicknames.' Jay looks excited now.

'What did you have in mind?' asks Hercus, who looks less than impressed with the idea of a nickname.

'Well, team name first? How about Team Mars.'

Quasar laughs. 'Lame.'

'Well, you give an idea then?' Jay snarks.

'Okay, then. How about The Storm Rovers.'

Jay snorts. 'Come on. Storm Rovers? May as well be Storm Troopers!' He smiles at his own joke.

'This is ridiculous.' Hercus starts tapping her foot.

'How about Ghostbusters?' adds Quasar, chuckling away.

'The Martian Man-Hunters,' I say, remembering an old comic-book I used to read.

'Oh, that's…perfect, actually.'

'Spot on.'

Actually, not your worst idea.

'And nicknames? If we're doing superheroes, I want to be Thor.'

'Really, Jay? You're more Bruce Banner, computer nerd, than Thor.' Quasar is enjoying this.

It's nice to see them sparring like this. It must be what friends do. I could get used to it.

'Okay, but seriously, how are we going to get that sword and how are we going to save our dads? We're already late on the original plan. Although clearly Eva had another plan.' Hercus brings us back to Mars with a thump.

'Yeah, Hercus is right. Enough messing around. We don't have time for it,' I say.

Jay and Quasar sit down at one of the tables. I remain standing, unsure of how to propose what we must do, worried about how they'll react.

'We need to find out where the sword is being held first. They have it locked away somewhere. I tried to break into the computer and find it, but it's heavily classified and encrypted.'

'I might be able to help with that,' says Jay.

'How?'

'Well, it might have been me that encrypted the location on the system. Mum doesn't have the skill to do that, so she asked me to.'

'Wow! That's amazing. Even T couldn't break down the firewall around the information,' I say.

'Who's T?' replies Jay, looking around for someone else.

'Oh, no one. It's nothing.'

No one? After all I do for you. How rude.

Jay arches an eyebrow.

'Just tell him, Eva.' Quasar has her arms crossed and is slowly tapping her foot on the metal cafeteria floor.

'T is my AI implant, who I programmed and designed, who talks to me sometimes when I need help or advice.'

'Where is he...implanted?' Jay's eyes go wide.

I point to my ear, placing my finger on the small bulge in my tragus.

Ouch!

'Sorry, T.'

'Ha! He can't feel pain surely?' Quasar jokes.

'No, but he likes being melodramatic.'

Well, excuse me! Melodramatic indeed. From the girl who is alllll about the drama.

'Right, so you have T in your ear. That was stage one. Let's get back to the plan.' Hercus taps her foot.

'I'd love to chat to you about it, Eva.' Jay looks like he just won extra rations in the Mars-Lotto. 'And wow, you programmed an AI, Eva? That's genius-level stuff! When did you learn code? One time I coded a —'

'Plan?' Hercus crosses her arms.

'Alright there, supreme leader! I have an idea.' Jay stands up. 'But it will be the ultimate betrayal. I could take down the encrypted firewall and the location will be easily searchable. Then, I could put it back up before anyone notices.'

'Won't your Mum go mad?'

'She'd go more than mad. But I'm fed up, cowering under her shadow, when I've done so much to help her, tech-wise, in all her roles. Even hacked her scores in the commander application process, to make her the outstanding candidate.'

'You did what?' I say, bristling with anger after how she spoke to me during the career consultation.

'Yes, there were a few others in contention, and the scores were all very similar. It would have been a close call, so she made me edge hers up a few points to make sure she got the role.'

'After all her lectures on following orders and commands and guidelines, and she cheated to get here.' Quasar shakes her head and walks to the viewing screen.

'Well, technically I cheated.' Jay slumps even more in his chair.

'Yes, because she told you to. We'd all do that for our parents if they asked us,' I say.

We all nod.

'This is all very outrageous and controversial and all. But it doesn't really help us right now. We need a proper, thought-out plan. And we need it before we leave this room.' Hercus pulls out a chair from under the table. 'Everyone, sit. There's a storm coming, so we need to be quick, but we also need to be prepared.'

At last. Someone with a bit of sense.

23

Trust issues

We sneak through the corridor, walking past the door to the main command centre, where commander Darshi, the last person on Mars we want to see, currently is.

'Quiet.' Jay snaps at Quasar.

'Well, stop talking then. That's louder than my footsteps.'

'Shhhh.'

'You shhhh."

Hercus gives them both the 'glare'.

Silence follows.

We continue to tiptoe, all the way to the far end of the corridor, Jay focused on the red dots on his wrist-pad.

'She's still in there. Four others too. Her office is empty.'

'Okay, let's go in.'

'Wait. I think I should do this myself.' He pauses. 'Yes, you go and get whatever you need and meet me at the rover bay door. Twenty minutes, max.'

'Are you sure you can do this yourself?' Hercus frowns.

'Trust me.'

'I do trust you. But we have a better chance if we all stick together and work as a team. I can't just leave Dad's fate in someone else's hands.'

'Okay, well here's what we can do.' Jay pulls us close and whispers instructions.

'Where is he?' Hercus checks her wrist-pad for the fiftieth time in the last minute.

'He'll be here,' I say, as much to comfort me, as them.

'What will we do if we're caught? We're already on an official warning from the break-in. Imagine what they'll do if they discover we're planning to break-out.' Quasar paces back and forth.

'We'll never be trusted enough to be engineers, or commanders, or astronauts. That's for sure. All our dreams, shattered.' Hercus shakes her head.

'You don't have to come,' I say to Quasar. 'Maybe you shouldn't. You're giving so much up, for our dads. You've got your own life and your own parents to take care of. Dad's right, I really am selfish.'

'Nah, we're all-in now. Team Martian Man-Hunter, forever!' Quasar smiles and holds out her fist.

I bump it.

Quasar does the same to Hercus, who shakes her head and stares intensely at the door that Jay should have come through about sixty seconds ago.

'He wasn't exact about the time. He'll be here.'

'Hey Herc, what's in that huge bag of yours anyway? Think Eva and I just brought some clothes.'

'Everything we'll need.'

'Like? A pop-up colony?'

'You'll be glad of it, later.' I've never seen Hercus this serious or worried. I wonder if she's regretting this now.

My foot is tapping automatically on the metal grid below and it's not until the noise makes Hercus tut, that I realise and stop.

Someone is approaching.

I wave at Quasar and Hercus to stand back from the door to our left, just in case it's not Jay and we need to make a run for the rover.

We hear movement on the other side. Someone speaking, too.

'You hear that, he's not alone,' says Hercus.

'Never trusted him,' adds Quasar. 'Let's make a run for it,'

'Wait.' I hold up my hand and move towards the door.

'Eva, come on. Your dad? We need to leave the sword.'

'It's okay. If we're going to do this, we need to trust each other. If he's told his mum, then its already game over, but we can't keep mistrusting him. He's never let us down before.'

Then Jay appears, a small card in his hand, muttering to himself.

'Sorry I took so long, but there's a lot of people to get past without looking suspicious. But I got it. We should be able to go in with this.' He waves a multi-pass. It looks like his mum's.

'And you're sure it won't set off any alarms?'

'Positive. Come on in. Let's get the sword.'

And we follow him through the door, into the secure weapons room. I'm not sure I've ever seen a weapon on the base anywhere, but this place is full of guns and knives, and other equipment for mining as well. And in the centre of the room lies a large black box.

'It's inside there. I think,' Jay shrugs, but we know he's done his research.

Together, we pull off the massive cover, and lay it gently on the floor. I peer over the rim of the box, and inside is the blade.

It's dull and unresponsive right now, like when I first saw it. Before I touched it. Before it touched me.

'Best not pick it up, Eva,' Jay warns. 'Remember what happened last time.'

I nod. We just need to get out of here with it, then I can worry about how I'm going to use it later.

'Give that to me.' Hercus swings the blade over her shoulder with ease.

'Okay, one last hurdle,' I say. 'Let's go steal a rover.'

24

How to Steal a Rover

We make it, hovering at the doors to the rover bay.

'Okay, last chance to turn around. Once we leave, I am not coming back without Dad.'

'Me neither,' says Hercus, looking up at me with watery eyes and nodding.

'Come on, Princess, don't get all mushy on us!' adds Quasar.

'The odds of us even getting out of the bay without discovery are…'

'SHUT UP!' We shout at Jay in unison.

And then we laugh. Our final laugh in the base, before I take my friends into mortal danger.

I bow my head in a moment of guilt and hope that I won't bring them to any more harm than I already have.

The others hesitate, like they're waiting to be caught at any moment…perhaps they want to be caught…it would save them from this potential one-way trip towards probable death.

But there's no one here. With the oncoming storm taking up everyone's attention, nobody is even watching four wandering kids. Plus, they'd never expect anyone to be crazy enough to try and drive a rover out into the worst storm in history.

It's not too late to turn around. It would be completely understandable.

But T's comment just strengthens my determination. Focus on the plan.

'Once I scan this pass, they'll know, and we'll have less than five minutes before they get down here and stop us. So, as we rehearsed – Jay, you grab the exo-suits, Quasar you get the O_2 tanks—as many as you can get on a trolley—and I'll get the food and water supplies.'

Don't forget the ropes. You will need them if you have to tether.

'Hercus, you get the ropes.'

They all nod.

'Okay, Jay…now.'

He swipes his mum's access card, and the doors swish open. We all move through and begin to gather the supplies. I grab one water and two food boxes – all I can drag and pull them towards the now open rover – Hercus was quick!

I pull the boxes up the ramp at the back of the rover, and into the tiny cargo bay. Already I can see it's going to be tight. I put my insulin bag down – can't forget that!

Jay approaches with the suits and hangs them quickly on the hooks, and last, Quasar is dragging a huge cart loaded with O_2 cylinders.

I rush down to help her. 'Jay, get the rover going.'

'I don't know how,' he shouts.

'Don't worry, I've got it,' says Hercus.

I leave them to it, helping Quasar to the ramp. 'The trolley won't go up; we need to load them individually.'

'It'll take too long,' Quasar grabs the first cylinder and climbs in.

167

'How long do we have, Hercus?' I place a second cylinder inside the rover.

'Less than a minute. Engines are on and ready to go.'

'Ah, Jupiter! Okay, one more each, Quasar, and then we need to go.'

'But that's only four cylinders – enough for maybe four sols if we're tight with it.'

'It will have to do.'

'The journey there and back alone will take two or three sols. And that's without the storm or any hold-ups.'

'It's fine, Quasar. Dad's party must have spare oxygen on site. All we have to do is get there.'

We load the last two cylinders, close the ramp, and Hercus edges us closer to the outer door.

'Okay, Jay – you're up.'

He swipes the access card on the rover dashboard display, which clicks, and a sudden depressurisation sucks the air from the rover bay. It makes the inner doors lock, so they'll not be able to get to us now.

Jay is in the driver's seat, clutching the steering wheel tightly. Our rover accelerates underneath the still opening outer door and we speed off down the 'main road' that leads from the base to the landing pads for the supply rockets.

As we pass them, I see the blackened carbon from the earlier rocket explosion, marking the surface and our artificial structures.

Finally, we pass the outer markers of the colony.

The coms continue to flash red, but nobody is touching it – I can just imagine the raging voice of Commander Darshi ordering us back to base. But we're committed now. There's no turning back. I'm off to save Dad.

I sit down, relieved to have managed it but, as I look at the faces of my friends, also wondering if I've made a huge mistake.

'Oh no.' Jay stares ahead.

'What?' I ask, trying to see what he's looking at.

'We have a problem.' He points to something on the virtual map. 'The bridge has collapsed.'

A large and wide canyon is directly in our path, flanked by two small hills. The only thing remaining of the old bridge is the large metal pillars at either side of the canyon. The middle must have fallen into the canyon at some point.

'Can we go around?' I ask.

'No. The rover won't manage the terrain or the steep incline of the dunes on those hills. It would add sols onto our trip to go the whole way round and we'd need to turn back towards base.'

'I suggest we do that,' says Quasar.

'How wide is the canyon, from our side to the opposite side?' I start trying to work something out.

'It's about twenty metres across and three-hundred metres deep.'

'We could jump it,' I suggest.

'Eh, nope!' says Quasar. 'Time to turn around.'

'Yeah, that sounds crazy, Eva,' adds Hercus.

'Maybe not.' Jay starts punching numbers into the control panel.

'What are you doing?' Quasar asks.

'Calculating the initial velocity required for us to jump it. There's a small, rising lip on the edge there that will act as a ramp for us to take off. If we can get up to the correct speed, we might just make it.'

'T, can you work that out for us?'

I relay what T says, once he's accounted for Mars gravity

and the angle of take-off. 'T says we need to go thirty kilometres per hour.'

Jay thinks. 'But the rover can only do—'

'Twenty-five kilometres per hour,' I interrupt. 'I know'

'That's that then. I'm turning us around.'

'No, not an option. T, could the rover go faster if we dumped some things?'

Yes, you'd need to lose about a hundred kilograms to reach the required speed.

'Okay, we need to lose some weight,' I say, looking around at the equipment behind us.

'Eva, we barely brought enough as it is.' Hercus looks worried.

I'm probably being too rash again, but we can't afford to go the long way round. I won't go back.

I have a brainwave. 'We can lose some O_2. If the rover keeps working, the MOXIE will keep producing oxygen.'

'But if the MOXIE breaks or the rover loses power, we'll have nothing to breathe, Eva. That's ridiculous.' Quasar stands in front of the oxygen tanks.

'I agree with her, actually.' Hercus stands beside her.

'Jay? What do you think?'

'I mean, in theory you're right. The MOXIE will keep us alive and if we don't use our suits much, we'll have enough oxygen to pop out of the rover for short trips, but it gives us so little back-up. If anything goes wrong, we suffocate.'

'So, you say dump the oxygen?'

'I'm not sure there's another way. The physics dictates we need to.' He shrugs and turns back to his panel.

'Well, I'm voting firmly against this crazy plan.' Quasar crosses her arms.

I turn to Hercus. 'Herc, we need to be quick. Our dads

are out there, alone, with this storm coming. They would do it for us.'

She walks back and forth for a moment. Then shakes her head. 'It is a stupid plan. And I can't believe I'm saying this, but let's dump the oxygen.'

'What? I am on a mission with three complete numpties?' Quasar shakes her head and goes up front to sit with Jay. 'I certainly won't be helping dump anything. Ridiculous.'

Herc and I roll the circular tanks off the back of the rover. One hits a sharp rock and hisses into life, thrashing across the red dust as it empties its cargo of precious oxygen.

'How's the weight, Jay?'

'Almost there. We need to lose twenty kilos more.'

'Let's dump some water then. That's heavy.' I can already sense Quasar's eyeroll, but Hercus agrees with me, and we throw that out, too.

'Are we good?' I ask.

'Yup. That's us, Chief. Strap yourselves in back there.' Jay gets the rover ready.

All I can hear down the coms is Quasar repeating, 'Crazy, crazy, crazy', so I switch her off. I'm already nervous enough.

'T, please tell me this will work.'

My calculations are accurate.

'You're one-hundred percent sure?'

I cannot be wrong, Eva. You know this, despite your best efforts to prove otherwise.

Jay starts to accelerate the rover.

'We're up to fifteen kph,' he announces.

The rover begins to jump and bump on the rocky surface.

'Twenty.'

I clutch the hand rests beside my seat tighter. Hercus closes her eyes.

'Twenty-five kph. About thirty metres from the ramp.'

I stare out of the front screen, but the sight of the fast-approaching canyon is too much. I close my eyes, too.

'Twenty-eight. Ten metres from the ramp.'

Come on, come on. Please give us this one. Please let me not mess up again.

The rover is jumping and juddering around so hard my teeth are clashing.

Then we're airborne.

The juddering stops and is replaced by a light feeling, almost like floating. I sneak a look out the screen and see the blue sun setting behind the mountains far away. Despite my belt I lift out of my seat, and then we reach the highest point and I drop back down.

'Nooooooo!' Hercus, who is furthest back, shouts.

I whip my head round and see the problem. The back ramp has been forced open, probably during the fast, bumpy run-up, and two oxygen tanks slide out disappearing into the canyon below.

We begin to fall, the landscape rushing up to meet us, and our rover's nose begins to point downwards. I see the red floor of Mars. But it's too far away. We're going to come up short.

We're not going to make it. I close my eyes.

The rover crashes hard.

But keeps motoring forward.

'WE MADE IT!' Jay's voice screams through the rover.

I open my eyes and see only dust in the screen, but we're definitely across the canyon and driving beyond.

Jay slows the rover to a stop, and we all whoop and bump fists, except Quasar.

I turn to Hercus. 'We just jumped over a canyon in a rover. That's pretty cool, huh?'

She shakes her head. 'Remind me NEVER to come off the base with you again.'

But Quasar punctures the moment. 'Yes, very good heroes, but we've lost two more oxygen tanks, so save that cheering breathe. We're gonna need it.'

'The co-ordinates are stored in the system, Eva, so I'll just drive in the general direction for now. When the storm gets closer, we might need to look at alternative routes that are more sheltered from it.'

'Thanks Jay.'

'I feel obligated to tell you, though, that I don't think this is the wisest course of action I've ever taken. In fact, statistically it's the poorest.'

'And I appreciate it. All of you. I know how much you are all risking for me, and my dad.'

'And Hercus' dad, and the other ten colonists who are with them,' Quasar adds. 'The workers who, as usual, are forgotten. I am here for them, as much as for your dad.'

'Of course,' I say, sliding back in my seat and closing off the chat for now.

I mentally re-calculate our O_2 consumption, as we now have two cylinders instead of six. Our only hope now, is that there are cylinders that are still intact in the mine and haven't been completely used up. It's a total guess, and I'm taking a huge chance, but I must do it. I'd rather die trying to save Dad than live without him.

25

Are We Alone?

'Mars is actually quite a beautiful place. I've never really appreciated it from our base. I mostly thought about the inside, rarely about the planet.' I stare out of the window at the landscape. We've already passed the first ever Falcon Heavy rocket that landed with humans, sitting just below the tall, spiky rock, Tesla Tower. It's part of my history.

'Dead dust and rock. Poisonous atmosphere. Enough solar radiation to ensure it stays lifeless for eternity. Yup, a real beauty.' Quasar rolls her eyes, but doesn't stop looking out of her window.

'You don't get it, Quasar, it's not about living things,' says Jay. 'The rock formations, the way the planet once was and how that's caused it to look like it does now, it's all history. Millions of years in the making. It's different from Earth, which is teeming with life, and all the better for it. That's why it's beautiful. The lifelessness that has made it fascinating to humans for hundreds of years is what inspired us to come here and explore.'

'We're not here to explore – we're here to inhabit, to

transform Mars to our will, to suit us, to make a second Earth for us to escape to once we mess up the first one. There's no beauty to that, just destruction.'

'So, who wants some more nutri-soup?' I ask, handing out rations for our dinner, and trying to diffuse the argument evolving between Quasar and Jay.

'Again? We had that for lunch – what else is there?' asks Quasar.

'That's it – or algal-jerky. And some cricket-chips.'

'Oh great! I certainly won't be touching the crickets. Barbaric.'

'You could have picked two boxes with better food in them,' adds Hercus.

I shake my head. 'Hardly had a chance to sit down and make a delicious food plan for us all, did I? How was I supposed to know they'd be exactly the same?'

'They have these great rice ones, don't they? And for special occasions, I've heard there's imported bacon. I'd love a bit of bacon right now,' says Hercus.

Quasar purses her lips. 'It's ridiculous to have meat products up here. Plant produce is by far the more energy efficient. Ninety percent of energy is lost by that one step more in the food chain and…'

We sit and suck on our nutri-soup, while Jay drives. For someone who had never driven a rover before he's already insisting only he drives, and we're only a few hours into the journey. Says he won't leave the wheel until he's mastered it.

'I think the sat-nav is wrong. I think I've worked out a better route.' Jay shouts back to us.

'Stick to the sat-nav for now,' I say. 'We don't want to get lost before we've even got close, especially if the storm closes in around us. We can only drive blind if we're following the sat-nav on auto-drive.'

'Yes, but I can save us around six hours with my route. O_2 is tight, so statistically it is worth it.'

I take a deep breath. Saving oxygen and getting to Dad quicker seems like the obvious choice, but it's risky. If we leave the path and get lost, or trapped, no-one will be able to track us.

'Okay, I have an idea. I wonder if Thunderchild could be inserted into the rover's motherboard and could help us more directly?'

'Good idea, using his logic algorithms he could help us navigate the route better than the sat-nav.' Jay seems excited by the prospect of the experiment.

'Okay but be careful with him. If you think it's not going to work, stop immediately.'

'Got it.'

'Sorry, T. Just going to take you out for a moment.'

Do I get a say in this?

'T, we need you. We really need you.'

Get on with it, then.

I carefully remove the chip from my tragus and pass it to Jay. He handles it delicately, which is a relief, and then slowly lifts the panel to the circuitry beneath. I can't see what he does next.

But it doesn't take long.

'There, all done,' he announces. 'Let me try and sync T with the speakers in here.

He presses a few buttons.

'T, can you hear us?'

Indeed.

His voice reverberates throughout the rover, clear and with a tone that is both familiar and new.

Oh, this is not…natural.

'Weren't you designed to talk via speakers on your AI body?' Jay knows EVERYTHING!

Well, you have a point. Perhaps I have become too accustomed to communication via vibrations alone.

'T, are Jay's directions good? Can we do it and save time?' I worry about every second we waste, imagining my dad alone, hurt, or dead in that mine.

Yes, his alternative map is mostly good. I will make a couple of alterations, though, to optimise our journey time.

Quasar's eyes flick between Jay and the speaker where T's voice is coming from. 'Can you even tell which one is which?' she whispers in my ear, then laughs.

'Fine. Let's do it then, Jay.' I try to sound assertive and certain, but neither is coming naturally. Truly, we are all out of our depth. Especially me.

'Strap yourselves in. Not entirely sure how smooth the surface is likely to be on this new route.'

'Do we have any music?' Quasar asks.

After eight hours of driving, we need to stop to charge the battery via the solar panels.

'I don't think the rovers are fitted with a collection, somehow,' says Jay, laughing.

Well, actually, I have some music in my memory.

'You do? What is it?'

Rock Ballads Forever. From the 1980s. I believe it's from Commander Knight's collection.

'Put it on,' I say, excited to hear something other than the hum on the rover's MOXIE.

A warm and comforting sound comes from the speakers and I'm seven again, playing with Dad in the living room, before I became burdened with my own fame and Dad's over-protectiveness.

'This is OK,' says Hercus. 'I think I actually like it.'

'Me, too.' Jay is bobbing his head up and down.

'Oh please. What a waste of battery. You're all acting like this is just a fun trip off the base, and not the life-threatening mission that it actually is.' Quasar moves to the back of the rover and lies down in her sleeping bag. 'Wake me when this ear-sore is over.'

'It gives me hope,' I say. 'Hope that we'll find them. All alive and just mining away. That what I saw on the video wasn't as bad as it looked. And we'll bring them back again. Or we'll be told off for doing this. Maybe grounded for a hundred sols. I'd take that if they were all okay. That one sol we'll all be able to dance to this in our apartment, or even in our hovel in The Pits. I don't care anymore; I just want one more moment with him.'

I could keep talking, but they're all staring at me. And when I stop talking, they all quickly look away.

'Sorry,' I say.

'No, don't be sorry. We'd all be the same about our parents.'

'Well, I wouldn't go that far,' says Jay, rolling his eyes.

'You love your mum though, right? Even if she's sometimes…'

'Horrible? Yeah, I still love her. She cares for me, in her own, unusual way. I know she'll be worried about me out here. It's tough, with it just being the two of us, and her moving from job to job. But it's kept us close I reckon.'

I find it hard to imagine anyone loving Jay's mum, but your parents are always your parents, even if it's hard to like them sometimes.

The music stops.

Sorry to interrupt, but we have a problem.

'What now?'

The solar panels are not charging the battery.

'Do you know why?'

There's zero photo absorption, like there's no sun, but the lux readings are high. And we need this charge because once we hit the storm, there will be no more.

'Okay, I'll go out and look,' I say, sliding into my exo-suit.

'I'll come, too,' adds Hercus.

'Jay, keep an eye on the weather map. I don't want anything sneaking up on us while we're out there. They might send out drones.'

'Yes, boss.' He salutes.

I laugh. 'T is the boss.'

'Okay, so it looks like a big dump of Martian dirt on the solar panels.' I stand on the roof of the rover, looking down at the three large panels. One beneath my feet, on the roof, and two that slide out from the sides of the rover, like wings.

'How?' asks Hercus. 'There's almost no wind out here. It doesn't make sense.'

'Weird but didn't Professor Labou once tell us it's like an electrostatic thingy?' adds Quasar.

'Oh, I know this one – it's because the atmosphere on Mars is so thin and conditions are extremely dry, dust particles become charged, making them stick to the panels.' Jay sounds so excited to inform us all. I actually remember that one, and it is a cool fact.

But Quasar is less impressed that he's improved on her fact. 'Yeah, basically what I said - hurry up and get them cleaned so we can get going again.'

'Why don't you come out and help?' Hercus peaks in through the window.

'No thanks. I have to stay in here and make sure Jay doesn't do anything stupid.'

Hercus and I sweep off as much of the dirt as we can with our gloves, careful to make sure there's no sharp pieces that could puncture them.

'Okay, that's them mostly cleared.' I hop down from the rover roof. 'T, how is the photon absorption efficiency now?'

Eighty-seven percent.

'That'll do for now.'

Hercus and I head back inside the rover. The other two are sitting in their suits, sweltering. The rover seems too hot.

Once we seal the door, we all remove our helmets.

'Why's it so hot?'

'Yeah, I noticed that, too?'

'Is it the battery heating up now that it's charging?'

Battery temperature is stable. It's a blockage in the MOXIE which is causing the issue. It will need clearing, or the unit will overheat, and oxygen generation will cease.

'Well, we'd best unblock it then.'

'How about you go this time, Quasar?' Hercus smiles.

'What do I know about MOXIEs?'

'Well, maybe you should have learned? Why are you here anyway? What skills are you bringing?'

'Leave it, Hercus. I'll go. You come this time, Jay.'

'No, I want to know what snide comment Quasar has for us now.'

Quasar goes even redder. She shakes her head and marches to the back of the rover and slumps down.

'Nothing? Good. I'll come with you, Eva. I don't think leaving me and her in here together is a good idea.'

The room becomes silent. I want to defuse the argument

but have no idea what to say. I need to keep them together, so we can get through this. It's not just about saving the miners and Dad now, it's about keeping my friends alive and getting them home, too.

'Helmets on.' It's all I can manage.

They all do it, though, and Hercus and I climb out again to clean the MOXIE.

26

Losing Oxygen

Hercus lies underneath the rover, occasionally asking me for a tool.

'She does nothing to help, and just sits around making comments all the time. She has nothing nice to say about anyone or anything,' Hercus says, using the private tether-com.

'She's not that bad. She's actually really nice when you get to know her better,' I say.

'I know her well enough. You didn't need to bring those two, you know, Eva. I would have come along and helped and been enough.'

'You're the best, Herc. You really are. But they were willing to help, and without Jay, we wouldn't have the sword.'

'True, he did help. And he knows some stuff, too. But Quasar is just dead weight. Using up our oxygen and food and bringing down morale. And we're only on the first sol.'

'Give her a chance. I promise you'll like her before we get back to the base.'

'There's more chance of us meeting a Martian, than me liking Quasar.'

'We'll see.'

'Hand me those tweezers, Eva.'

I slide under the rover and hand her the tool. The movement makes my stomach twinge. Actually, it's worse than that, enough to make me wince. 'You see what's blocking it?'

'Yeah. But it's weird. There are small rocks wedged in there – really far up. It's like someone pushed them inside the CO_2 intake valve.'

'Someone?'

'Yeah, I know how it sounds. But them being here is not natural.'

'Just get them out. We need to rest while the panels charge, and then get moving when the sun sets and drive through the night. We might get ahead of the storm and maybe get some sun in the morning.'

'Maybe. Right, that's it cleared.'

'Don't tell the other two about this.'

'What, about it being wedged in by someone?'

'Yeah, I'm trying to keep everyone's spirits up. If they start thinking something, or someone is messing with us, it won't help that moral situation you mentioned.'

We both slide out from beneath the rover and look all around.

The Martian landscape is beautiful. Dunes and rocks and valleys. But also, unknown. We really don't know what's out there. And my mind keeps coming to one conclusion.

We are not alone. Aliens, ghosts, or some other lifeform. Something else is here.

We climb back on board, and I realise the time. 'Hey, have any of you guys seen my insulin case? I need to take a dose.' I lift all the small boxes and cases of food, looking for it.

'What does it look like?' Hercus asks.

'It's red, with the image of a needle on it. It put in next to the O_2 cylinders when we came on. Luckily, I remembered to grab it before we left, I can't believe I nearly forgot it.'

'What would happen if you didn't have it?' Quasar asks, stepping side to side, nervously.

I stand up. 'Quasar don't mess around with me. You know I need it, or I'll get very sick. My glucose levels will go so high, I'll be in a lot of trouble.'

She looks worried.

'Quasar? What is it?'

She backs away towards the cockpit. 'Don't be mad.' She slides in beside Jay and slams the cockpit door closed, separating them from me and Hercus.

'What are you doing? Why would I be mad?'

'I think…I think I threw out a red case when we were trying to lose weight. It was next to the water and oxygen, wasn't it?'

I stare at her in the front of the Rover, shifting around nervously. I should be mad; I want to shout and scream.

But I don't. That was my call to dump the weight and try that jump.

'It's fine,' I say, relaxing and sitting down.

'It is?' Quasar asks. 'But you said it would cause you a lot of trouble.'

'It will. But it's not like I haven't been high before. I will just need to cope.'

It isn't fine, it's the complete opposite of fine, but even as the fear rises inside me, I understand that panicking everyone else isn't going to help.

'I'm so sorry.' She slides the door and sits next to me. 'You know I wouldn't have done that if I knew what was in the case.'

'I know. We've got to keep focused on our mission. No point in us arguing over something we can't do anything about now.'

I don't say anything to them, but I'm already feeling hyperglycaemic. If I don't eat too much over the next few hours, it won't go crazy high.

I can't afford to be sick right now. Dad needs me.

'We should send the drone-copter ahead, to scope out the landscape and weather ahead,' Jay suggests.

'Agreed. Send her up.' It might also see what blocked the MOXIE and covered the solar panels in dust. I have my suspicions but neither Quasar nor Jay needs to know that. Yet.

'How far do we have to go, T?' I know we'll hit the storm at some point, but I want to be as close to Dad's location as possible before that.

Approximately fifty kilometres. The storm is getting close now. Should be with us sometime today.

'So, we'll be driving through the storm? There's no way to avoid it?'

Not unless you can drive beneath the surface of Mars, or fly above the clouds?

Quasar laughs. 'He's funny. How did you programme him to be funny?'

'I didn't – he learns human traits by listening and imitating.'

'Still pretty cool, though?'

'Pretty annoying.'

Well, really. I can hear you...

'I know, T.' I smile.

'So, what we're saying is that we could make it to the mine

opening today, but if we drive into the storm, we could get lost or delayed?'

'Yes,' says Jay. 'And an added problem is that when we enter the storm, we'll no longer be able to use the solar panels to power the Rover. Whatever we have entering the storm is all we will have until we make it to the mine.'

'So, we have no time to lose, today. Drive, drive, drive,' I say. 'T, we need you to fly the copter-drone in front of us and give us warning for the storm...and anything else you might spot.'

Affirmative.

The Rover trundles along, Jay pushing the speed a little more than previously, and my teeth bang together more than once.

Quasar, Herc and I are strapped into the equipment bay at the back of the rover, slipping into uneasy naps before being violently awoken by a bump or two.

'Hey, are you two okay?' I ask, the guilt of dragging my friends along again wriggling in my tummy.

'Absolutely, Eva.' Hercus never gives an inch.

'Oh, top of the world. Wouldn't want to be anywhere else; we've got storms and sand, and Jupiter knows what else ahead of us.'

'If I had to do it again, I don't think I'd have forced you to come along.'

'Nobody forced us, Eva,' says Hercus.

'She's right. We came because we wanted to help. And it did sound fun.' Quasar smiles, that mask that covers everything going on beneath.

They are worried, whether they admit it or not. And I'm terrified. Not just of losing Dad, but that I'll lose one of them in the process.

EVA?

T's voice booms through the speakers in the back of the rover.

'Yes, what's the update?'

The first wave of the storm is approaching.

As we drive forward, small gusts of wind sweep over us, bringing heaps of sand and dust, and muddying the landscape from view. It shifts and turns, sparkling in the air and then …

'STOP!' I shout, pointing out the window.

Jay slams the brakes, skidding us to a halt.

Dust whips around the window in front, blotting out anything more than ten metres from the rover.

'Did you see that? There's someone out there. A person. Or a figure or something.' I'm sure of it.

'I didn't see anything.' Jay leans forward and peers into the edge of the storm.

Quasar and Hercus pop their heads into the driver seats. 'What's going on?'

'Eva thinks she saw someone. Or something?'

'I did.'

Quasar presses her nose to the window. 'I can't see any—'

BANG!

Something hits the back of the rover.

Our heads jerk to the location of the noise.

'That wasn't just me, was it?' I ask, not sure if I'm hoping I imagined it or not.

'No, we all heard that one,' says Hercus.

'We should just drive.' Jay is poised to hit the accelerator.

'No.' Every part of me wants to speed off, but I can't keep running from the ghosts forever. And maybe, just maybe, it's the one who is my mum.

And then I remember what Mum-Ghost said about the sword.

'Hold on.' I suit up, and carefully take the sword from the

unit we've been storing it in, worried that it could activate at any moment.

Maybe I'm feeling weak, or my glucose is off the scale, but it's heavy, and my arms shake as I hold it and move to the exit. The pain in my stomach doubles. I need stronger painkillers.

'Seal off the driver section,' I say. The door seals Quasar and Jay in the front of the rover.

'Eva, don't go out there. We need every second moving forward to get to our dads.' Hercus is now in her suit, too. She tilts her head and puts her hand on my shoulder.

'I have to see what it is. I just have…a feeling.' I hit the button and the external rover door slides open.

We're both whacked by a sudden spray of dust and dirt.

I step out, immediately feeling unsteady in the poor visibility and strong winds.

'Tether up,' Hercus reminds me.

'Yes, nearly forgot.' I tether to my friend who in turn tethers to the side of the rover.

I walk to the back of the vehicle, lifting the sword, ready for whatever comes next.

But there's nothing there. Nothing that I can see.

We walk the whole way around the rover and still nothing.

'Let's go back inside.'

I agree with Hercus and follow her to the door. As she steps inside, the door closes, the tether between us snaps and I'm hauled backwards into the storm, away from the rover.

My stomach lurches, as my feet leave the ground. I grip the sword hard and hope for the best.

For about twenty seconds of terror, the winds swing me back and forth, up, and down, and I wonder if this is the end. How can the wind be this strong? And then I think of Dad and start swimming my arms towards where I think the ground might be.

And it starts to work – I move in the direction I want to. But then the wind seems to release me. And I fall.

When I land on my back, I drop the sword and cradle my sore ribs.

The coms in my helmet crackle, but nothing clear comes through.

'Hercus? Quasar? Jay? T?' I repeat their names several times, but I get no answer.

I can see nothing now, just red sand and rocks and then…

The sword begins to glow beside me.

And then an outline approaches, growing in intensity.

A ghost.

27

The Great Dust Storm

'Mum?'

Look below the surface.

Mum-Ghost opens her hand and gestures to the ground.

'For what? What's below the surface? Is it Dad?'

She nods. **And remember the blade. It is the downfall and the saviour of Dad. His fall and rise. The only way to save him.**

'That's what you said before. Do you mean he's below the surface and the sword will help him come back up?' I recall the feeling of flying high above Mars when I last let its power take over me.

Her image begins to fade.

'Tell me. Help me.' I shout it, but she's gone, leaving me alone.

But as she disappears the storm eases a little and I'm able to see further around me.

I stare at the ground, wondering if Dad is down there somewhere – but that doesn't make sense. The mine is supposedly fifty km away. The last time we checked, his signal was still coming strong from the mine.

Maybe she isn't being as helpful as I want her to be. Maybe she's leading us off-course.

But she's different from the other ghosts. They chill my bone marrow and freeze my neurons. They make me more scared of anything, except losing Dad, or being stuck on this planet.

She's my mum. Or at least the face of my mum.

I wish I had T right now, to play the recording of her voice. I need that reassurance right now to keep going, to trust her ghost. But he's stuck in the rover dashboard and I'm alone.

But then the rover appears a few metres from me, and jerks to a sudden stop. I rush over and watch the side door lift open.

Hercus grasps my hand and hauls me inside with more power than the storm. 'What happened?'

'The storm pulled me away. But I'm back, and I'm okay, I think. We need to get moving because we're still too far away. Time is running out before the worst of the Great Dust Storm arrives – that was just a prologue.'

Jay spins round in the driver's seat. 'I'm not sure how far we—'

'Drive, Jay. We have no choice.'

'Alright, fasten your seatbelts. This is gonna be bumpy.'

The odds of successfully navigating the rover fifty km through this storm are approximately—

'SHUT UP, T! You're nearly as bad as Jay.' Quasar winks at Jay.

The heart of the storm arrives.

When I was outside the base, rescuing Dad, and lifting the sword, the dust was difficult. Now, it's impossible. And impassable.

'We need to stop, Eva. I can't drive in this anymore. We could hit a rock at any time and crack the hull or the windows. It's too risky.'

'But it won't pass, will it? Not until it's too late, for the miners and us?'

Storms of this magnitude tend to have peaks and troughs, and this is just peak of the first wave. I don't think it will last too long and visibility should get a little better, and we can proceed.

'Can't we use radar or something?' asks Quasar. 'These things have it installed, right?'

Yes, the old RIMFAX equipment for detecting water beneath the surface is still installed. But radar uses a lot of power, five to ten watts, which we can't spare, and the antenna is pointed downward.

'So, we're just stuck here?' asks Quasar.

Yes. We must wait.

'Well, let's use the time productively,' I suggest. 'Let's have a look through the maps of the mine on the computer system.'

Jay punches a few words into the keyboard and a 3D, but very rough, map appears on the window.

'They've gone quite deep in places, look at all those shafts…they look almost like precisely carved rooms…' Hercus frowns.

'They do look very square. There's no way Dad and the team could have dug that.'

'I agree,' says Jay, who peers at the image and looks very confused. 'The entrance tunnels drilled by us are all a certain shape, rough at the edges. These have been made by someone else'

'Someone? You mean not us?'

'Yes.'

My thoughts immediately stray to the ghosts. Are they the ghosts of a people who once inhabited this mine? That perhaps lived in those smoothed rooms, under the mountain. The thought of Dad trapped with those ghosts makes my mouth dry and my heart thunder. Is that what those dark shapes were that we saw on the video link?

Look below the surface.

'You said the antenna was facing down, T?'

Affirmative.

'Well, let's look down.'

'Eva, I'm not sure—'

'Just try it. Trust me.'

The three of them exchange a look. The same one they use when I mention the ghosts or the sword and ask them to trust me.

Activating RIMFAX. It will take a few moments to boot up and for the scans to be complete. It's very old, almost obsolete software. I would recommend it be deleted entirely upon return to the colony.

My stomach grumbles as we wait. I've avoided eating to keep my glucose levels from going crazy high, but I'm not sure how much longer I can hold out. The dizziness is intense, and the thirst is overwhelming. I hope none of them notice how much I'm sipping my recycled water.

I have some results.

A 3D drawing begins to appear, showing the scan of the ground beneath us.

Many of the tunnels and pockets from the mine map are visible at the very edge of the scan, but still too far to reach from here on foot.

But only ten metres below us is a slowly descending surface tunnel.

'We're right on top of our way in!' Jay gives Quasar a

high-five. He holds up his hand to Hercus, but he's left hanging.

'So, we need to drill down.' Hercus looks absorbed.

'T, does the rover have any drills attached? You know, for collecting rock samples etc?'

Well, yes. But not powerful enough that they can go that deep. In all probability, they would overheat just a few metres below the surface and blow the fuses. And the power drain would completely empty the rover's battery.

'How certain are you, T?'

60%.

'60% is good enough for me. If we get below the surface, into this tunnel, we wouldn't need the rover anymore. We could walk the rest of the way to the mine – fill our suits with as much oxygen as they can carry - it's not so far now, and we'd be out of the storm.'

'And how about getting home?' asks Quasar, her eyes wide.

'There's the other rover. The one my dad and his team brought. We return in that.'

'But how do we know it's still functional?' Jay stands again and begins to pace in the cargo bay. 'It could be drained, too. It could have no resources or battery or anything, and then we'd be stuck. This rover is our lifeline. I don't fancy leaving it if we don't have to.'

'I'm with Jay,' says Quasar.

'Hercus?' I ask. 'What do you think?'

'It's risky. We might not even get through the ten metres with the drill. And T seems to think it's a bad idea.'

'So, none of you agree with me?' I close my eyes and flop my skull against the headrest. 'This is impossible.'

'We just have to wait out the storm.'

Hercus is right. They are all right. Probably. But I can't sit and do nothing. If we wait and get to Dad and the miners too late, I'd never forgive myself. Never.

'You have five minutes to come up with a better idea than mine, while I go out and align the drills. If not, we go down.'

'No, Eva. This is a terrible idea.' Hercus stands in front of the exit. 'I won't let you do this. I know you're a do-er. I know you act first, think later. And I love you for it sometimes. It's such a strength, but it's also your biggest weakness. This is too much of a risk, even for you. We didn't have a choice with the canyon jump, but we do have other options here.'

My body tenses hard. I could never take Hercus, but I'm also not waiting.

'Move.' My teeth grit. 'Now.'

She shakes her head, and then Jay stands beside her.

I glance around for something to help me fight my way out. And I see the sword. As my eyes move to it, Hercus second guesses me and moves for it.

But I'm quicker and I grab the hilt and hold it in front of me.

Sparks fly.

The hilt begins to warm. The blade colours, like a rainbow.

'Eva, put it down.' Hercus has both her palms facing down. 'Please.'

'I will not. We are drilling, and if you try to stop me… well…just don't try to stop me.'

She nods and steps back.

'Get in the cockpit, all of you.'

They nod and slowly move into the driver's seats. I close the door.

'T, lock the cockpit. And the manual controls.'

I am not sure—

'Just do it. You are supposed to help me.'

Eva, I can't help but—

'T, Dad will die if we don't help him soon. There's a whole group of miners who need us. You must trust me. This is the right thing to do.'

He doesn't respond verbally but I hear the door click.

I open the external door and walk out, clinging to the side of the rover with one hand, dragging the sword in the other.

It's morphing colour and shade even more dramatically and variably now, like it's building in power. I can sense it, too.

Lightning strikes in the distance.

I lay the sword down and open the side compartment that contains the drills and storage containers for rock samples. I pull the containers out and chuck them into the storm.

Then I pull the long arms that hold the main drill down and aim it directly beneath the rover.

I tap into the rover coms. 'T, begin drilling. Give it all the power we have.'

Eva, I really must insist—

'JUST DO IT.'

And it begins. Rock and dust spray upwards from the penetration points, but it's little difference out in this storm anyway. I catch a glimpse of the sword again, beginning to fade in colour and luminosity, maybe because I'm not holding it.

I don't want to lose it under a heap of sand, so I pick it up and use it to lean on. One hand on the hilt, one on the side of the rover, to keep me steady. I know my glucose levels must be all over the place. My mouth is so dry.

Lightning strikes again. This time much closer.

'T, how close was that?'

Twenty metres. I'd advise coming inside Eva. It is not safe, especially as you are touching two metallic items.

I look at the sword, then the rover. I can't let go of either.

'I have to stay here in case the drill jams.' I'd do anything for a sip of water – it hurts to swallow.

And then I notice a small change in the external sounds. It's so noisy with the storm, but the shrill, tearing noise of the drill has stopped.

'T, what's the status with the drills?'

The drills have overheated, as I predicted, and the fuses have now blown. Luckily, we did not use all the power from the battery in this futile effort.

'Futile?' I bang the side of the rover with my glove. 'FUTILE!'

Eva, I suggest you take a few calming, deep breathes and return—

I lift the sword high above my head and swing the blade towards the ground as hard as I can muster.

Just as it meets solid rock, my body is hypersensitised with a feeling I've only had twice before.

And both times it nearly killed me. And others.

Lighting strikes for a third time, connecting with my blade at the same moment as the tip slams into the ground.

The floor of Mars begins to crumble.

And both the rover and I slide down into the sinkhole that's been created.

The vehicle drops first, crashing down into the darkness below.

And as I follow, I see a clear image of my mother's ghost beneath me, smiling and saying, 'Well done.'

28

Farewell, Thunderchild

The rover is dead. And Thunderchild with it.

Jay pronounced it a minute ago.

It was like watching a friend dying, as the last flickers of the rover's battery life disappeared. T might have been salvageable, but his chip seems to have fused to the motherboard of the rover because of the massive electrical current from the sword. We'd need to weld it off and we don't have the equipment here. Or the time.

He kept us alive these last two sols, as we asked him a million questions to help us. He helped us survive the storm and sheltered us from the worst.

He's been my friend, sometimes my only one, for so long now.

As it sits there, cold, and still, a wave of grief almost buckles my legs. It's just an AI chip. A set of algorithms I rewrote. But it got us to the cusp of finding Dad and the other missing miners. I didn't know if I'd ever see him again. Even as we got closer, he seemed so far away. But you carried us here, T, through the harshest of conditions a human could possibly face.

And for that, Thunderchild, I will be forever grateful.

Sleep well.

The tunnel we've arrived in is warm, dark, and damp. The roof is only just out of Hercus' reach, and it's wide enough for the four of us to walk together. Just.

The water on the walls looks like it's moving, so there must be a source somewhere nearby. I can't help but wonder who built all of this. And why? And more importantly, where are they now?

Everyone else seems fine physically, although Jay isn't moving all that smoothly, but we're all a bit shaken.

'Listen, I think we need to discuss what happened up there.' I haven't been able to look them in the eye since we descended.

'Don't worry about it,' says Hercus, avoiding looking at me at all.

'I am so sorry. I just get so caught up in the moment and I can't lose him. He's the only family I have.'

'Seriously, just leave it,' adds Quasar.

'Do you want to know what happened?'

'We don't care.' Jay is the first one to look at me since we fell. 'I thought you cared about us, too, that we were friends, but it's obvious you only care about one thing, and you'll do anything, at any cost, to get it.'

'But I wouldn't. I mean…not deliberately. I thought…'

'Enough.' Hercus shouts. 'We have enough problems without this.'

Thanks to RIMFAX, Thunderchild, the powerful sword, and the ingenuity and genius of my three quick thinking friends, with a dash of my own stupidity, we have made it to the mine.

Well, about 100 feet below the mine, but still, this natural, ancient tunnel has saved us time and our lives. We'd never have made it through the storm on the surface.

It's warm now in our suits, padded against the extreme temperatures on the surface, lined with hydrogenated boron nitride nanotubes (BNNT) to reduce our radiation absorption. We are surrounded by geothermal vents which not only cook us but steam up our visors.

'This is impossible!' shouts Quasar over the coms.

'Impassable, perhaps. Difficult, yes. But not impossible. In fact, our odds are better down here than they were on the surface…'

'I don't need to hear this right now, Jay!'

'I don't need to hear your hyperbolic exaggerations of survival chances either, but I don't shut you down.'

I push past the arguing pair, up a long, steep incline. 'How close are we to the mine?'

'About half a kilometre this way. We should have enough oxygen to get there. Let's hope they have a supply on their rover.'

'Or breathable air in the mine?' suggests Hercus. 'Like in the Pits back home?'

'Ummm, guys…' Quasar's voice trembles through the coms.

Our heads jerk round in unison. Behind us, crawling and slithering along the walls, ground, and ceiling of the tunnel, are hundreds of oxide vipers.

Even through our suits, we can hear the hissing…or is it the vibrations of the hissing…?

'Turn on your all your lights,' I say, tapping my wrist-pad to turn on the helmet and wrist lamps. 'It interferes with their infrared vision. Then, we could pull out those support pillars and bring the roof down?'

'Are you mad?' Quasar's eyes are wide through her visor.

'It would stop the vipers behind us – they'd struggle to follow us then. We can't exactly outrun them. Do you have a better idea?'

Jay shakes his head. 'Probably not better, but maybe you could use the sword?'

I stare at it, fastened to the side of my suit. 'What if I crushed us, too? I can't seem to properly control it.'

'I agree, maybe leave the sword out of it this time.' I'm so grateful to Hercus for making the decision.

She points. 'Right, Eva, we'll take out the pillars simultaneously. I don't know how long it will take for the roof to come down, so but we've got to make a run for it as soon as we remove them.'

'Got it.'

'Jay, Quasar, get as far down the tunnel as you can just in case more of the cave falls in than I think.'

'I'm not sure about this...'

'Quasar, trust me. It'll be fine.' Hercus gives her a warm smile. The first I've ever seen her direct to Quasar.

They run off. The vipers have spotted us and are starting to crawl out of the cave. They're sluggish after being in the dark, but they're getting livelier, and quicker. We shine as much light on them as we can and although a few retract, others slither further out of the shadows.

'It's now or never, Herc,' I say. She nods and we dash to the pillars, and I pull hard. It doesn't budge.

I pull away at the rock around it, trying to loosen it. Vipers hiss at my feet, overhead, and on the walls around us, looking for a place to strike and sink their fangs and venom into us. 'Hercus, it won't budge.'

She has already hauled her pillar from its roots and chucks it right at the swarm of vipers on the floor of the cave.

'Hold them off with both lights, I'll get the pillar.' She chucks me her wrist-pad and I shine both lights, only partly stemming the tide of snakes sweeping towards us.

I hear the soft fall of rock from the roof. Hercus pulls at the second pillar. It loosens from its holding.

'Now, go,' shouts Hercus. 'I'll catch up. This is definitely going to crash down as soon I pull it.'

'Not without you!'

'Don't get stupid. I'm much faster than you. I'll catch up. Go.'

A viper lands on my shoulder and I jerk it off as its fangs snap at the air. A second one lands on my helmet and bites hard. I punch it away, lucky that didn't penetrate the metal, and start running, knowing I won't get so lucky again.

I glance back to see Hercus pull the pillar free. Then she stops. And so do I as I realise what's happening.

The vipers have filled the space between us and Hercus could never follow me without being bitten a thousand times.

I scream. 'Please, don't. Just run. We can outrun them.'

But she just smiles.

And then the cave roof comes crashing down between us.

'Hey, where's Herc?' Quasar sits on a rock, along with Jay, resting after their sprint along the tunnel.

I shake my head.

Jay stands up. Quasar lowers her head.

'What happened?' Jay's voice trembles down the coms.

'She just...she...saved us.' I fall to my knees.

Jay shuffles awkwardly over to me and places a loose arm

around me and pats my shoulder with his other hand. I gaze at Quasar with wide eyes and tears slide down her cheek.

Then she joins us, and we stand there in a strange, silent, awkward, mourning embrace. I wish Herc was here to squeeze us.

And I'm simultaneously guilty, because I've just lost the best of my friends, and the superficial hugs don't come close to bringing light into the dark abyss that's developed in my chest. All I can see is Hercus, smiling sadly, as the walls crashed around her. The image will haunt me forever.

'We have to go back,' I say.

But hisses already come from behind us, and it's clear that despite bringing the roof down, the vipers have somehow slithered through.

'We need to go. We must go on. The vipers will catch up with us soon,' Jay replies.

I release both, standing stubbornly on the spot. I should go back, but the growing number of snakes between us make it impossible.

We start marching up the tunnel, away from the snakes, slowly climbing.

'She did it, though.' Quasar walks alongside me. 'She stopped the vipers. Her plan worked.'

'It should have been me. I couldn't lift the pillar, which is why she was behind me. She had to lift both.'

'That's not your fault, Eva.'

'Maybe. But I shouldn't have run when she said.'

'Then you'd both have been killed.'

'Plus, maybe she survived,' adds Jay. 'I mean it's Hercus. If anyone could make it, it's her!'

We walk in silence. I glance over and notice Jay staring at Quasar.

'What's wrong?'

'Nothing. Except, Quasar has a small tear in her suit.'

I stop. 'Where?'

'It's fine, we patched it up while we waited for you. I was just checking it's intact.'

'How much oxygen do you have left?'

'About thirty minutes, give or take.' She shrugs.

'But that won't be enough, unless we quickly find Dad's rover, with a spare tank.'

'Well, I wouldn't say no to it, but our first priority is finding your dad.'

'Not anymore,' I say. 'I'm not letting anyone else die. We're getting you to that rover and then, once you're safe, I'll go and get my dad. Mars is taking too much from us. First T, then Hercus...it won't take both of you, too.'

29

No More Training Required

The silence in the tunnel is broken by a series of long howls.

We spin around and look for the source but see nothing aside from the occasional red glow of the geothermal vents.

'Seriously, what now? Like, you couldn't make up this much crazy stuff happening to us.' Quasar begins to quicken the pace. 'Come on, I am done with exploring Mars. Let's save these people and get back home.'

'Hard agree,' adds Jay. 'These bionic legs were not built for this amount of walking!'

'Oh yeah, that's why you're walking like a cowboy,' jokes Quasar.

I notice him moving alongside Quasar and we climb the steep path leading to, hopefully, Dad's mine.

I move my lips to talk to T, but then remember…

'Are we in range to try them on the coms, Jay?' I ask, hoping to hear Dad's voice, to be reassured he's alive and well.

'Yeah, I would think so. We get a few hundred metres of range with the coms, but who know knows with the thickness of the walls in here.'

'This is Eva Knight. Is there anyone out there?'

No reply.

'Is there anyone from the Mariner Base team out there? This is Eva Knight, and we're here to rescue you.'

Static and silence.

I keep trying, but the climb burns, and the howling continues, it becomes more and more like the shrieks of angry sirens.

'What was that?' Quasar's voice trembles. 'Over there.' She points just ahead of us.

The tunnel's still climbing and the glow from the geothermal vent is dulling with each step, towards a dark convergence that looks like a doorway - huge, ancient, and carved.

'I can't see anything,' Jay eventually replies and starts walking again.

'Wait.' Again, Quasar stops and puts her hand on his chest.

With a growing brightness, white shapes begin to float through the doorway towards us. Slow at first, and faint. But speeding up and appearing clearer and clearer, their forms becoming apparent.

They circle us, but don't come too close. Finally, the largest of all the white beings arrives, standing directly in front of us.

The leader says something but it's no language I've ever heard. Quasar and Jay look puzzled, too. They move closer together and hold hands.

'We mean no harm,' I say, stepping forward.

The leader grows in size. I hold up my hands and take a step back.

'We're here to rescue my father. And anyone else alive. May we pass?'

The leader tilts the part of him that's probably the head. Then speaks again, but we still don't understand. They repeat themselves - the tone seems angrier.

'Look, we need to pass. We're sorry to trespass on your... well here...'

The ghosts close in, forming a tighter circle. There's no way to escape without facing them now. These ghosts, or dense array of electrons, as T used to call them. I really could do with his advice right now. And I wouldn't even ignore it.

Probably.

'Eva, use your sword,' Jay mutters.

At my side, the blade rests, inert. It's hard to imagine the excess of destruction it's caused every time I've drawn it. I hesitate, worried it could bring down the whole tunnel and crush us all.

But I'm not losing anyone else without a fight - maybe destruction is what we need right now.

The moment my hand touches the hilt, the now-familiar sensation crackles through my arm and permeates across my body. The scarring has been getting darker, thicker, and more branched with every use of the sword. And it's weird, I feel it's also changing me on the inside, too. Like the way I see things is changing.

The passage brightens as the blade goes through its phases of many colours. Small sparks start to flicker from the tip.

I manoeuvre myself so I'm back-to-back with Jay and Quasar. The ghosts have stopped approaching but remain tight in their circle. Nowhere to run.

'Do they mean us harm?' I ask the other two.

'Eh, yeah they do.' Quasar replies. 'Get them, Eva.'

I lift the blade but pause. 'Wait, these things could be sentient. They could be lifeforms, like us. I can't just attack them because they speak a different language or look threatening.'

'Eva, they are freaky Martian ghosts!'

'I've got to agree with Quasar here. They don't look friendly, whatever they are.'

There's a long moment and nobody moves. The crackle of my blade is the only noise in this silent tunnel, deep beneath the surface of Mars.

I know what Dad would do.

I lower the blade.

'No, Eva. Don't—'

And then they attack. A co-ordinated surge, like a pack of oxide vipers crushing their prey. My reflexes kick in, and I lift the blade, swinging it at the alien assailants.

Quasar shouts out. Jay falls to his knees.

But I don't have a moment to see what's happened, I just keep swinging the blade at them. And it's working.

Every time I move it in their direction they back off, closing in only on the opposite side. They sense the power of the sword. I don't want to kill anything, even if it is a ghost. But if I'm forced…

I won't let my friends be hurt. I won't let Dad and any other survivors die.

Summoning all my strength, I raise the blade above my head, holding it with two hands. I close my eyes and breathe deeply. In and out.

I'm flooded with that all-powerful feeling, but this time I'm in control. I'm calmer and thinking solely about protecting us, not attacking, not killing, or causing destruction. I think of my friends and continuing our mission.

When I snap open my eyes I'm floating a foot off the ground. But I don't panic. This is normal and I am in control. As I swing the blade in a circle, a bubble forms around the three of us, the walls made of electricity, pulsing and sizzling, but connected in a protective dome.

'Eva? What the heck?' Quasar is kneeling beside Jay, who, I now notice, looks in a lot of pain. He's clutching one of his knees.

'What happened? Can you help him? I need you to follow me.'

'I'll try.' They stand up together and Jay throws an arm around Quasar's shoulders. They hobble up towards the large, ancient doorway.

Still in the bubble, I stop and turn. 'Do not follow us or try to hurt us. We mean you no harm.'

But several of the ghosts take that as a signal to attack. They rush the electrical shield and instantly disintegrate into thousands of small flakes of ash. Or at least that's what it looks like.

The others back away, losing interest.

I turn and follow my friends into the dark chamber beyond.

30

Skeletons

'Eva, I've seen some crazy stuff, but that was something else. You were floating!' Jay is sitting on a rock, resting. His face glossy with sweat. Quasar sits beside him with the same, awestruck expression, and for once, silent.

'I honestly don't know what happened. I've never been able to control it like that before. It's always been so full of emotion, or panic, or anger. But I was so calm. I knew it would help protect us.'

'Well, however you did it, I'm glad you did. Those things were awful. The biggest one put their arm right through my suit and inside my body, like it wasn't there. I hope they all can't do that.' His eyes betray the pain of the memory. 'They twisted my knee ligaments or something.'

'How is it?' I ask.

'I'm struggling. I don't know how much more walking I can do. It was already difficult. These bionic legs are the only reason I'm still standing.'

'Just rest, Jay,' says Quasar.

I want to agree with her, but we need to move. Dad might be on his last breath. 'We might lose others if we delay.'

'Eva, he needs to rest.'

'Yes, you're right. I know you're right.'

'I understand. If it was my mum, yes even *my* mum, I'd be powering on.' Jay grimaces. 'Go.'

'What about your oxygen level?' I ask Quasar, checking my own on the external wrist-pad.

'Not much. You?'

'Okay, but we need to hurry. Find Dad and the miners, find their rover, oxygen supplies and hopefully a functioning MOXIE. Otherwise…' I don't finish my sentence. There's no need.

'Eva, what if you find Hercus' dad? What will you say?'

'I'll tell him brave his daughter was. How she gave her life for ours and how proud he should be.'

'I'll try and remain in coms range, so keep in touch. I wouldn't want you to be alone in here.'

'You got it, boss.' Jay grimaces.

'But what if those ghosts come back? 'You've got the sword, but Jay …' Quasar looks unusually serious and worried. 'I'm going to stay here with him. He won't be able to fight them off.'

'And I can share my O_2 with you,' says Jay, squeezing Quasar's shoulder.

I know they're right. There's no way we can all continue, and this is my journey now. 'I think they'll leave us alone for a bit. But straight on the coms if you see them. Got it?'

'Aye, aye, Captain.' Jay salutes.

Quasar rolls her eyes. 'Nerd.'

'And proud!' He nudges her.

And I'm alone, striding forward. We started with five of

us. Now it's just me. I should never have brought them. Everything that's happened – it's all on me.

The chamber is dark, echoey, and cold. The external temperature (according to my suits sensors – I miss T!) is much lower than the tunnel we've just come through.

Weirdly, the oxygen levels are actually quite high in this place – eight percent. I could take off my helmet for a few minutes and not die. I consider it for a moment then decide that maybe I'll save that experiment for another time.

The ground is easy-going, like I'm on a smoothed path, and I can't help but wonder if those ghosts were the architects of this intricate underground place during their lives. Perhaps they died here and want to protect it. After all, we're the aliens here.

I try the coms again, but no response.

Hope of seeing a light or hearing a voice is slowly dwindling as I move through this large chamber. I shine my wrist-light from side to side and use my helmet-light to illuminate the path in front of me, but there's not much to see, except piles of rocks from years of weathering? Or mining? But how is that even possible? Wish Jay were here - he'd know. Or T. I already miss him so much.

I spot the odd site of pooled, frozen water. Our scientists would go nuts if they saw this. I'd love to explore it more myself if I had the time. T would tell me it's my obligation as a colonist on a foreign planet to take and return samples. Ah, T.

I do a quick search any other signals via my wrist-pad. Someone from the mining team might have damaged their coms and be using morse code, or alternative frequencies, but nothing. I also scan for electrons, or the ghosts, but again nothing. Eerily silent.

'Eva, are you okay?' Jay's voice comes back through the coms when I return to our original frequency.

'Fine. There's nothing here, Jay. I don't understand.'

'Keep in touch, Eva, we're going to start following you soon. Don't go too far.'

A few hundred metres ahead, I see a white figure on the ground. I run over, my heart leaping as I recognise a colony spacesuit. But it's completely still. The helmet visor is smashed. I dare not look inside.

Instead, I look at the name on the arm. Wěi. I didn't know Professor Wěi very well, but his daughter Cindy seemed nice. Never spoke to her much, but she'll be crushed when she finds out about this. I imagine how I'd feel if I'd stayed at the base and found out Dad had died this way…

I wipe the thought from my mind and continue, eager to find Dad. He is alive, I know it. He'd never give up on me. He'd fight to stay alive so he could return to me.

He is alive. He is alive.

The path begins to widen and even though it's dark, I can feel the chamber opening around me. That sense of space, even if I can't see it. I can no longer see the sides of the chamber when I shine my light either way. But ahead I do spot something.

Two large rovers, with their cargo and equipment trailers tethered behind. Their power must be cut as their spotlights and headlights are both off. As I creep closer, I keep seeing movement out of the corner of my visor. But when I light up the place where I saw it, there's nothing.

'Quasar? Jay? There are two rovers here. Get here ASAP, there's probably oxygen inside.'

No reply, but hopefully they heard me.

Maybe I'm being paranoid. Maybe I just want to see someone, anything moving. Instead, I see two more bodies lying between the two rovers. I'm so jumpy now and keep turning in circles to check all around me. The calmness of the tunnel has completely gone now, replaced with a loop of thoughts and an image of seeing Dad lying face down in his suit, like Wĕi.

'Hello?' I say over the coms, but there's no response. I wonder if their coms may be broken, so I check my wrist-pad again for the oxygen concentration – nine percent. Okay, let's do this.

I unclip my helmet, shouting the moment it's clear of my mouth. 'HELLO!' As my voice echoes around the chamber, I slam the helmet back into place, but not before taking a small breath of the oxygen-low air. It feels like a serrated knife to the lungs. The cold mixed with the lack of oxygen and abundance of other toxic gases, makes me gasp and then double over. I twist the helmet to seal it back in place and take a long, slow breath from the suit's oxygen-rich air and it brings instant relief.

My shout is still bouncing off the walls, but I can't hear any response, even with the auditory sensitivity on my suit cranked up to the max, to catch the faintest sound. I don't want to miss anyone.

But still nothing. And now I have to do it. I must find out who those two bodies are, to check if one of them is Dad. I couldn't bring myself to look at Wĕi, but if that's Dad lying there, then I need to see.

I step towards the rovers, but trip on something, and fall forward. Luckily, I get my hands down to break the fall before my visor smashes on the hard ground. My feet are tangled in a wire extending from the rovers to two large spotlights – the same ones I saw behind Dad in his transmission. I look from them to the rovers, trying to work out the angle, to see where the call took place. The computer he called from may have more of a recording of what happened here.

When I get to the spot, I do find a laptop. And it seems to still have some battery power. As I open it, I see movement again, but I can't catch it with the light. It's very fast and I am definitely not imagining it.

I am not alone.

I do a long slow circle, shining both wrist and helmet lights around as much of the chamber as it can reach. As I do that, I spot a few more spacesuits, but I don't want to look any closer.

I really don't want to look, but I must.

The laptop needs a password. I try Dad's birthday. Nope. Mine. Yes!

As I log in the video transmission resumes recording. The command centre on the base suddenly flashes up live and I see the face of Corporal Deremenko staring back, eyes wide and mouth open.

'Corporal, it's me, Eva Knight.'

'Eva? You made it! What's the status? We've all been so worried.'

I consider telling him. 'Sorry, no time. Has there been any contact since you first lost Dad?'

'None. When it cut out, when you were with us in command, that was the last one. Have you found anyone?'

'There are…bodies…'

'Oh.' The Corporal covers his mouth. 'I've messaged the commander. She'll be here imminently. Don't go anywhere.'

A long, piercing howl disturbs the silence of the chamber.

'Sorry, I have to go.' I close the laptop.

It came from quite far away, but I don't have time to waste. I head to the rovers, stopping only to check the two bodies. Neither is Dad. I am horrified by my feelings of relief.

They're someone else's family. But I have to bury the guilt for now.

I open one of the rovers and switch the power on. The headlights immediately illuminate the chamber, and it takes me a few seconds before I can open my eyes. As I do, the full scale of the mine is clear.

Hundreds of smaller tunnels lead off this huge chamber, with four larger ones at each corner. I entered through one of them and I can now see some of my path back. In the centre of the chamber is a huge hole where small puffs of steam or smoke rise. For some reason terror rises inside me.

I jump across to the second rover and turn on its lights, too. Beneath the rubble, it's clear this room was once grand and beautiful and built by intelligent life.

I can now see ten bodies lying on the ground.

Dashing across the cavern, I check off each body. None of them are Dad. Then I approach the last one. I check the name tag, to avoid looking at a dead face.

Armstrong.

A shaky breath escapes me.

Hercus' dad.

I make myself look at him in case he's somehow alive, even though his wrist-pad assures me he has no pulse. Sliding up the opaque sun-visor, my helmet-light shows me…

A skeleton? But …

He was alive two sols ago. If anything, he should be better preserved down here as it's so cold and there's so little oxygen. I check the other dead. They're all the same. All the tissue eaten away, and empty eye sockets stare back at me.

A crackle from the coms makes me jump. 'Eva, we're coming – we saw the lights. Will be there in a few minutes.' Quasar sounds worried. 'But Jay can't go on much further. I'll get him to the rovers, put him inside and come help you.'

'Okay, see you in a minute.'

A scream booms through the chamber.

'Quasar?'

'Eva, it's Jay. Something bit Quasar. Her suit is torn. We need you. NOW!'

31

All is Lost

'I'm coming!'

I see them both lying on the ground, Jay moving his wrist-light from side to side at whatever is attacking them.

And then I spot one. An oxide viper. I should have known.

I turn up the lux on my wrist-light and point it at anything that moves. The vipers dart away from it.

I kneel and help Jay up to lean on one shoulder, and Quasar on the other. The escaping gas is visible on the leg of her suit.

We limp together, four working legs between the three of us, towards the rovers. Quasar is losing consciousness and I have to let go of Jay.

'Sorry, just sit tight for a few minutes. I'll come back.'

'What?' he shouts. 'Don't leave me here alone.'

'It's the only thing I can do.' I remove Quasar's wrist-light and throw it to him. 'Hold them off. I promise I'll come back for you.'

I pull Quasar onto my shoulders, a firefighter's lift they called it at the Academy. And I can run now.

My legs ache and burn, and I stumble twice on my way back. But luckily the vipers don't attack me. But if they're not going for us, they're going for Jay.

I push Quasar inside the closest rover, close the door and jump into the driver's seat. And accelerate.

Rocks and equipment crunch beneath the spinning tyres, but none of that matters.

'Eva, hurry. One of them got me.' Jay's voice is weak.

'Hold on.'

But we're going too slow, so I ditch the cargo and equipment carriages behind us. They crash to the ground, equipment scattering everywhere, but people, not things, are all that's on my mind.

Jay is up ahead. A swarm of vipers closing in. I turn up the lux on the lights and the Martian snakes scatter. Diving out the rover door, I grab Jay and help him inside, locking the door behind us. With the rover sealed, I remove my helmet and grab a first-aid kit, searching for the anti-venom.

But I can't find any. Only empty containers. And no needles.

'Damn.'

Jay and Quasar have curled up close to each other. I can see both their visors are steaming up and, glancing at their flashing red wrist-pads, I see their core temperatures are rising.

'Hold on.' I dive back into the driver's seat and turn, accelerating towards the other rover.

I jerk to a stop and rummage in rover 2, finding a small bottle and one needle. They'll have to share the needle, but it's the best I can do.

I administer the life-saving liquid into their legs, near the bites. Then I patch up the tears in their suits. The steam begins to dissipate, and I can see both have either fallen asleep or passed out. The rover battery shows about six hours of power, so I leave them to recover in relative safety and move back to rover 2.

Suddenly my energy levels drop, and I am shattered. I need to rest, but I can't now. The pain in my stomach is an eight out of ten, and my glucose levels are super high without my insulin, but I need to keep eating or I'll feel faint.

I fight the urge to close my eyes for even a second. I'd fall asleep in an instant.

I start driving to the closest of the four large doorways off the chamber. With my helmet off, I take deep breaths to try and calm myself and shake the tension from my shoulders.

Checking the rover's log for the mission details, I see that there were eleven people out here. I've found ten bodies. But not Dad. Yet. There is still hope.

I try to stay alert, focusing on every detail of this new tunnel, but my mind is wandering. Every recent memory of Dad, every stupid decision I made that hurt him, every argument, they all flicker through my brain like a highlights reel of Eva's Regrets. And it's not just Dad – the faces of my friends, all now lost, dead or injured, play out too.

The first tunnel was a bust. Completely empty. I don't even think the expedition team came down here.

I return to the chamber and try the second tunnel. Same result.

In tunnel three I pass lots of drilling equipment, and lights (not working) and support pillars, but no people. I keep going. This is the last place he could be as we arrived through the fourth tunnel.

Well, he could be anywhere. In one of the small tunnels,

outside of the mine, or even in that huge hole in the middle of the chamber…

Please, no!

But I am clinging to a small glimmer of hope that this is the one.

Then the rover begins to power down.

'Hey! Wait, the readout says you've two more hours of power.' I punch the control panel.

But it keeps changing into low power mode – which means no driving, and grinds to a stop. At least I have oxygen and it will stay warm for a short while, before cooling right down.

I climb into the equipment hold, behind the driver's area, and sit on the floor, pulling my knees up to my chin, and rock back and forth. Using the wait to think.

Okay, so I haven't found Dad, but maybe that's a good thing. No news is better than bad news, right?

But no-one answers. T is long gone.

I measure my glucose, and my connected wrist-pad beeps to indicate my levels are dangerously high.

'What else is new?' The sweat on my forehead is sliding down into my eyes now, then on to my nose and mouth. It drips onto my lips. Tastes sweet.

Sweet sweat. I laugh at myself.

I put on my helmet and somehow stand, my legs feeling like jelly. I stumble into the door but can't get it open. I'm struggling to grip the handle. I can't see very well. Everything is fuzzy. But I keep walking.

Must find Dad.

Then I stumble, and fall.

And pass out.

32

Team Mars

I wake inside rover 1, hearing Jay and Quasar chatting.

I jerk up and see them across from me. 'What happened?'

'Hyperglycaemia. Coupled with mild hypoxia and toxic metals in your blood. Lucky to be alive, I'd say.' Jay smiles, but it's more a grimace. 'We're all lucky to be alive.'

I sigh. 'Thank you. But we're not all alive. Dad is still missing, probably…well, it doesn't look good now…and Hercus… she's gone.'

'Nope, not yet, kid.' Hercus enters from the cockpit, carrying a protein bar and some water, handing it to me, with a big smile on her face.

'What?' I can't help but think I'm hallucinating. I close my eyes and reopen them. She's still there. 'What?'

'Surprised then?' She sits next to me.

I nod, unable to come up with the words.

'I'd give you a long, heroic story of how it happened. But we're short on time. So, let's just say, I got back to our rover, took refuge, found replacement fuses for the drill on the rover and used that to break through the collapsed rock from the roof.'

'But I thought the rover lost power.'

'It did. But that big hole we made when we came down with the rover, well, it let in some light, and that charged the rover enough to power the drill for about five minutes. That was enough to get started, and I dug and chiselled through the rest myself.'

'Oh Herc.' I grab her and pull her into a tight hug, despite the pain in my stomach. 'And how did I get here?'

I turn to Jay and Quasar, who shrug.

'I came and found you,' says Hercus. 'Wasn't hard to follow your tracks. Your rover driving is hardly very smooth.'

'But the vipers and the ghosts…'

'No sign of them,' she replies, shrugging. 'Now come on, we need to find your dad and mine. Can you walk?'

'Yes,' I say, automatically, but my body feels like doing anything but walking. 'But Hercus. I need to tell you something.'

'What is it? We're low on everything right now. Oxygen, power, water, you name it.'

'It's your dad.'

Her face falls. Her shoulder sag and her legs seem to buckle as she crumples into her seat. 'Don't say it.'

'I'm sorry, I—'

'DON'T!'

'Found him.'

'Do not tell me.'

'Hercus, he's dead.'

'No.' She starts swaying back and forth, her arms crossed. 'No. No.'

'I'm sorry,' I say, gently.

'I didn't fight through all that for him to be dead. He wouldn't die. He wouldn't give up.'

'I'm so sorry.' And I force myself up to hug her, but she's away before I get to her, putting on her suit.

'Where are you going?'

'To see for myself.'

'You don't want to see it, Herc. Trust me.'

'I'm going. You won't stop me.'

'Shall I come with you?'

'I'm going alone.' She moves into the equipment bay, closing the inner door and then exiting the rover. We watch from the window as she moves from body to body, seeing what I saw.

I take a few moments to get to my feet and become steady. The rover feels like it's swaying.

'Take it easy, Eva,' says Quasar, softly.

'My Dad is out there somewhere. I know he's alive, I just feel it. But I don't know where.' I can't take my eyes away from the hole, steaming away in the ground. It's the only place I haven't searched.

'I mean, he could be down there. It's just that I get a bad feeling about that hole.'

'Me, too,' adds Quasar, getting up. 'I think I saw something about it earlier.' She walks over and picks up some RIMFAX printouts. 'Yes, look. Here's a scan of the hole. The Endless Pit, it's been called. And no wonder. Look how far down it goes.' She hands me the printout.

'I wish I could ask T.'

Jay looks to Quasar, then back at me. 'Well, you can actually.'

'What?'

'Hercus managed to get his chip out of the rover. She

brought it here.' Quasar picks it up from the cockpit and tosses it to me.

I catch it and kiss it. 'Oh, T! I just hope you work. I hope you somehow work.

And I slide the tiny chip into my tragus.

'T?'

Nothing.

'Thunderchild?'

Well, hello there.

I laugh. And then I'm sobbing. Uncontrollable, happy sobbing.

'I wish I could hug you.' It's all I can manage between the snorts and the gasping breaths.

As an AI, I have no requirement for human contact or affection. That said, I appreciate the sentiment. I, too, am glad to be at one with you again.

I smile.

'What's he saying?' asks Jay.

'Nothing. Just being the usual pain in the butt.' And I laugh again.

So, what ridiculous situation do we find ourselves in now, Eva?

33

The Endless Pit

Hercus returns to the rover.

It shakes as she re-enters and through the inner door to the equipment bay, we can see her throwing things around. Her helmet comes off and is hurled at the wall.

'Someone should go in,' says Quasar.

'I agree,' adds Jay, both of them looking to me.

How do I console her? I'd be the same if I had just seen Dad as a skeleton. If all my efforts were for nothing.

'Okay, I'll go.'

I make sure Hercus spots me, before joining her. When she sees me, she does seem to calm a little.

'What the hell has done that to him?' She steps right up to me as I enter.

I can only shake my head.

'It's not fair.' She paces away from me. 'It's just not fair…'

And then she's turning and leaning over to put her head on my shoulder. She shakes as the tears flow. I grab her tight, imagining being in her place and knowing I'd be as wrecked.

After a minute, she stands up, takes a deep breath, and

wipes away the tears. A few snuffs later, and she picks up her helmet. 'Well, nothing to be done for my dad now. But we can find yours.

'Quasar, if you're okay, bring that winch with you. Herc, grab those flares. I'll get the sledgehammer and pegs,' I say.

Jay drives us to the edge of the Endless Pit where we get out with our equipment and lay it down next to the abyss. The feeling of vertigo makes me take a few steps back, but it's more than that – there's something wrong with this place. I sense it in my bones.

'Jay, keep those lights shining on the pit. Let us know if you're running low on power, so we have warning if it's going to cut out.'

'You got it, Chief.' He salutes from the cockpit.

'T, how deep did the scan show this was?' I ask.

RIMFAX did not find the bottom. But it's more than five hundred metres. That's where the scan ends, at the end of its range.

'Okay, the ropes on these winches are five hundred metres, which according to T is as far as the scan goes, but we won't know how far it is to the bottom from there.'

'Wait, so you're going to dangle five hundred metres over the edge and then what?'

'We'll see when we get there,' I say.

'You could take a supplementary rope,' suggests Jay. 'Then you could tie it to this one and it will give you another one hundred metres or so.'

'Good idea,' I say. I step closer to the edge, watching the eerie steam-slash-smoke drift up. 'T, what's the temperature on that steam?'

It's very hot. Fluctuating between eighty to ninety degrees Celsius. It will be much hotter further down. The suit should reflect most of the heat, but there is a limit, and I'd imagine that limit will be passed if we go down five hundred metres.

'T, are you going to suggest I don't go down there.'

The thought had crossed my mind.

'Well, don't. Nice to have you back, by the way. Any idea how much oxygen Dad would have if he's down there?'

Without spare oxygen, it would be minimal. There is hope as the air may be breathable down there.

Hercus is the only one of us with any real strength left, so she assembles and anchors two winches on solid frames, using the sledgehammer to pin down the frames with wedges.

'There,' she says. 'That'll hold us for sure. And the extra weight of someone else on the way back. If we find anyone.'

I nod. 'Thank you.'

Quasar looks down into the Endless Pit. 'So, we have two winches. We have three of us. Who's the unlucky one who misses out?'

'I'm going,' I say.

'And I'm going, too,' adds Hercus.

'Oh shoot! Well, alright, I suppose I could let you two go.' Quasar looks over to Jay, who is shrugging in the cockpit. 'And someone needs to keep an eye out up here. Hoppy in there isn't going to be much use on his own.'

'Heard that,' he replies over the coms. 'I'm more use with one leg, than you are with two.' He frowns back down at us.

And we all laugh. Gallows humour, Dad calls it. I hope I get just one more laugh with him.

But the laughter stops, as one long, screeching howl fills the chamber. It seems even louder next to the Pit, with the endless vibrations and echoes.

'No! Not now,' I shout. 'Do not come any closer or I'll…' But then I realise that the sword is not with me. 'Where's my sword?'

Hercus looks to Quasar, who looks up to Jay. 'I haven't seen it since the tunnel,' he says, shrugging.

'It must still be in rover 2. I need to get it.'

'Don't worry, I'm on it,' says Jay.

'I'm coming, too,' says Quasar, who jumps up and grabs the handrail on the side of the rover.

Rover 1 accelerates off towards the tunnel where I passed out earlier to recover our only weapon against the strange creatures in this place.

'We need to hold them off until Jay returns,' I say. 'Once I have that sword, I can deal with them.'

'How do we 'hold them off'?' Hercus asks.

I shake my head. 'Distract them maybe? Try and talk to them? We spoke to them in the tunnel earlier and they didn't attack immediately.

'What happened?'

'Well, they eventually attacked Jay and Quasar until the sword managed to create an electrical bubble thing around us.'

Several howls come from one of the large tunnels.

'Did you annoy them?' she asks.

'Kinda. I didn't mean it but a few of them ran into the bubble and they…well, they kind of evaporated.'

'Evaporated?'

'I'm not sure if that's the right word. T?'

The 'ghosts' are a dense array of electrons, circling the atoms that beings are composed of, as I have told you many times, Eva. They do not 'evaporate' like liquid element; they can have their ionic bonds broken and they can disperse into individual particles. Often the reaction causes a small release of energy know as nuclear fission, like when you split atoms in a lab.

'T says they disperse.'

'Right, so what do we say to these ghosts to keep them distracted. Tell them some jokes. Why did the Martian cross the road?'

I smile. I am so grateful for these few extra moments with Hercus. And this time I'm not going to lose her.

'Hercus, if I die before we find my dad, will you promise to keep looking?'

She turns to me, a sad look in her eyes. 'I will. We are saving one dad today. Or we will die trying.'

'Fingers crossed for option A,' I say.

I'm glad to hear it. I'm really looking forward to not dying again.

34

The Final Battle

The ghosts come like before, in one huge circle, slowly constricting.

There must be thousands of them now, a whole colony. Heck, a whole civilisation. In this chamber, they look even bigger and brighter and more powerful.

Hercus moves closer to me. 'If I wasn't so terrified, this would be amazing.'

The sharp pain in my stomach continues to pulse and I'm feeling light-headed again. 'Not now.'

'What is it?' Hercus grabs my elbows, looking parental.

'Take your pick! Just keep me upright, and alive, until Jay returns with the sword.'

She nods and digs her feet into the ground, taking the stance we were taught during self-defence lessons.

The swarm closes in. It's hard to tell their expressions or emotions, I would guess this current look is angry. Anger at the 'death' of their friends earlier. At us invading what seems to be their ancient home.

As the ghosts get closer they become more solid-looking, blocking out nearly everything beyond them.

'Hello.' I hold up my hands, hoping they understand the meaning. The all shrink back and retreat. 'Sorry, I don't mean to threaten.' My voice sounds like it's muffled under a blanket right now, the ghosts are so dense. I'm not even sure they can hear me through the helmet, although that one did, back when the I found the sword.

They begin to move in again, perhaps spotting the lack of a sword in my hands. I try again. 'Sorry, we are not here to harm you, or trespass. We just need to get my dad back. We think he's down there.' I point into the pit.

And again, they all shrink away, this time looking even more scared, like what's in the Pit terrifies them more than me and the sword.

'We are friends. We mean no harm,' I repeat.

But it's no good, whatever I say they keep coming. 'They've worked out we have nothing, Herc.'

'Time to run?'

'Yup.'

'Go straight for that patch there – it's a little less solid and that's where Jay and Quasar went. Three, two, one…'

As we run, and we meet the first layer of the ghosts, it's like gravity has gone haywire. Herc and I are pushed with such a force, it feels like hundreds of times the pressure on Earth. Every movement forward, so easy a moment ago, is now like lifting a rover.

Their touch is like ice on the skin – stinging and numbing and very uncomfortable. They seem like a half-solid, half-gas being, meaning they feel like running through a thick liquid, like jelly or something.

I struggle and have to get low, digging my feet into any grip I can get on the smoothed ground. The lower I go, the more progress and eventually, I'm almost horizontal with the deck, driving forward like an Olympic sprinter running through water.

I turn to see Hercus making much better progress – she's almost through the densest of it.

And then I slip.

The force of the ghost circle is pressing me backwards towards the edge of the Endless Pit. I scratch and tug and try to hook my hand or foot onto anything as I slide, but the floor is too smooth. The ancient, alien architects have done their job too well.

I'm about five metres from the edge, but with no grip, there's nothing I can do to stop this. I can barely see Herc now.

My heart is thundering hard.

Think, Eva!

I'm going to fall, nothing can stop that, but the ropes are still there, and I think they're in reach. I grab the tether clip from my belt and wait until we pass the winch, reaching out and grabbing the rope.

But my glove slips and I'm past the rope, untethered.

Two metres until the drop.

'Help!' The time to panic has come. I thrash at the ground, or anything, to slow me down. I close my eyes.

I don't want to die.

And then I've stopped.

Music booms through the chamber.

'What is that?' Hercus yells, pushing through the ghosts, coming into view again. 'The ghosts have got … thinner.'

It's coming from Rover 1.

'It's Dad's favourite song! Oh, my sols! I can't stand it when he plays this over and over. It's called Life on Mars.'

'Whatever it is, the ghosts hate it!' yells Herc, as rover 1 bursts through the ghostly mist.

Quasar is there with the sword, and she passes it out to me. 'Eva, we have some bad news.'

'What's wrong now?'

'Oxide vipers. A LOT of oxide vipers.'

Jay angles the rover headlights and I see them, swarming towards me. The ghosts coming from one side, the vipers from the other.

Rover 1 pulls to a safe distance.

Gripping the sword in both hands, I focus my mind on being calm.

I think of the time when Dad gave a me a telescope for my eleventh birthsol. He said that if I looked in it, I could see the Earth. But that I could also see all the stars in the sky. One of which was Mum.

The sword erupts in a cascade of sparks, the colours multiply and change faster than ever before. I raise the blade above my head, and I concentrate on it forming a protective bubble.

It works, this time the dome grows and covers more and more area around me. As it reaches the snakes or the ghosts, they are destroyed instantly.

I concentrate hard on maintaining its size. I don't want to kill them all. I just want to protect myself and my friends. I walk in the direction of the rover and as it passes into the dome the ghosts who'd been attacking it start to disperse.

'Guys, where's Hercus?' I realise I've not seen her for several minutes. I've been so consumed with the sword; I've not been looking out for her. Light from the sword sweeps the chamber and I see her. She's hanging onto the winch frame. It looks unsteady.

I run towards the Endless Pit, trying to maintain my focus

on the bubble but it begins to spark out in places and gaps appear in the protective dome.

The ghosts surge in from above, the snakes do the same from the holes near the ground. But I don't have time to seal them. I must get to Hercus.

My body won't go any faster, holding the sword high, so I lower it to my side, and I run faster. But the dome is disappearing. And I see the ghosts and vipers closing in on me, and just ahead, on Hercus.

'Eva!' Her voice is full of desperation. 'Help.'

And then the frame wedges fly up from the group, the frame comes loose and the whole mechanism, along with Hercus who is grasping it, lifts up and falls into the Endless Pit.

It's like it happens in slow motion. Her face becomes wide with terror, but no matter how slow it is, I am not fast enough to reach her.

And then she is gone. She doesn't even shout or scream. Her fall is silent.

I'm struggling to breathe. I bend over and lean on the sword hilt.

And now a full chamber of ghosts and vipers focus upon me. They think I've lost my power, that the protective dome has broken.

I am broken.

And now, they will break.

I raise the blade up in the air and give every last joule of energy I have into summoning a tall tower of electricity. It rises from the tip of the blade all the way to the top of the chamber, so high we'd not been able to see it until now.

For a split second, I spot what look like mosaics created by the ancient race. They were probably very fine beings, once. But now they've killed my friend and I have no restraint.

I bring the blade down and slam it into the ground. The smooth floor acts like a conductor and the electrical surge reverberates throughout the entire chamber, cutting every viper into small shreds and dispersing the ghosts in a small explosion of energy. The atoms of the ghosts rise towards the ceiling in the blast, the bodies of the vipers strewn across the ground.

The smell, the sight and the sound of vengeance is sweet.

That was for Hercus.

35

Descent

Particles of the dispersed ghosts float through the air, like falling snowflakes.

I've never seen snow fall, except in movies. It would be quite pretty if it wasn't for the fall of Hercus.

Dead oxide vipers lie all around us, like they're sleeping, and we've fallen into the middle of their lair. Luckily, they'll not wake.

The three of us stand in silence, none of us quite believing that we've survived. But the mission is far from over.

I turn to the Endless Pit, staring down into the dark abyss.

Quasar stands beside me, putting her foot onto the edge of the precipice and giving me momentary vertigo. 'Your dad isn't making it easy for us, is he?' she says. 'He couldn't just be sitting up here waiting for a rescue. He had to be in the absolute belly of Mars.'

'I've got to go. I can lower myself, but I need someone to wind the winch back up for me, Hercus and Dad.'

'I can do that. Team Martian Man-Hunter forever!'

I nod and tether myself to the one winch that remains intact.

I tug on the rope, jerking the tether, and jumping up and down a few times to let the winch mechanism take my weight a few times.

'Okay, it feels stable.' I stand on the edge, facing down into the dark void. Occasional gusts of scalding air circulate up from below, steaming the outside of my visor.

'Dad used to hate me being reckless. I bet he won't complain now.'

I jump.

I sway back and forth for a minute, my legs dangling and my arms holding the lowering mechanism tight.

My legs swing in the dark, but I take a deep breath and relax. As I do, my body stills and the swaying stops.

I touch the trigger and I fall. So quick, so hard, that I release it in fright and jerk to a stop, about twenty feet down. The rim of the Pit is still visible above, but only just.

I press the trigger much more gently this time and descend at a less panicked speed until I'm in near darkness. I try to turn on my helmet light, but it's dead. My wrist-light, too.

My helmet visor is completely steamed up, so is no real use now. But I'd better keep it on for now to protect from the heat.

A hissing rises from below.

Please, not more vipers.

I touch the hilt of the blade at my side, I don't want to use it in such a confined space.

Suddenly, I stop. I try to find more rope beneath me, but I only swipe at air. I'm hanging, suspended in nothingness. I fight my every instinct to go back, fight to stay focused.

What is that noise?

It sounds like a drill, like the one on the rover …

The RIMFAX!

It uses radar to measure depth, and I can do the same! Well, sort of.

I yell as loudly as I can, 'DAD? HERCUS?' The Pit fills up with my voice, echoed and amplified hundreds of times. Hearing your own voice is the worst. I sound so…American. Dad would hate it, he's so Scottish. I would give anything to hear that voice again. Just one wee word.

Obviously, I can't work out the exact depth; I'd need T for that, but I can tell it's pretty far. Further than I want to fall.

'So, what choice do I have? Wait here and get winched back up. That might be hours without coms to tell them. Or fall, and probably die? Or at least break my legs and be no use to Dad.'

It is not a great choice. Logically, the correct choice would be to wait and return to the surface.

I close my eyes and sway. The condensation on my visor makes it pretty much impossible to see anything anyway, and I'm so hot, it's like I'm being cooked inside my exo-suit. I check my readings: temperature, percentage of gases in the air, and the pressure – 120 degrees with seventeen percent oxygen. That is almost within breathable limits. But far too hot to bear for more than a few seconds. Where is all the heat and oxygen coming from?

If only I knew for certain that Hercus was alive, or that Dad was down there, then it would be easy. Then I remember Quasar and Jay at the top and everything they've endured to get me this far.

They might not hear me, but I open the coms one last time. 'Hey Jay and Quasar. You've both been awesome. Really brave during the whole mission, and always followed me, even though it would've easier to not. You are good friends. Keep each other safe if I don't come back.'

I unclip the tether clip and fall.

36

Goodbye, hello

My leg breaks.

The crunching sound is loud and clear. The pain is delayed for about a second, but when it comes, I scream, and grip the gravel around me, burying my fingers in deep.

My teeth grind and my jaw is clenched shut.

In a half faint I grab the emergency morphine from my belt pouch and slam the long needle into my thigh.

I'm on my side, with my broken leg beneath me. I glance at it and gag when I feel the angle of it through my suit.

The pain is slowly disappearing, replaced by dry retching. The image of my shattered leg bones is making me want to vomit.

I sit up and swing my wrist-light around me to assess my new situation. I've hit the bottom of the not-so-endless-pit and it's smooth too, like the tunnels. There's a decent-sized hole in the base of the pit with a door. And that's when I see her. Hercus is just a few feet from it.

My ribs burn as I drag myself to her. I'm struggling to breathe but I move, centimetre-by-centimetre towards her.

'Hercus?'

Nothing.

'Come on, Hercus. Come on.' I throw myself beside her and manage to sit up, burying the pain.

I stare into her visor, looking for signs of eye movement or anything.

I shake her by the shoulders. 'Hercus?'

Nothing.

I start chest compressions, counting them out like we learned in class. I hoped I'd never have to do it.

Nothing.

Hercus Armstrong died at the bottom of the Endless Pit.

She doesn't deserve to die, while I live. While anyone else lives.

I turn and drag myself towards the door. It looks unnatural, like it's been forced in place. Maybe Dad and his team built it.

But something about it tells me I'm wrong. It doesn't look...human built.

I bang on it. Thumping my fists on the metal, the vibrations creating a deafening noise which I'll bet even Jay and Quasar could hear.

I keep punching it. 'Open this door right now!'

It opens.

Bright lights flood out and give me spots in my eyes. It takes a lot of blinking to be able to stand the intensity.

I see a dark shape approaching, the outline of a person.

'Hello, Eva. I've been waiting for you. Come.' The voice is female, and familiar.

My stomach lurches as I'm drawn up into the air. I'm...floating...

'Don't be afraid,' says the voice. 'I am levitating you.'

'Who are you?' My body lowers and gently lands on a couch, or bed.

I blink and can see her face.

'Mum?'

'No, I'm not Mum. Though I understand why you think that. I took on her likeness to gain your trust.'

'Are you the ghost who's been speaking to me?'

'I have been speaking to you, but I'm no ghost. I just use their electrons, their life force, to give myself a shape to talk to you.'

'What are you then?' I shake my head and this time when I look, my vision has cleared.

But I can't believe what I am seeing. Before me stands... well, someone who looks like me...like my mum...

'I am Celeste. Your sister,' she says.

I must be hallucinating. 'I don't have a sister.'

Her eyes widen. 'They never told you?' She shrugs. 'I'm not surprised. Dad always was overly protective.'

'Where is Dad? Is he here?'

'Yes.'

Suddenly everything seems worth it. I even smile. 'Wait. What? And he's safe? He's alive?'

'Yes.'

And with those words, my whole body suddenly relaxes, and I drift off to sleep.

37

Sister, Sister

I wake in a large, circular room. It's very clean and white. White walls, floors and even the various machines and equipment storages. There is a control panel in the centre of the room, with a smaller circle of white seats around it.

Above the control panel is a ladder which leads up a narrow, long tube, probably into the upper floors of…whatever this is.

'Relax now, Eva. I have healed all your ills, but you must rest.'

'My ills?'

'Yes, I have healed your injuries, removed the toxic metal contraption, and restored your glucose levels to homeostatic ranges.'

'I'm healed? Wait, what are you? You said you're my sister, but you're an alien, right?'

'Well, I'm a hybrid now, but I was once pure human.'

'How did you become…not pure human?'

'That's a long story. And a painful one. But right now, we need to talk about Dad.'

'What's wrong with him? I want to see him. Now.'

'He won't survive leaving the medical pod that I have placed him in. His injuries were severe. Your technologies are not advanced enough to keep him alive. But I can.'

'I don't understand.'

'I'm taking him away. Back to our Titan base, and then onwards to our home world.'

'But I've come to rescue him.'

'No, you've come to rescue me. I've been leading you here with the Ergon Blade this whole time.' The sword lies beside me.

'Wait, what? You said it was to save Dad?'

'No. I said the blade would be his fall and rise. He fell into the pit and now he will rise with me, in this spaceship.'

'Wait, this is a spaceship?'

'Yes. I crashed here years ago, having lost the Ergon Blade that powers my ship, Andromeda - it's her heart if you like. And so, while the other basic systems have kept me alive in here since, I couldn't take off without it.'

'So, you used me. You risked Dad's life, not to mention all my friends.'

'Yes.'

'Don't you feel anything? Don't you care about killing people?'

'There are many of you – bred for quantity, it seems. I was unaware a few losses would matter. It is our way to think of self-preservation first as so much time and energy has gone into perfecting each one of us.'

I think of Hercus … A few losses. But I bite my tongue, now is not the time to let my anger get the better of me. 'Is there any human left in you? Anything that feels or cares at all?'

'Enough. Enough to understand why you are so angry

and scared right now. But small enough to not let those emotions override my logical, evolved sense of self-preservation.'

'I can't let you take Dad. I won't let you.' I haul the heavy blade up and the pulsing energy begins to ride through me.

'What will you do? Try to kill me? I could easily stop you. Take Dad? In both scenarios, you will die. As will your friends above.'

I raise the blade. Forks of electricity shoot out, striking the roof, the circular control panel in the centre of the room and the medical pod on the right, lighting up the bed where Dad lies motionless.

The moment I spot him, I drop the blade and the fight leaves me.

I only care about one thing.   I run across the room, leaping a box of cargo, and I can't help staring at my healed leg. It feels totally normal. I pull at the handle to the large pod, about the size of our home in The Pits.

But it won't budge.

'Open it.' I tug at the unyielding handle.

'No.' She hasn't moved.

'Open it, now.' I bang on the clear, blue-tinged screen separating me from the pod. Dad lies just beyond on a bed, inside a cylindrical machine, like the MRI machine that we have back on the colony. I can't see his head, which is furthest inside the tube, only his legs and feet. An android stands still as a statue nearby. Most of the panels look blank and powerless.

'Let me see him!'

'Eva, he cannot come out of there. He would die in minutes. We may have the medical equipment on Titan to heal him, but it's likely he'd need to be augmented, like me, if he is to survive.'

'Augmented? You mean all spliced up with DNA to make him less human?'

'Well, you put it crudely, but yes, that is what would happen. But it's that, or certain death as a human.'

'Why do you even care about him?'

'I may be different from what I once was. I've changed a lot. But some things remain. Love is stronger than any genetic correction.'

I bang my fist on the screen again, but it's solid and my hand aches.

'Can I go in and see him?' I place my palm against the screen, my fingers digging, like roots trying to burrow their way through concrete.

'It's a sterile environment, designed to prevent any infection. He's already so weak, that any microbe could be fatal.'

'I just want to touch him…to hold his hand…to get scratched by his beard one more time…'

'I'm sorry, Eva, but no.'

I spin round. 'Do you feel nothing? Really? Hercus died for this. All to save Dad. And I won't let you take him away or deny me being close to him.'

I want to pick up the blade and use its power to threaten her, but by the time I spot it on the floor where I dropped it, it's too late.

The blade floats up into my sister's hand.

'How did you do that?' I shake my head.

'There is much you don't understand yet, Eva. You are young and have much to learn. And you will. We have foreseen it.'

'You've foreseen what exactly?'

'You will do great things.'

'I don't want to do great things; I just want my dad back.' I move towards her.

'Stop.' The blade glows, much brighter and more powerful than I've ever seen it before.

For a moment, I'm terrified she's going to direct it at me.

But then she thrusts it into a slot in the centre of the control panel.

Immediately the ship begins to vibrate, everything powering up for the first time since she landed here.

She's focused on the central control panel, which is now flashing furiously with information and schematics and what looks like star charts and maps.

She swipes her hand right, and a projected skeleton appears above the panel. As she swipes, a new layer is added; first ligaments and tendons, followed by organs and muscles, then the central nervous system, and finally, the skin and external features.

Only then do I realise it's Dad.

'He is a great candidate for augmentation.'

'A great candidate for augmentation? That's my dad! That's your dad!'

'The genetic relatedness means he is far more likely to accept the augments, yes.'

'No, that's not what I meant…doesn't he get a say in this? Don't I?'

'Of course, our medical ethics dictate that. But for now, preservation of his life is the overriding factor.'

'Well, I don't consent!'

She ignores me, and instead taps the central panel, mapping a route through space to some distant galaxy. She's so intent on it, I take my chance.

I spring up onto the control panel and grip the handle of the blade, pulling it hard. It begins to slide free, but I'm thrust upwards, stopping suddenly in mid-air. I'm floating about ten feet above the white floor, my head just under the roof.

My sister stands below, hot with fury. The first real change in emotion I've seen from her since I arrived. And not a welcome one.

Her wrath seems to give out heat, the ship warming up, and the vast whiteness of the room slowly changes to a dark crimson.

She jerks her right arm backwards and I feel a tug on the blade, but I hold it firm.

The ship is quietening now that it's lost its power source, the electrostatic sparks coming from the blade becoming louder and louder.

She jerks her arm back again, this time more forcefully, and again the blade is tugged, and almost comes free from my grip. I swing my other arm round, despite a howling pain in my ribs and hold on for dear life.

38

The Exchange

My sister flicks her wrist and I fall to the floor.

The impact is worse than being twisted in the air. I struggle to take a breath. The blade lies beneath me, and I remain still, a dead-weight over it.

'Eva, I need that blade. It's all that matters to me. I can't be stuck here for one more sol. I must return to my people.'

'You're with your family,' I wheeze out.

'Maybe once you were.' She holds out her hand. 'This is my final offer: Hand over the blade, and I will transport you to your colony, along with your friends outside, safely.'

'What about Dad?'

'He must come with me. I don't know how else to say that.'

'I can't give him up. My friend died to save him. I can't just let him fly off with you.'

'Then let me save your friend.'

'She's dead.'

'Maybe by human standards. If you give me the blade, I

can restore her in here, and then return you all to your colony. Is this agreeable?'

I hesitate because I can't lose Dad. But if I can save Hercus, and Jay and Quasar…this is…impossible.

She stares at me, the ship's floor, walls, and everything else, returning to its original white colour.

Her anger is subsiding.

I pace back and forth, avoiding her gaze, still gripping the sword with all my strength.

'I need haste. As does your dead friend. The longer she is dead, the less chance I have to save her.'

'What do you mean? Can you save her or not?'

'I will resurrect her. That is all I can say. How much of her previous self remains is another matter.'

'No-one should have this much power. To bring people to life, to take away people I love, to make me choose between them.'

'I'm not asking you to choose, Eva – give me the sword and everyone lives.'

She's right. But giving up on Dad is impossible. What will life even be like back at the colony without him? It was hard when he was around, but now it will be bleak. And worst of all, I had him all those years and kept pushing him away and defying him.

And I'll never get to tell him how sorry I am for that.

'Okay, I've decided.'

I drop the blade at her feet. 'It's yours. But you had better keep my dad alive because I am coming for him. It might not be for a while, but I'm going to come after you, and I am going to get him back. This is not the end for us.'

'Of that, I am sure.' She smiles. Then slowly she bends down, picks up the blade with so much care and love, much more than she seems to show me or Dad.

Then she plunges it back into its slot on the control panel and the ship comes to life again.

'Andromeda, reborn.' She says it like a person has come to life.

'And now you will keep your side of the deal. Save Hercus and return all of us to the colony before you leave Mars.'

'Absolutely.' She flicks her hand at the door that leads to the bottom of the Endless Pit. It swishes open, and with a second flick of her wrist, Hercus' still body floats into the ship and comes to rest in a second medical pod.

I rush over to see her, but the screen comes down quickly and I'm left staring through the blue barrier.

The medical android in this pod gets to work quickly. He injects Hercus with various things and then her body jerks as the defibrillators slam down upon her chest repeatedly.

'I don't understand – if you can use telekinesis or whatever on Hercus, why not use it to just levitate out of here yourself?'

'Good question. My power was limited without the Blade. As was my reach. It took all I had just to project myself upon those ghostly forms to get you and the Blade here.'

I turn away unable to watch Hercus' resuscitation and move to Dad's pod. He remains unmoved in the cylindrical machine, but the medical android is moving back and forth across the room, keeping him alive.

I wonder if this is the last time I'll see him. All my promises to rescue him, and now he's being taken to Titan, then some other galaxy. But I will try. I will become an astronaut – nothing will stop me now. I will cross space, as much space as is needed, and I will find him again.

'Hold on.' Her voice brings me out of my thoughts, and I realise the ship is about to take off.

I grab a handrail and the vibrations make my teeth crack together and my bones ache. My ribs worst of all.

Eva, I would suggest strapping into one of the chairs.

I stumble over the circle of seats around the control panel and put on the seat belt.

The roar of the ship's external metal scraping against rock gives me shivers. We must be buried far below the surface.

'Remember Jay and Quasar,' I shout.

She nods and the ship suddenly jerks upwards, making my head flick backwards and straining my neck. My body feels like it's being crushed into the seat by g-force. I can't reply. My head is spinning, and I want to throw up, and my ribs feel like they've been crushed by a meteor.

And then it stops.

Suddenly my breaths come back in rapid, short bursts and my body feels normal again.

'Hold on, we're going to land next to your friends, who appear to be taking refuge in a rover near the entrance to the mine.'

I nod, glad to hear that they are both safe and alive. I glance over to Hercus' pod and still see no movement, but at least the defibrillator has stopped pounding her chest.

'Will she be the same?'

'She will be alive, and that is as we agreed.'

I narrow my eyes, wondering just what I've signed Hercus up to. If I've saved her life, but that she might not wake up, like Dad. Or she will just be…different.

'Tell me one thing. What are the ghosts? You said you used them to project yourself. But what or who are they?'

'They are the ghosts of the ancient Martians, who once lived near your colony, millions of years ago. They were brutally slaughtered by another invasive species that came to Mars at that time. I believe they are most angry with you because much of your base is built upon their old cemetery and homes. It is unwise to disturb the dead, which is why they haunt you.'

'But it's just me? Why can't anyone else see them?'

'You are Martian. They are not. They may choose to reveal themselves to some humans, some of the time. Sometimes they can't help it, like when they are angry. But mostly they remain hidden to all but true Martians.'

39

The Rise of Dad

The ship lands and I unbuckle. I've still got my exo-suit on, so I waste no time in running outside when the door opens, desperate to get to Jay and Quasar and make sure they're okay.

I bang on the rover door and see Jay's face appear. I manage to smile at his expression.

He holds up two fingers and disappears, I assume to put on his exo-suit.

The door slides open.

'Did you find your dad? And Hercus?' He leaps out and hugs me.

I spot Quasar over his shoulder, slumped in a chair, unconscious.

'Long story. How is Quasar?'

'She's okay, I think. We tried to bring you back up, but just got an empty rope. We feared the worst. Then, we went back to the rover, and I gave her the anti-venom, and she fell unconscious. I drove to the entrance that the original team entered through, to see how the storm was. How did you get back up and out of the Endless Pit?'

'You wouldn't believe me if I told you. But we have a ride home so let's grab Quasar and go.'

'We have a ride? Who?'

'Later.'

We hold an arm and leg each and carry Quasar to Andromeda, which sits silently just outside the entrance to the mine.

'Holy Jupiter! Is that a…?'

'Yup, it is. It'll take us back to the colony.'

'Eva—'

'I know, and I promise I'll tell you everything. But we need to get going.'

Jay looks around with wonder at every single thing we pass and nearly faints inside the ship, especially when he sees my sister.

'Who is that?' He secures Quasar into one of the seats.

'I am Celeste. Eva's sister.' She seems to glow when she smiles at him. It's not human. Or even Martian.

'Eva's sister?' He falls back onto a seat.

It hits me that I never used her name or connected her to the wee girl that went missing all those years ago. Maybe I didn't want to give her any humanity since she is taking Dad. Or maybe I didn't want to feel anything more for her. I want to ask if that's the name Mum and Dad gave to her, or something else that's 'evolved' about her. But I'm not sure any answer would make me happy.

'Strap yourself in,' Celeste tells Jay, and she returns to the control panel to fly us home.

She turns to me. 'Home?'

'Home.' I don't sit this time, moving to the screen outside

Dad's pod, so I can spend the last few minutes I have with him. Maybe forever.

'I doubt your sensors would detect my ship in the middle of this storm, but I'll land a short distance away anyway.'

I nod, my mind split between Hercus and Dad's medical pods. 'Will he be able to speak to me before you leave? Can he be woken up?'

'Perhaps. I will ask the system.' She taps the touchscreen on the control panel a few times.

My foot is tapping. I can't stop fidgeting.

I shrug, get up and start pacing between the two pods. I glance at my sister, the alien, to see if she has an answer yet. But she ignores me.

I notice Quasar sleeping with her head on Jay's shoulder, and I smile at them. An unusual spot of happiness in my broken emotions.

As I feel the ship lowering to land, a sudden urge to break my deal with Celeste starts to play on a loop in my mind, threatening to overwhelm me. I could steal the blade, use it to save Dad, to remove him from the pod and bring him back into the base. I want to defy my half-alien sister and do the one thing I really want: to save Dad. But I need to listen, to curb my instincts, to do what I have agreed to. I tell myself he is too gravely injured for our basic colony medicine. He is beyond human help.

The ship comes to a stop and the almost-silent engines become completely quiet. The main door slides open, and a ramp slowly lowers to the Martian terrain below. The air is full of dust and rock, but none of it penetrates the inside of the ship, probably some kind of advanced forcefield or protective bubble.

'Go.' Celeste points to the door. Jay and Quasar stand.

'And Hercus? How will I get her inside if she's all connected like that?'

She snaps her fingers, and the medi-droid starts to push Hercus from the pod towards the door. She is still unconscious upon the wheeled bed.

'Our medical beds have an oxygen bubble around them – a small parting gift. It will last thirty minutes. You can push her bed inside your base comfortably in that time.'

Jay and Quasar move towards it and push it to the edge of the ship. Quasar turns. 'Coming?'

I shake my head. 'You go ahead, I'm going to say goodbye to Dad.'

She nods. Jay stares for a moment, about to speak, but then turns and helps push Hercus off the ship.

I return to his pod and place my hand on the screen that separates us.

'Can I touch him one last time? Hold his hand and say goodbye. Please, you spoke of love earlier. If there's any love left in you, please let me do this.'

Celeste nods and the door slides open. The bed slides out alongside me.

Dad looks so peaceful. The artery in his neck is throbbing healthily, and his ever-present frown is having a well-deserved rest.

I hold his hand, then I cover the joined hands with my other hand. 'Dad. I don't know if you can hear me. Probably not. I wanted to rescue you. I thought that was my purpose. But I need to let you go. I see that now.' I swallow and turn to see Celeste looking on with mild interest. She doesn't hurry me.

'If this is goodbye, and I promise you I will do everything I can to make sure it is not forever, then you need to know that

I'm going to be okay. I think. I will manage without you, so don't worry too much. Don't cry or miss me. I've not been easy, have I? Always challenging you and doing things we both know I shouldn't. I guess you just wanted to protect me, and I pushed hard against that.'

Everything about Dad is soft and relaxed, unlike how he could ever be when awake. He always had so much on his mind, so much weight to carry. And now, at least, he won't.

'But now I must leave your protection, you'll be relieved to hear, but you've been the very best dad to me. The best dad a Martianborn human could ask for. Sleep well.'

I give him one last look, then stand. The pod begins to retract, and Dad disappears behind the screen again.

'You could stay with him, you know?' Celeste is standing closer than I realised. 'You could come with me and be one of us. First stop is Titan, but there's an endless possibility of worlds out there for you. Not just Mars, or Earth, or anything so small as the Solar System.'

I could. I realise that I want to. For Dad. But also, I've spent most of my time on Mars wanting to leave. A month ago, I'd have done anything for a chance like this. But thinking about what she's done, how's she tricked me – she's killed all those people for this sword – I can't go with her, even if it means leaving Dad.

'No, this is my home. I've spent my whole life running away from that, from who I am, and it's time for me to accept that. I have friends who were willing to, and did, give their lives for me. I can't abandon them. Mars is my home. For now.'

As I turn away, curiosity stops me from leaving.

'Celeste, what happened that day? When you went missing?'

She remains silent, as though trying to remember a

memory from a past life, not just a few years ago. Part of me doesn't want to know the answer. I should hate her. But she's also my sister and was once just like me. A girl lost on Mars.

'My new family picked me up, on the verge of death. I had no oxygen left, and they took care of me, and offered this new life, a major upgrade on my human life, stuck on Mars, the daughter of two people who obsessed more about themselves, than me.'

'Did you not feel bad leaving Mum and Dad behind? They never got over it.'

'I did. For a time. But as time passed, I was able to move on. And remember, without me disappearing, you may never have been born to replace me.'

'To replace you? So, I was just a substitute for their missing daughter?'

'Most likely. Perhaps I will ask Dad when he is transformed.'

The word 'transformed' reignites my earlier rage, but I know it's no use. My decision is made. I must leave Dad to whatever waits for him next. I try to think of it as a new adventure for the man who loved adventures. And maybe he can bring some humanity to these aliens and make them better. To care more, like he does.

'Will I ever see you again?' I don't know why I ask. I don't want to see her ever again.

'I've built a deep telepathic relationship with the ancient Martian ghosts, and so if you ever need me, simply ask them to pass on the message and I will see what I can do, if I'm in this part of the galaxy.'

Great, speaking to the ghosts again - the last thing I'd want to do.

'It's time to leave, Eva. Go and be great. Don't let any human keep you grounded. You're an alien, a Martian, so keep shooting for the stars. Perhaps one day I'll see you out there.'

I take one last look at Dad. 'Take care of him. Or I will come after you, to the stars and beyond.'

And I turn away from my dad, and my sister, and return home.

A New Age

_____

I've moved pods.

Packing up the old one was harder than I thought it would be, putting Dad's personal things into storage boxes. His clothes and uniforms have already been given to new owners.

Nothing gets wasted up here. A constant recycling of air, and water, and absolutely everything.

Including nasty rumours and gossip.

I've heard it all over the last few days; that I killed all the expedition party myself with my powerful, alien sword. That I'm a terrorist, determined to destroy Mariner Base and have us shut down. Even that, mostly from the younger kids, I'm some kind of Martian god with the power to defy anyone.

I quite like that last one.

The pod is in the command wing, which seems like an unfair reward for what I've done, but my new neighbour makes sure it never feels that way.

Commander Darshi is next door – my new guardian. She still despises me, but now she has to legally take care of me, and I really enjoy how much she hates having me sitting at the dinner table with her every evening.

Although I must admit, she was really nice about Dad and the others who died at the memorial service. I almost believed she had a heart. A tiny one, but there's something else there now that I've never seen before. I will never like her, but she might be a bit more human than I thought.

The service was tough. Reliving all those deaths, watching the families all devastated. Hercus was a mess. I tried to comfort her, but she's struggling to adjust. And it felt weird lying about Dad, but I couldn't tell them the truth. They just assume his body was unrecoverable.

I stare up at the ceiling, lying comfortably on my bed, a copy of the astronaut training programme's practice entry test, next to me.

Some sols I feel like I can't get out of bed. I've been speaking to counsellor Io twice a week, to help with my nightmares and dealing with all that happened. There was just so much death, and I just wish I erase all the memories of what happened, but I can't.

Other sols, I feel like I can take on the entire Solar System and all its genetically enhanced aliens myself. Life is a yoyo right now and adjusting to the new normal is hard.

I get up to leave – I'm going to be late again. I'm already grounded for the rest of time, but no point in giving Darshi another reason to punish me.

As we move quickly through the corridors, the usual scared or angry stares come back. The telescreens show the latest news from Earth. The headlines sting.

Have the Martians lost their minds?
Is Mars still a new frontier, or is the reward no
longer worth the risk?

**Ex-Commander Knight, and crew, die on Mars in
mysterious circumstances.
Daughter, Eva Knight, possibly to blame.**

Dad's been gone a week. Hercus barely talks to anyone, and Jay and Quasar spend all their time together.

'At least I still have you, T.'

Yes, always here. Whether I like it, or not.

I laugh and my cheek muscles ache due to a lack of use.

'Come, let's go inside and talk to these kids.' And I open the door to the nursery, watching the faces of the young Martianborn staring up at me.

'I am Eva Knight. I am the first Martian…' And I launch into a talk about all the benefits of being Martianborn and the virtues of Mars. The young ones have their eyes fixed only on me, their legs crossed, mouths wide open. I quite like it.

Careful Eva, I sense you may be enjoying yourself.

I smile as I continue to talk. T is right. This is home. For now.

But one sol, I'll be the first to leave Mars, too.

In five years, I will be an astronaut – I don't care if they all say it's impossible. I don't care if Darshi doesn't think I'm up to it.

I will prove them wrong. I will make my father proud. Then I'll find him.

Nothing is going to stop me now.

(PROBABLY NOT!) **THE END**

Acknowledgments

Where to start?

Firstly, and most importantly, my family, especially Helen, my wife, who always supports me, whatever daft things I do or say, or try and has been 100% behind me in all my writing endeavours.

It takes a lot to put up with me 24/7 and she deserves as much credit for this book, and WriteMentor etc, happening as I do!

To my kids, ~~Luke and Leia~~ (only kidding!), Eva and Xander, who bring some much needed light into my life. They continue to inspire me each and every day, and give meaning and purpose to the stories I tell. I love you both, infinity plus one!

To my non-writing friends and family, who support me from afar and always ask how the writing is going ('mehhh' is the usual response!) and who I know will be buying this book and supporting me and my writing going forward.

To my many, many writing friends in the huge community that we've built with WriteMentor - thanks to all of you for your constant support and well wishes, even when things weren't going so well for me, writing-wise. I am always grateful and appreciative of all your support. Thank you!

To Jennifer Jamieson, who illustrated the beautiful cover for this book, and has been wonderful to work with throughout this whole process, constantly making my small, nagging alterations and being generally such a lovely person.

To Emma Read, who has been with Eva on this adventure from the very start - reading the very first drafts as it was composed, through to editing the most recent drafts and doing big development and line edits on the manuscript. Your constant questions and 'sense checks' have moulded this story into something less self-indulgent and more readable over the last couple of years - thank you!

To Emma Finlayson-Palmer, who provided the final read through and proofread for the manuscript. I appreciate the delicate touch you always take with your comments and changes, and how you encourage and highlight all the better points of my writing. It's always a joy to work with you, and you've certainly helped polish this story.

A LOT of other writers have read the manuscript in various iterations and I fear I will miss names - so, so sorry if I have - but to mind, thanks to Melissa, Florianne, Carolyn, Ian, Daisy, Tom, Michelle, Estelle, Debbie, Natalia, Jonny, Helene, Selina, Helen, Zeshan, Angela to name a few.

To Rachel Faturoti, who gave GoM a sensitivity read and gave such encouragement.

To Vashti Hardy, who gave such a wonderful cover quote for the novel, and is always a source of inspiration and encouragement.

To my Scribbler buddies, who did the CB course with me back in 2015 for their constant support ever since.

To my TWP writing buddies, for all the laughs and support since 2017.

To the many bloggers and reviewers who are supporting me with early reads and reviews and helping to get word of the book out to new readers.

To Jo, at Book Jive Live, who let me read the opening chapter of GoM out live to an audience for the first time.

To Sara Grant and the Undiscovered Voices team who

have all championed my writing for years, and who gave GoM an honorary mention in their 2020 anthology.

To Sally Doherty, who has been a constant source of advice and help during the publication process - can I just ask a quick question?

To Alex Page, who's constant encouragement on DM's and Zoom calls about this story have helped me to keep going with it. I can still picture your face when I told you the pitch and your enthusiasm that followed.

To Jo Clarke, who kindly agreed to help reveal the cover for the novel, all those months ago, on Twitter, and helped it get the most amazing reception, well beyond my wildest dreams. Thanks for taking a chance on an indie author.

And finally, to all of you, the people who have bought my book, read it, and are continuing to read, even the acknowledgements - you are the one who matters most, ultimately, as I write the book for you, to help you escape our ordinary world, to put ourselves in the shoes of someone else and live their life and experiences.

They say, as readers, that we live a thousand lives instead of just one, and I love that view.

Reading is a special thing, and so thank you for choosing my book from the thousands out there.

Picking up the book is a small step, but reading it is a huge leap, so I thank you, to Mars and back!

About the Author

Stuart is a writer and secondary school teacher, who has undeterred passion for helping people, whether it's his students at school, or the writers who have joined the Write-Mentor community.

He has a Masters Degree in Creative Writing and founded, and now runs, WriteMentor. In 2020 and 2022 he was placed on the SCWBI Undiscovered Voices **longlist** and named as an **Hononary Mention** for his novels 'Ghosts of Mars' and 'Astra FireStar and the Ripples of Time'.

Stuart's ethos focuses on making writing more accessible and affordable, something that is at the heart of everything he does and motivates him to make WriteMentor helps as many people as possible.

He makes sure WriteMentor is always open, warm and welcoming and, as a writer himself, he understands what you need to help pick you up as well as improve to take that next step in your career.

Stuart was included in **The Bookseller's** 2021 list of **Rising Stars** in the publishing industry.

You can find out more about Stuart and his forthcoming books by going to his website, https://stuartwhiteauthor.co.uk, or by signing up to his newsletter: https://stuartwhite. substack.com

facebook.com/swhitewriting

twitter.com/StuartWhiteWM

instagram.com/stuartwhitewm

tiktok.com/@stuartwhitewm

amazon.com/author/stuartwhitewm

Printed in Great Britain
by Amazon

17240036R00160